TWELVE
TO
MURDER
A MAC FARADAY MYSTERY

BY
LAUREN CARR

TWELVE TO MURDER

Published by Acorn Book Services

For information call: 304-995-1295
or Email: writerlaurencarr@gmail.com

Designed by Acorn Book Services

Publication Managed by Acorn Book Services
www.acornbookservices.com
acornbookservices@gmail.com
304-995-1295

Cover designed by Todd Aune
Spokane, Washington
www.projetoonline.com

ISBN-13: 978-0989180467
ISBN-10: 0989180468

Published in the United States of America

To my son, Tristan.

So young. So smart. And so very dear to my heart.

TWELVE
TO
MURDER
A Mac Faraday Mystery

CAST OF CHARACTERS

(in order of appearance)

Janice Stillman: Talent agent to some of the greatest child and teen stars in Hollywood until she retired. Lenny Frost was one of her biggest stars.

Austin Stillman: Janice's husband.

Derrick Stillman: Janice and Austin's son. He manages his mother's comedy club, Lenny's Comedy Cafe. In his youth, he was Lenny Frost's best friend. That was a long time ago.

Mac Faraday: Retired homicide detective. On the day his divorce became final, he inherited $270 million and an estate on Deep Creek Lake from his birth mother, Robin Spencer.

Archie Monday: Former editor and research assistant to world-famous mystery author Robin Spencer. She is now Mac Faraday's lady love.

Robin Spencer: Mac Faraday's late birth mother and world-famous mystery author. As an unwed and pregnant teenager, she gave him up for adoption. After becoming

America's queen of mystery, she found her son and made him her heir. Her ancestors founded Spencer, Maryland, located on the shore of Deep Creek Lake, a resort area in Western Maryland.

Police Chief Patrick O'Callaghan: David's late father. Spencer's legendary police chief. The love of Robin Spencer's life and Mac Faraday's birth father.

David O'Callaghan: Spencer police chief. Son of the late police chief, Patrick O'Callaghan. Mac Faraday's best friend and half-brother.

Dr. Dora Washington: Garrett County Medical Examiner.

Deputy Chief Arthur Bogart (Bogie): Spencer's Deputy Police Chief. David's godfather. Don't let his gray hair and weathered face fool you.

Chelsea Adams: Paralegal for Ben Fleming. First and current love of David O'Callaghan. Suffering from epilepsy, she has Molly, a service dog trained to sense and warn of seizures.

Ben Fleming: Garrett County prosecuting attorney. He's one of the good guys.

Gretchen: The Stillmans' neighbor across the cove. Possible witness. Her apple muffins are to die for.

Tonya: Spencer Police Department Desk Sergeant. Mac is paying for her classic T-Bird.

Lenny Frost: Has-been child star and teen idol. Now he's a second-rate stand-up comic, drug addict, and alcoholic.

Carson Drake: Second-rate actor. At the height of Lenny's fame, he was tasked with keeping the famous teenager happy with drugs, women, and booze. When Lenny's star fell, so did Carson Drake, which is why they say he kidnapped the celebrity.

Gnarly: Mac Faraday's German shepherd. Another part of his inheritance from Robin Spencer. Gnarly used to belong to the United States Army, who refuses to talk about him.

Molly: Chelsea's service dog. A white German shepherd trained to sense and warn of seizures.

Zachery Harris: Author. His book about Lenny's kidnapping was a big hit with lawyers specializing in lawsuits.

Sheriff Christopher Turow: Garrett County Sheriff. Had been in office three months when Lenny took the patrons and employees at Blue Whale Pub hostage.

Deputy Parker: Sheriff Turow's deputy.

Edith: Cook at the Blue Whale Pub.

Carl: Owner of the Blue Whale Pub.

Bernie: Elderly patron of the Blue Whale Pub. He just wants to watch the baseball double header.

Hap: Elderly patron of the Blue Whale Pub and Bernie's friend. They call him Hap because he is always happy.

Sela Wallace: The mysterious woman who has some role to play in all this.

Special Agent Alex Fredericks & Special Agent Richard Saunders: Agents with the DEA—Drug Enforcement Administration. They're hoping their special investigation is not messed up by all this murder.

Sally Riggleman: Comic at the Comedy Cafe. She's funny.

Zoe Reese: Derrick Stillman's assistant at the Comedy Cafe.

Special Agent Sid Delaney: FBI agent. Mac's source for FBI info.

Special Agent Jeb Winkler: Retired FBI agent. The Lenny Frost kidnapping ruined his career.

Jeff Ingles: Manager of the Spencer Inn, the five-star resort owned by Mac Faraday. Mac likes to keep Ingles' life interesting.

Officers Brewster & Fletcher: Officers with the Spencer police department.

People are more what they hide than what they show.

—Unknown

PROLOGUE

Stillman Mansion on Deep Creek Lake, Maryland

"Austin is back this year," Olivia said in rhythm with the pace she had set for her power walk.

Two paces behind his wife, Roland took note of the white stone mansion along the chilly lakeshore. The mansion looked closed up. All was quiet, as it was with many of the estates along the lake in the early spring. With each passing day, the quiet was giving way to the snowbirds coming in to roost at their summer homes in the resort town of Spencer, located in the corner of Deep Creek Lake in western Maryland.

The middle-aged couple walked briskly on the running trail along the lake while noting the stillness of the mansion. The only tell-tale sign of change from its winter hibernation was the yacht at the dock in the back. It had not been there the morning before.

"I wonder if Janice will be throwing her week-long Fourth of July bash with all her has-been clients this year?" Roland asked.

"I can tell you right now that I'm not going if that loser Lenny is there." Feeling her heartbeat slowing down, she picked up her pace.

"Come on," her husband said with a laugh, "Lenny Frost isn't that bad. He's really kind of funny."

"He's crude," she shot at him from over her shoulder.

Roland was going to respond that he felt sorry for the least popular of Janice Stillman's former celebrity clients when a black Porsche almost hit the couple rushing past them and turning sharply into the driveway of the white mansion.

"Do you two ever take a break?" the young man shouted at them when he threw open the door and climbed out of the sports car.

"Never," Olivia answered with a frown at Derrick Stillman's apparent lack of self-discipline that was displayed in the stagger in his pace and the fact that he had clearly slept in his clothes. Judging by his disheveled appearance, she concluded he hadn't been sleeping at all.

"Well, you can work out for me, too," Derrick said.

"Party last night?" Roland asked.

"Date." Derrick ran his fingers through his dark curly hair. "I was going to come in yesterday with my folks, but when I met Maddie the other day—" Clutching his stomach, he groaned.

"That must have been some date," Olivia said in a bland tone.

"I've had better." With his steps slightly off balance, he made his way to the front door.

"Come along, Roland," Olivia ordered.

The couple continued on their way. They had only made it to the other end of the property when Derrick's screams stopped them. The young man was running out the front door and dropped to his knees in the yard when they made it back to the driveway.

Olivia rushed over to Derrick, who had his face buried in his hands. "What's wrong?"

Shrieking, he pointed to the door. Roland ran inside.

"What happened, Derrick?" she demanded to know. "What's going on? What's in there?"

His face white, Roland came running back outside.

Olivia's heartbeat was racing. "Roland…"

"They're dead," he said in a panicked tone while taking his cell phone out of his pocket. "Both of them. Janice and Austin. I can't believe this would happen here…in Spencer."

"Who—" she asked with tears in her eyes.

"Janice wrote something in her blood," Roland said before turning his attention to the cell phone. "I'd like to report two murders."

"Her killer," Derrick spat out. "I saw it, too. Lenny. Why else would Mom have written out his name in her blood while she was dying? Lenny Frost did it. He killed my parents."

CHAPTER ONE

For the first morning in the three years since he had inherited two hundred and seventy million dollars, retired as a homicide detective, and moved into his late mother's stone and cedar mansion on the tip of Spencer Point, Mac Faraday was finally going to be allowed to sleep in.

But who or what could possibly keep a multi-millionaire from sleeping in if he wanted to?

Gnarly, that's who.

Gnarly was another part of Mac Faraday's inheritance from his birth mother, Robin Spencer, the world-famous murder mystery writer. The German shepherd was a morning dog who woke up at the crack of dawn. When Gnarly got up, Mac Faraday—under threat of being trampled to death by a hundred pounds of paws and claws—had to wake up to let the dog outside to check the perimeter and conduct other canine business.

This weekend, Gnarly was gone.

Mac expected to sleep in to his heart's delight—until his body refused to sleep one minute past six o'clock. Suddenly, he was staring up at the ceiling and cursing Gnarly for making the early morning wake-up such a habit that he couldn't sleep in—even though he could.

Gnarly, Mac grumbled at the absent dog, *I'm going to kill you.*

A long slender leg slid over from the other side of the bed to drape itself across his bare hips. "Are you up?" the gentle voice whispered into his ear while stroking his chest.

"What are you going to do to me if I am?"

"Come over here to my side of the bed and you'll find out."

He rolled over to gaze into Archie Monday's emerald green eyes. His late mother's lovely assistant was not technically part of his inheritance. However, Robin Spencer had deemed that Archie was allowed to live in the guest house for as long as she wanted. She was no longer living in the cottage. She now resided in the main house—in Mac's bedroom.

"There are advantages to being an early riser," he noted while reaching for her.

ଔ ଯ ଔ ଯ

Mac woke up a second time to the sweet scent of freshly brewed coffee coming into the bedroom. He moved to the center of his king-sized bed to allow Archie room to slip in next to him and hand over one of the mugs she was carrying.

"A guy could get used to this." He rested on the pillows stacked up against the headboard before taking the mug she offered to him.

Pulling up the shoulder of her red robe that had fallen to reveal her slender shoulder, she flashed him a smile. "Are you talking about the coffee in bed or not having to get up to let Gnarly out… and then in…and then out again—"

"And then back in again," Mac said before taking a cautious sip of the hot coffee.

"Come on, you miss him," she insisted.

He reached up to touch her cheek. His fingers lingered on a blonde lock that threatened to touch her eyebrow. "Not as much as I miss you when you aren't around." He chuckled. "Gnarly doesn't bring me coffee in bed."

"Only because you don't allow him on the counter," she joked before setting her coffee mug on the night stand. She slipped under the covers and curled up against him. "I bet you don't know what day it is."

"Yes I do," he replied. "It's Saturday."

"I don't mean the day of the week. I mean what day it is."

Not quite understanding, Mac furrowed his brows.

She lifted her head from his shoulder to gaze up at him. "You really don't remember, do you?"

Mac held his breath. "Give me a hint."

She sat up. "A year ago today you asked me to marry you."

"Has it been a year already? Are you sure?"

"Yes, I'm sure," she said. "A woman doesn't forget those type of things."

"I thought—"

"I'd forgotten?"

"No," Mac said, "I didn't think it was really official until I gave you the ring and we set the date."

Her eyes narrowed to green slits. "Okay then. Let's make it official. Let's set a date." She folded her arms across her chest. "New Year's Eve. At Spencer Church. We'll bring in the new year as Mr. and Mrs. Faraday." Her eyes locked with his.

"Well…" he replied in a soft tone.

"What?"

"I think that's a great idea…" His voice trailed off.

"But?"

"I was planning for us to spend New Year's in Paris." He hurried with his explanation when he saw her throw back the covers and climb out of bed. "It was going to be a surprise. We were going to have dinner at that little café that we discovered. I thought you would love to see the Eiffel Tower in Paris with the New Year's fireworks—"

"Really?" Her tone was filled with doubt.

"Really." He asked, "Don't you want to see the Eiffel Tower?"

"I've seen the Eiffel Tower."

"Not on New Year's Eve."

"Actually I have, as a matter of fact."

"Well, I haven't," Mac said. "I want to go to Paris this New Year's Eve."

"I want to get married."

"We will," he said.

"Sure."

The sarcasm in her tone, combined with the pout on her lips, told him that she wasn't buying it. "Why don't you believe me when I say we're getting married?"

"How is it that I knew when you asked me last year that this was going to happen?" She stopped and took a deep breath.

He watched her hold it for a moment before letting it out in a sigh filled with exasperation. When she spoke, her tone was calm, which frightened him more than when she was agitated. Now she was being reasonable. It's hard to argue with a reasonable woman, especially when she's as smart as Archie Monday.

"When you asked me to marry you, you were afraid of losing me," she said.

"Which made me realize how important you are to me," Mac said. "I don't want to not have you in my life."

"And you do have me in your life." She slipped back onto the bed next to him. "Mac, I love you so much—"

"Why does this sound like a kiss off?"

"It's not a kiss off." She reach up to touch his face. "I'm just releasing you from your obligation."

He grabbed her hand from his face and held it tightly in his. "What does that mean?"

"You're proposal last year was made in the heat of the moment," she said. "If you were serious, if you really were ready to get married again, then you would have given me a ring and we would have set a date. I'm not stupid. Every time I have brought up a possible date, you have a reason why we can't do it—"

"Legitimate reasons."

"Then why haven't you bought me a ring?"

"I've been busy."

"For a full year?" She laughed. "Mac, I'm not dumping you. I'll continue to live here in the mansion and in your bed for as long as you'll have me. I love you, damn it. But as for this game of us pretending to be engaged…" She shook her head. "I'm not a fool."

He grabbed her by the shoulders. "I love you, Archie."

"I don't doubt that." She gazed into his blue eyes. "But you're not ready to get married again. Have you forgotten? I was here when you first moved in three years ago. I saw how hurt you were by your first wife leaving you for another man after raising two children together. I listened to you talk about Christine—about how she had changed—how she wasn't the same woman you had married—and murder cases, how people change. Isn't that a big fear you have about me—about us? That right now we are perfect for each other, but what about a few years down the road? I think you're scared of going through all that again, of being hurt to the core again the way Christine hurt you—"

"I'm not afraid of anything," Mac said forcibly.

"I know you, Mac," she said in a soft voice while brushing his cheek. "It's okay. I'm not going anywhere, but I'm not going to push you either. When you're ready to get serious about our getting married, I'll be here—right by your side." She pressed her lips against his.

When she pulled back, Mac was trying very hard to piece together what had just happened.

It felt like he was being dumped. The pain in his chest told him that he was. But then, she was smiling at him with love in her eyes—only there was hurt in their deep emerald pools, too.

Her love and kindness cut him to the quick worse than any hurtful words she could have tossed at him over his failure to follow through on the engagement after his proposal.

Her lips were moving and words were coming out of her mouth. "Mac, your phone is ringing," he finally heard her say while picking it up from the night stand and handing it to him.

His fingers felt numb when he took it and checked the caller ID. It was David O'Callaghan, the chief of police. "Yeah, David…," he said into the phone.

"Mac, I know you were planning a special weekend with Archie, but are you able to come in? We've got a serious situation here."

"How serious?" Mac asked while grasping Archie by the shoulder as if to keep her in his bed. At the moment, he felt desperate to hold on to her.

"Two bodies. Multiple gunshot wounds. Middle-aged couple found by their son."

"I'll be there." Mac felt her watching him while he took note of the address and location of the house.

When he hung up, she asked, "Is there anything I can do to help?"

"Wait for me." He tossed the phone down onto the bed and took her into both of his arms and held her close. The top of her robe fell off her shoulders to reveal her soft tender skin. As always, her scent excited him.

"I'll always wait for you." She gazed into his eyes. Their lips were barely touching. "I'm a fool for you, Mac. Haven't you figured that out yet?"

"No," he said, "you're no fool. I love you and I do intend to marry you."

"And I want to marry you," she said. "So what's the problem?"

"No problem here."

"Prove it, Mac Faraday."

"That's what I intend to do, Archie Monday."

CHAPTER TWO

Spencer's police chief was waiting in the driveway of the Stillman estate when Mac pulled his red Dodge Viper sports car in the driveway behind the black SUV cruiser. "SPENCER POLICE" was painted on the side in gold block letters.

It didn't escape Police Chief David O'Callaghan's notice when Mac slammed his car door shut. "Sorry I interrupted your hot weekend alone with Archie…sans Gnarly."

Realizing his sign of impatience, Mac apologized. "It's not your fault. Things were going south before you called."

"Oh?" A grin crept to David's lips. His blue eyes, identical in color and shape to those of his half-brother Mac, danced with amusement. In appearance, there was practically no denying that the two men were dipped from the same gene pool. They shared the same body build and facial features. The only real difference showed in Mac's dark hair and coloring in comparison to David's blond hair and features.

"Don't tell me the perfect couple is having a fight," David said to Mac.

"It's not a fight."

"Nothing to be ashamed of, Mac," the smooth, cultured tone of Dr. Dora Washington responded from behind as she passed him on her way up to the front door. "The most compatible couples do fight. It's those who don't that you need to watch out for."

With her medical bag hanging from her shoulder, she led them up the walkway to the mansion's front door. With her long, midnight-blue hair cascading to the middle of her back in a single ponytail and the striking features of a high-fashion model, Doc often caught people off guard when she arrived at a scene to probe dead bodies. Yet, within seconds of hearing her speak, they would be further taken aback by how brilliantly smart the beauty was.

"The reason?" She continued to tell them from over her shoulder, "Couples who fight air their differences and work out their problems. Those who don't let issues fester until suddenly someone's top explodes from their pent up anger, usually at which point it is too late to fix." She turned around to flash Mac a wide grin filled with bright white teeth. "Considering how good of a shot Archie is with that pretty pink handgun she carries, be thankful that you two can air your differences while they're little more than petty problems. I'd hate to have to come out to Spencer Manor after Archie has blown your head off for leaving the toilet seat up once too often."

"Mac, haven't you learned yet that when you live with a woman, you need to put the seat down?" Deputy Chief Arthur Bogart asked while holding the front door open for the medical examiner to step inside. Even at sixty-five years of age, the silver-haired officer had the frame and strength of a body builder. His thick mustache stretched across his face when he grinned.

"That's one of the things I love most about Bogie," Doc said while sneaking a coy grin in the deputy chief's direction. "He's such a gentleman."

Bogie's cheeks turned a deep red.

Before Mac could respond, David asked, "Is that what you and Archie are fighting about?"

"We're not fighting." Mac changed the subject. "Is there any sign of forced entry?"

"None," Bogie said.

Mac pointed to the security company sign in front of the house. "How about the security system?"

"Son says it was off when he arrived an hour ago," David said. "The security company is sending over a rep to check it out for being tripped and will send us a report of when it was activated and deactivated."

"Where's the son?" Mac asked.

"Being checked out by the EMTs." The police chief pointed to the emergency vehicle at the end of the driveway. "He was hysterical. They're sedating him."

"Well, let's get a look at the crime scene." Mac brushed past Bogie to go inside the house.

One of the deputy chief's bushy silver eyebrows rose up into an arch after Mac crossed the threshold.

"They're fighting," David mouthed to him.

"About Doc's comment about me and the toilet seat—"

"Bogie, do I look stupid to you?" David cut him off with a chuckle.

Once he stepped inside, Mac noticed Doc Washington kneeling next to a body up on the landing of the stairway located across the spacious foyer from the front door. The man's legs were sprawled down the first few steps that were coated in thick blood that had turned a reddish brown. His feet were encased in tan leather boat shoes. Blood splattered the wall several feet up behind where the medical examiner was kneeling.

"Poor guy. It looks like he didn't know what hit him." Shaking her head, Doc dug into her medical bag for a thermometer to take the man's liver temperature in order to determine how long he had been dead.

Taking in a deep breath, Mac made his way up the stairs. As his head cleared the landing, he saw what he expected.

The victim looked like every other man. The guy you see every weekend doing yard work next door. His hair was cropped short to his head and liberally mixed with gray. His bloody body was clad in khaki pants and a blue button-down shirt.

Mac didn't know anything about him—even his name— but he assumed he had been a fine man…and a good father. Otherwise, why would they need to sedate his son?

"His name is Austin Stillman," Bogie told them from the bottom of the stairs. "Fifty-nine years old. Senior partner of a public relations firm in Washington. They handle a lot of businesses and politicians." He gestured to the back of the house. "His wife's body is in the kitchen."

"Looks like he was coming down the stairs when he got it in the chest." Mac noted the size of the holes in his chest and the pattern of the blood on the walls and stair landing. "There's a second splatter pattern lower on the wall and here on the floor." He glanced over his shoulder to where Bogie was at the bottom of the stairs. "The first two shots were at a high angle from down there. That dropped him and sent the splatter up high on the wall because he was standing. Then, the killer came up the stairs and shot him in the head while he was down to make sure he was dead."

Bogie searched the floor around his feet. "No shell casings. Killer could have taken them with him. They found none in the kitchen, either."

"The holes could be twenty-two caliber. I'll have to extract the slugs to make sure." After extracting the thermometer, the medical examiner noted the reading and the time on her watch. Instantly, she came up with the time of death. "He's been dead fourteen to sixteen hours. That would put the time of death at between seven thirty and nine thirty last night."

"Hey, Bogie," David called from somewhere on the main floor below them, "where's the victim's son?"

"The last I saw him, he was in the back of the EMT truck being sedated," Bogie answered.

His cell phone to his ear, David came hurrying into the foyer from the back of the house. "Chelsea just called. She's watching a live report on one of the news shows. A reporter is interviewing the son right outside this house. If Fleming sees this, he's going to have a cow—" His voice rose to a yell. "He's telling them what he saw when he found the bodies! He's giving a blow-by-blow—"

Bogie bolted out the door.

David cursed and turned to Mac. "He should have been locked up in the police car and taken down to the station for a statement."

"Which proves that it pays to know people," Mac said. "If your girlfriend wasn't the county prosecutor's paralegal, you wouldn't have gotten the heads up that one of your suspects was making his case and pointing fingers right outside the house."

"Is that why you used your friendship with Ben Fleming to get her a job working for him?" David asked him. "So that we would have eyes and ears inside the prosecutor's office?"

Mac flashed him a coy smirk.

"Still doesn't make me immune from getting chewed out by the prosecutor when his jury pool is muddied by leaks to the media," David said. "We can only hope Ben and his wife were at brunch or some shindig while that was airing. Who let the victim's son loose anyway?"

"Don't blame me," Mac said with a shrug, "I just got here. Can I see the wife's body?"

"Damn it," David muttered while turning around to lead Mac back to the kitchen.

"Sounds like someone is having a bad day," Mac replied.

"At least my girlfriend isn't mad at me." David threw open the swinging door and stepped aside for Mac to enter the gourmet kitchen.

The layout of the Stillman's kitchen was more spacious than the one at Spencer Manor. The appliances were black and the cabinets were white. The tile floor was stark white as well. The granite counters were pitch black.

The bright white color of the floor made the red of the wife's blood jump out at Mac when he almost stepped on Janice Stillman laying face down right inside the door. Her head was a matter of inches from the door frame. She had three gaping holes in her back and one in the back of her head.

As Mac stepped around the middle-aged woman's body, he saw her right hand positioned above her head with her index finger resting in a line of blood, which was part of a pattern. Kneeling, he studied it more closely. "What's that?"

Releasing the door to let it close, David replied, "What does it look like?"

Mac looked at the bloody hand and the letters clearly spelled out in her own blood: L-E-N-N-Y. "Lenny? Who's Lenny?"

"Lenny Frost," David said. "According to the neighbors, Janice Stillman had been a talent agent in Hollywood before coming out east with her husband and son. Many of her clients were child stars or pop singers and teen idols. Now they're on reality shows. When her husband opened up the public relations firm in Washington in the 1990s, she let them go and moved out here. About ten years ago, she opened up a club called Lenny's."

"Lenny's Comedy Café," Mac said. "I've been there. He's raunchy."

"He's also got a horrible temper," David said. "Bogie pulled up his rap sheet when we saw this. He's got a long line of assault charges. While the club has Lenny's name, she owns it."

Mac looked up from the blood to ask, "Now that she's dead, who does it go to?"

"Good question. Derrick. Her son. Their only child is the heir apparent."

"Then he has motive," Mac said.

"He claims he has an alibi," David said. "Bogie has a call in to his date. It seems Janice Stillman bought the club as an investment for Derrick after he graduated from business school and to help out Lenny when his acting career went into the gutter after she left him."

"And this is how he pays her back?" Mac scratched his ear. "Didn't he win an Academy Award?"

"Supporting actor for playing the kidnap victim in the first Mickey Forsythe movie," David pointed out. "He was eight years old. I'm sure if you look through your mother's photo album you'll see some pictures of him and Robin. They both won Oscars for that movie. She won for best screenplay. Now Lenny's a second-rate stand-up comic."

"How the mighty fall." Mac stood up.

In the stark-colored room, the aluminum foil swan set in the middle of the island stood out like a silver bird in a black and white sea. "They'd gone to the Spencer Inn for dinner." He picked up the foil package and sniffed it. "Chicken cordon bleu with hollandaise sauce."

He turned back to the body. Her feet were pointing into the center of the kitchen with her head toward the door.

"She was killed before she had a chance to put this in the fridge, but she was running away when she was shot in the back." He pieced the scene together. "They went to dinner at the inn. The killer came in to wait for them." He went around behind the island and gauged the angle of the shots to the woman's back. "The murderer hid behind the island. When she came in to put away the doggie bag, he waited for her to get to the island before making his move. Leaving the leftovers on the island, she turned and ran for the door, but she only made it halfway across the room before he shot her in the back."

David picked up the scene. "Of course, the husband heard the shots and came running downstairs."

"The killer ran to the bottom of the stairs to kill him when he hit the landing." Mac was still staring down at the letters written in blood at his feet. "After shooting him in the head to make sure he was dead, the killer came in to finish the job here."

"Hey, Chief…" one of Spencer's police officers, a young man known as "Brewster," startled the two men when he opened the kitchen's deck door to shout in to them. "We got a witness." He pointed to the lakeshore. "The neighbor over across the way may have seen the killer coming in."

Mac followed David out onto the deck and around the corner of the house to where Officer Fletcher was taking advantage of a white-haired little woman's offer of hot apple muffins.

"Good morning, Gretchen." David bent over to hug the elderly woman before taking one of the muffins she held out to him.

"Davey Boy," Gretchen grinned. "I haven't seen you in ages. As soon as I heard there was a murder here I popped these muffins into the oven. I knew you and your men would be hungry." She peered closely at Mac while holding out the basket of warm bread to him. "Is this Robin's boy?"

His mouth full, David nudged Mac with his elbow. "Take one. Gretchen is the best baker on the lake. She used to have a bakery in McHenry. Most popular place in the area."

"Baked holiday pies day and night through the winter," Gretchen said.

"Around here, Thanksgiving wasn't Thanksgiving without one of Gretchen's pumpkin or apple pies."

When Mac took a bite of the warm muffin, he could see that David wasn't exaggerating. Gretchen could give Archie a run for her money when it came to baking. The elderly woman eyed him while he chewed and swallowed the first bite of her muffin. "Thank you," he mumbled around the baked good. "This is a nice treat."

"So you're Robin Spencer's little boy?" she asked. "The one she based Mickey Forsythe on?"

"I'm not Mickey Forsythe."

"That's not what I've heard."

"Robin wrote her first book back when I was a toddler being raised by my adoptive parents," Mac argued while David finished off his muffin and started on a second one. "Mickey Forsythe was a total figment of her imagination."

"You look like him and you have a dog just like Diablo."

"Diablo is less demanding and better behaved than my dog," Mac said.

"Gretchen," David cut her off when the little woman was about to interject with her next line of argument, "did you see anything last night?"

"I think I saw the killer breaking in," she said in a hushed voice. "But I didn't know at the time that that was what he was doing."

"Tell me about it," David replied.

"It was seven thirty last night," she said. "My show was over, and that's the time that I go to bed. So, just like always, I went to take Percy outside." She told Mac, "Percy is my dog. He's a little Maltese. Tiny thing. Nothing like Diablo. My Percy, bless his heart, is as dumb as a stick, but I still love him."

David gestured for her to get to the murder.

Thrusting a second muffin into Mac's hand, she said, "So last night, I take him outside and we're standing out there in the dark when I hear this bizarre noise. It was like one of those rock guitars going through a whole lot of notes all at once—like they used to do with pianos when the guy would sweep his fingers across the keyboard real fast." Her eyes grew big. "Well, I don't play a guitar and I know none of the neighbors are into rock guitars, except maybe Derrick Stillman. So I look over there and that's when I see that Mr. Stillman's boat is docked in the lake and there is a light on the back deck…and he was standing right under it—plain as day."

"He who?" Mac asked. "Derrick Stillman? Their son?"

"No," Gretchen said with a shake of her head. "This young man had bright red hair. You couldn't miss it on account that he was standing right under the light. He was playing with his cell phone. He put it into his pocket and then he pulled up the hood on his hoodie, and I saw him use the key to unlock the door and go inside."

"Bright red hair," David repeated.

"Like fire," Gretchen said. "Like that comic friend of theirs that they had here last year. The obnoxious one."

"Lenny Frost?" Mac asked.

Gretchen shrugged. "Maybe. I remember people telling me he was famous." She confessed, "He was too far away for me to see his face, but I saw that hair all right. Couldn't miss it."

"One of the things Lenny was famous for was his bright red hair," David noted in a low voice while Mac and he went back to the house after thanking Gretchen for the muffins and ordering Fletcher to get her statement.

"If you were going to break into a house to assassinate two people," Mac asked, "wouldn't you make sure your cell phone was off and put up the hood on your hoodie before entering the scene?"

"Why, Mac, what are you saying?" David cocked his head at him.

Stopping, Mac turned to him. "If this case was so easy, why did you call me in?"

"I wanted your opinion."

"About what?"

A sly grin came to David's lips. "What do you think?"

"You want to know what I think?"

"That's what I just said."

"I was a homicide detective for twenty years. I investigated more than two hundred murder cases." He looked over at the deck doors leading into the kitchen where Doc Washington was examining Janice Stillman's dead body. "In all those cases I investigated, the only place I ever saw a victim spell out the name of her killer with her blood was in the movies."

CHAPTER THREE

In the upscale resort town of Spencer, Maryland, where many of the residents were listed in "Who's Who," the small police station resembled a sports club. Its fleet of cruisers was comprised of top-of-the-line SUVs painted black with gold lettering on the side that read "SPENCER POLICE." Located along the shore of Deep Creek Lake, the log building that was home to the department sported a dock with a dozen jet skis and four speed boats. For patrolling the deep woods and up the mountain trails, they had eight ATVs. Like the cruisers, all of the vehicles were black with gold trim.

After following David to the station, Mac jumped out of his sports car to meet the police chief at the door of his cruiser. "Someone else had to have written Lenny's name in Janice Stillman's blood. I called Doc and she agrees with me that the victim would have bled out too quickly to have written it."

"Either that, or Lenny killed her and wrote his own name in order to make us think that." David led the way across the parking lot to the small police station.

"Is Lenny Frost that smart?" Doubt filled Mac's tone. "The guy has made a career out of making bad decisions. People like that don't think that far ahead."

David pressed his way through the door. "They also tend to do dumb things to solve their problems—like murder."

Mac's comeback disappeared from his train of thought when he stepped inside to hear a baritone voice say, "Not only do I feel violated, but I feel—these monsters stole something from me that I'll never get back. I spent four days handcuffed to a bed. I couldn't go anywhere. They didn't just take away my freedom, but they made me realize the true meaning of a word I have heard uttered so many times without realizing what it really meant. Victim. And I swear, with God as my witness, that I will never again be a victim."

Mac and David stopped to watch the image on the flat-screen television that was perched high on the wall in the corner of the room, almost to the ceiling. The officers kept the news tuned in and muted. With the media reporting on their murder case, Tonya, the desk sergeant, had the sound turned up. While the screen filled with quick changing images of a red-haired young man at various stages of his life, the announcer recounted the highlights of Lenny Frost's life:

"Speaking in a manner that sounded eerily like Andrew, the role in the first Mickey Forsythe movie that won him an Academy Award, Lenny Frost told Barbara Walters about being kidnapped and held for a million-dollar ransom. Little did Lenny dream that his life would go on to mirror his award-winning role. At the age of seventeen, he was abducted. The whole nation searched for him, and four days after his disappearance, his abductor abandoned him in a deserted cabin in the mountains outside of Los Angeles and Lenny called the police. Lenny, who had been heavily drugged during his captivity, was able to tell the FBI, who investigated the case, that he had overheard his kidnapper, small-time actor Carson Drake, phoning his partner with the news that he had received the ransom. Leaving Lenny handcuffed to a bed, Carson Drake was last seen going off to meet his mysterious accomplice. His car was found hidden on an isolated mountain road."

The television screen was filled with a publicity shot of a handsome young man with dark curly hair and chiseled facial features. "Carson Drake has become Hollywood's D.B. Cooper," the journalist announced, "with strong debates about the kidnapper's fate." A film clip showed the diminutive actor in what appeared to be a situation comedy with a canned laugh track. He had the build of a teenager.

"He doesn't exactly look like a legendary criminal to me," Mac noted.

"Billy the Kid was only five feet eight inches and weighed one hundred forty pounds," Tonya said.

"To this day," the newscaster continued, "Drake has never been captured by authorities, his partner was never identified, and the million-dollar ransom paid by the studio was never recovered. Some believe he was killed and his body was disposed of by his co-conspirator. Others believe it was the other way around and Drake left his car behind to make it appear as if he had gotten lost and died in the mountains. As for Lenny Frost—"

The image on the screen was of a teenaged boy with bright red hair whose face glowed with rapture over being at the top of his chosen profession.

"—it is easy to understand the effect these traumatic occurrences would have on a young man. Even an adult would have difficulties. To have lost the love of his life and to be the victim of a kidnapping—all before the age of eighteen. A brilliant actor with a genius IQ, Lenny Frost had the brightest of futures, but then—"

"Seems the media has already identified their prime suspect," Tonya said while hitting the remote to mute the broadcast. "Lenny Frost hasn't seen this much media attention since he got kidnapped."

Tonya had lived on the lake her whole life. Many suspected the long hours that the desk sergeant put in at the station served as an excuse for not going home where two of her three grown children had returned with their offspring after a short time spent in the outside world. She had three dogs that she doted on more than her kids. She claimed the dogs were more self-sufficient.

"Genius IQ?" Mac asked about the comment he had heard on the broadcast before she muted it.

"I didn't know that either," Tonya said. "They reported that his IQ is one sixty."

"I'm impressed," Mac said. "What was that about the love of his life?"

"Kate Coleman," David said. "Gorgeous pop star. Long dark hair and big doe eyes." He sighed. "I admit it. I had a crush on her. Lenny was two years younger than her. He was fifteen years old and dating Kate Coleman. I think they were the pop world's power couple for a good year."

"Then she drove her car off a mountain road in the Hollywood Hills," Tonya said. "Kids envy these child stars—all the fame, glitz, and money—but when you look at how they turn out—like Lenny Frost..." She shook her head. "It's very rare that you hear of one who comes out right on the other end."

"Look at Lenny Frost now," Mac muttered while glancing up at the montage of images of the young man who had so much, only to have lost it all. "A genius with no idea how far he had to fall."

David shook his head. "Lenny and I have the same birthday. We're the same age."

With a start, Mac noted David's youthful features and slender, fit build.

The image on the television screen shifted to a present-day interview with Lenny. The fresh-faced teenager had given way to a muscular man with a hard face marked with deep lines. His eyes were dull and sunken. The bright hue of his hair had been washed out until it turned the color of rust.

"Proof that it's not the years, it's the mileage," Tonya said.

David studied the image on the television screen. "When I was in high school, a lot of guys were jealous—envious—of Lenny Frost—being that young, driving fast cars—"

"I heard about the time he led the police on a car chase through Hollywood in his Porsche at one hundred and five miles an hour," Tonya said with a scoff of disgust.

"When you're seventeen and you have to mow lawns for your gas money, you can't help but admire someone like Lenny Frost who has girls all over the world throwing their panties at him." David gestured at the man on the screen who looked at least fifteen years older than him. It was hard to believe they had been born at the same time.

Mac turned to Tonya to ask, "Why would a woman throw her underwear at a man?" After she responded with an exaggerated shrug of her shoulders, wide eyes, and raised eyebrows, he turned to David. "Why would a man want a woman to throw her underwear at him? How is that a good thing?"

Not having an answer to his question, David gestured at the image of the has-been celebrity on the television screen. "Think about it. Lenny is the exact same age I am and he's already reached his peak. Awards, women, money, status—"

"Used underwear," Tonya interjected.

"—It's all gone. It's one thing to reach for it—but to have had it and lost it all before you were even old enough to drink—"

"Speaking of drinking, Lenny has been in and out of rehab like the center had a revolving door." Tonya handed David a sheet of paper. "Back to business. Report from the security firm that monitors the Stillman residence. The alarm was never tripped. The system was turned on and activated at the door leading into the garage at six seventeen. The rear door was opened and the security passcode was input at seven thirty-one. Then the alarm was reactivated on the keypad at that door."

"That jives with the time the witness saw someone with red hair and a loud cell phone on the back deck," Mac said. "The witness saw him let himself in with a key."

"Could have been a master key," David said.

"Not only did he have a key, but the killer also knew the security passcode to turn the system off."

"Which means we're not talking about a common household burglar," Tonya said. "The security company says the code was changed less than a month ago."

"This wasn't a burglary," Mac said. "Nothing was taken. It was an execution."

"The assassin turned the system back on after letting himself in so that the Stillmans wouldn't get suspicious when they returned and saw that it had already been turned off," David said. "He actually laid in wait inside the house to ambush them when they came home."

"Which happened at eight twenty-seven," Tonya said. "The front door was opened and the security passcode used to turn off the system. It was never turned back on."

"Eight-thirty," Mac said. "That's when the murders happened. The killer was inside and waiting for a full hour to blow them away when Janice went into the kitchen to put away the leftover chicken cordon bleu."

A loud snort from the direction of the sofa drew Mac's attention away from the police sergeant.

Stretched out and lying on his back, the hundred-pound German shepherd took up the whole sofa. His hind legs were splayed apart. His front paws were bent up and actually folded across his chest. The dog's head was tilted back so far that his fangs and some of his teeth were displayed to resemble the underside of a shark.

Gnarly was sound asleep and seemingly unaware that while he was snoozing, someone had tucked a cigarette into his mouth.

"What's *he* doing here?" Mac gasped out.

Tonya's grin turned into a smirk before she giggled out, "Lady Tala's mother ended their romantic weekend together early."

"Why?" Mac asked before turning to the sleeping dog to demand in a low voice, "What did you do?"

Gnarly let out a snort, took in a deep breath, and continued sleeping.

"Gnarly is," Tonya referred to her notes. "and I quote— the horniest dog I have ever seen in my life. If Lady Tala isn't pregnant after the last twenty-four hours with him, she never will be. I can't take it anymore. They had me up all night with their lovemaking. I'm going home, steam cleaning my sofa, and getting some sleep. End quote." With a laugh, she tossed the notepad onto her desk. "She also said to thank you for the use of your pure-bred German shepherd, even if he is a horny beast."

"Way to go, Gnarly." David patted Mac on the shoulder.

"I thought Molly was Gnarly's girlfriend," Tonya's voice had an accusatory tone when reminding them of Gnarly's friendship with Chelsea Adams' service dog, a white

German shepherd trained to detect epileptic seizures in time for her mistress to take medication before their onset.

"She is," David said.

"Fay is Archie's friend. Her husband left her for another woman," Mac explained. "She doesn't have a job and her husband got almost everything—except his prized champion German shepherd. So, she asked if Gnarly—"

"You pimped out Gnarly," Tonya finished. "How much are you getting for Gnarly's services?"

"Nothing," Mac said, "and it was Archie who pimped him out, not me, and she volunteered him to do it as a favor."

"Obviously," David said, "Gnarly had no complaints about doing this favor."

"Don't you even get one of the puppies?" Tonya asked.

"The last thing I need is a son of Gnarly wreaking havoc at Spencer Manor."

David looked down at Gnarly, who was still sound asleep. "Looks like he's having a better weekend than you are, Mac."

"Are you having a bad weekend, Mac?" Tonya asked.

"He and Archie are fighting," David said.

"Really?" Tonya picked up another note. "She didn't sound mad when she called earlier. She wanted to make sure that you would be home for dinner. She's making your favorite. Tuscan rib eye, garlic mashed potatoes, parmesan tomatoes, and a decadent bottle of Italian red wine." She winked at him. "She didn't tell me what she has planned for dessert."

Guilt stabbed Mac through the heart while he reached for the message from the desk sergeant.

"Make-up dinner followed by make-up sex," David said.

"What did you do to her?" Tonya narrowed her eyes to peer at Mac. Her maternal tone demanded a response.

"I did nothing to her," Mac said before muttering under his breath. "That's the problem."

He found an empty desk in the squad room to plop down and stare at Archie's message. It was his favorite meal. Something about Archie's Tuscan rib eye, the way she made it special for him, made him want to hold her and never let her go.

This is killing me. Maybe that's the idea. In the right hands, kindness can be a fatal weapon.

"Hey…" David snapped Mac out of his thoughts. He swung around the chair next to the desk and straddled the back. "Just heard back from Bogie about Derrick Stillman's alibi."

"What was it again?"

"Date." David referred to his notes on his notepad. "He said he spent the night with some woman in Georgetown. Madelyn Preston. According to his story, he left her apartment at three o'clock and drove straight out here to his parents' summer place."

"Georgetown is three hours away," Mac noted.

"Not exactly a quick trip to bump off your folks while picking up a cup of sugar from the corner store," David said. "If he was with her in Georgetown, he couldn't have murdered his parents here in Spencer."

"Does his alibi check out?" Mac asked.

"Police can't find her to ask," David said. "Her apartment is a sublet. The apartment manager has no information about how to get in touch with her. The woman on the lease is in the navy and stationed on an aircraft carrier in the Mediterranean. The Georgetown police will keep trying to track Preston down to verify Stillman's story."

"It's still early," Mac said.

"Do you think we should issue a warrant for Lenny Frost?"

"We can't not issue one," Mac said. "At the very least, someone is trying to frame him. He must have some idea of who that someone is." He laid the message sheet on top of the desk.

David's eyes followed Mac's to the phone message from Archie. "Care to talk about it?"

"No," Mac said in a firm tone. "Do you think I'm a coward?"

David chuckled, "Why would you even ask that?"

"I'm not talking about walking into a gun fight," Mac said. "It's…" His voice trailed off. He swallowed. "Archie is a very perceptive woman."

"You're right there."

"She called me on something." He shook his head. "Hit the nail right on the head."

The two men sat in silence. David watched Mac stare at the message sheet as if to burn the image into his mind.

"I want to marry Archie," Mac finally said in a voice that was barely above a whisper.

"What's stopping you?" David's voice was equally soft.

"I loved Christine, too," Mac said. "I had no doubt in my mind back then that it was right. Twenty years later…" He raised his eyes from the message sheet. "If Archie was to do to me what—"

"Archie isn't your first wife," David said.

"Christine wasn't the same woman I married when she cheated on me and left me with nothing. She'd changed. I've seen so many cases of couples who change and…if that happened with Archie and me…"

"So you're scared. That's what's stopping you. Fear."

"Yeah," Mac said with a nod of his head. "Archie says she understands—"

"They all say they understand," David said, "and they do. They sincerely try to be patient. But eventually they become frustrated. Friends are getting married and having babies, and they want to start a family and their clocks are ticking. Before long, the frustration turns into resentment, and how can two people stay together when they resent each other?"

Fighting the urge to get up and run away from the conversation, Mac shifted in his seat. Reaching over the back of the chair, David grasped his arm as if to hold him there to hear what he had to say. Mac turned. They locked eyes.

"Listen, Mac, I can't tell you what to do. You already know Archie is the best woman any man could ever want, and you are damn lucky that you're the one she's fallen in love with. I can't tell you whether to marry her or to leave her. You're the only one who can answer that. The answer to that lies in the answer to this one question." He held up a finger in front of Mac's eyes. "What's stronger? You're *love*, or your *fear?*"

Staring into David's eyes, Mac picked up a hint of intensity, a sense that he knew this topic intimately. "Are you talking from experience?"

David let out a hollow laugh before answering, "Do you know why Yvonne took that network job and moved away?"

"Your fear outweighed your love for her?"

Releasing Mac's arm, David stood up. "I've got to go put out that BOLO on Frost." He turned the chair around to return it to its proper place.

"Any regrets?"

"I'm with Chelsea," David said, "and Yvonne is married to some rich dude and living in Connecticut. We're both where we belong." He patted Mac on the shoulder. "I need to go put out this notice to be on the lookout for Frost." He hurried out to issue the order to police dispatch.

Mac picked up his cell phone to call Archie. The background on his phone was a picture of her in the rose garden at the manor. Her pretty face was surrounded by rosy blooms. She looked like a wood nymph—his wood nymph.

Tonya came into the squad room. "Gnarly is out cold," she said. "We've got a visitor out front and his nose hasn't even twitched." She placed a business card in the center of Mac's desk for him to read. "Where's the chief?"

Mac turned off the phone and returned it to the case on his belt. "Putting out a BOLO on Lenny Frost." He picked up the card to read the name. "Who's Zachery Harris?"

"A writer. He claims to have information about the Stillman murders."

"Send him in." Mac clipped the business card to his notepad and picked up a pen. "Tell David. He's going to want to join us."

"Sure thing, Mac." She turned on her heels before he stopped her.

"Can you do me a favor, Tonya?"

She turned back to him with a wide grin on her face. "Anything for you, hon."

Mac's cheeks felt warm when he asked, "Can you call the florist and have them send a dozen... no, make it twelve dozen long-stemmed white roses to Archie at the manor today? I have an account there already."

"*White* roses?"

"White," Mac said.

"That must have been some fight," Tonya said. "If I were you, I'd send a box of chocolates, too."

A grin crept to Mac's lips. "If you think she should get chocolates, order them. Order a box for yourself, too, and put it on my account."

"You don't have to offer that twice," Tonya said. "What do you want the note to say?"

"See you tonight."

"Do you want me to dog sit?" Tonya asked.

"Nah, I'll send Gnarly to Chelsea's place," Mac said. "Let Gnarly spend the night with his other girlfriend."

"Molly's going to smell Lady Tala on him and she's going to be ma-ad."

"They're *dogs.*"

"I'm just saying…" Shaking her hand, Tonya waved both of her hands. "Once Molly gets a whiff of another dog on her man, there's going to be big trouble in paradise."

"Gnarly's a German shepherd," Mac said. "He can handle it."

☙ ❧ ☙ ❧

Zachery Harris looked like the stereotype of a writer: slender with shaggy hair in need of a haircut and glasses on a thin face. He had the look down to his baggy khaki slacks, button-down shirt, and a corduroy sports coat with patches on the elbows.

When Mac stepped into the interview room, Zachery had his recorder resting in the middle of the table and his notepad out. After closing the door, Mac turned off the machine. *"I'm* interviewing *you*, not the other way around."

"Actually, this is for my protection." Zachery reached for the device, only to have Mac move it out of his reach.

"I'll give this to you when we're done." Mac set the recorder aside and sat across from him. Tapping his pen on the notepad, Mac sat back to regard the writer. It was a coin toss as to whether he had information to give them about the murders or was seeking it for himself. Mac guessed that if the writer had anything to offer, it wasn't much. It was too soon. The media didn't have enough details, even by way of rumors, to generate tips from the public. "You told the desk sergeant that you had information about the Stillman murders."

"I have a boatload of stuff for you," Zachery said.

"How is that?"

"Janice Stillman used to be Lenny Frost's agent back in Hollywood," Zachery said. "She was the one who got him that movie that won him the Oscar. She made him the teen idol of the nineties."

"I know all that," Mac said. "Now tell me something we don't know."

"Why he killed her," Zachery said.

In all his years of being a police detective, Mac had become an expert at keeping a poker face in order to not betray his emotions.

It's easier to control an interview or interrogation when the witness or suspect has no idea if the detective believes or is doubtful of what he's hearing. Keeping your body posture and face void of emotion keeps the subject on edge so that he doesn't know which direction to go in the interview to achieve his objective.

Even with the announcement that Zachery knew the motive for the Stillman's murder, Mac kept his face blank. "Why do you think Lenny Frost killed his former agent?"

"He did, didn't he?" Zachery was practically panting for Mac to confirm his suspicion.

"If you have information about these murders and you don't tell us what you know, then you can be arrested for obstruction of justice and impeding an investigation," Mac said. "So don't sit there asking me questions. I'm asking the questions. You're answering them. Now, why do you think Lenny Frost killed Janice Stillman and her husband?"

"Because she had him kidnapped and held captive for four days for a million-dollar ransom from the studio."

"She had her star client abducted?" Mac asked.

With a smirk, Zachery said, "How do you think the Stillmans got the money for her husband to set up that public relations firm like two years after the kidnapping? And how would she have had the money to buy that club where Lenny worked for her? It's blood money that came from Lenny's blood and sweat."

"She engineered his kidnapping?" Mac asked.

"Are you familiar with Lenny Frost's kidnapping?" Zachery asked.

"Fill me in."

"It's all in my book." Zachery reached into the valise he had set next to his chair and whipped out a hardback book with a picture of a handsome teenaged young man with fiery red hair on the cover. The title read: *Kidnapped: The True Story of the Lenny Frost Abduction.* He slapped the book down on the tabletop. "Read it."

Mac set the book aside. "Give it to me in bullets."

"Lenny was fifteen when he got the starring role in that television show and made all of the teen magazine covers overnight," Zachery said. "From child movie star in the eighties to teen idol of the nineties."

"Were you a fan?" Mac wondered if this writer had been obsessed with Frost. *Why was he so passionate about this case? Why wasn't he writing about current events or important cases? Kidnapped teen stars?*

"Kind of." Zachery plunged ahead. "Two years later, Lenny was snatched while out partying with his friends—Derrick Stillman being one of them. One minute he was drinking and dancing, and the next minute he was gone. The studio paid the ransom, and after the ransom was paid, Lenny called the police from a cabin in the hills. Lenny identified Carson Drake, his assistant on the crew of his show—"

"I thought Drake was an actor," Mac said.

"So you are familiar with the case." The corners of Harris's lips curled. "It's all in the book. The whole truth about how it happened." He slid the book toward the detective.

Mac continued to ignore it. "Tell me."

"Drake had a family to feed," Harris said. "Between jobs he would work on the crew of Lenny's show. Drake was Frost's assistant. They became friends. He trusted Lenny... and Janice Stillman."

"I'm assuming his trust was misplaced."

"You'd be surprised by how they manipulated him," the writer said in a whispered tone that sounded like the two of them were hatching a conspiracy. He inched the book closer to Mac's elbow. "The way I laid it out, you'll think, 'How could someone be that gullible?' Truth is, when you want something badly enough, whether it be success, fame, or even revenge, you'd be surprised by how blind you can be to the truth." He flashed Mac a grin. "Or to what lengths you would go for revenge after being the victim of said manipulation."

Mac finally picked up the book. "Is that the purpose behind your book, Harris? Revenge?"

"I consider it justice." Harris took the book and Mac's pen from his hand. "Consider this yours to keep. Read it. You will find it enlightening."

"I'd still prefer you told me the condensed version."

"I'll be more than happy to give you the highlights, but you'll still need to read the book to get the full story." After signing the inside front cover, Harris slid the book back across the table to Mac. "After the kidnapping, neither Carson Drake nor the million-dollar ransom was ever found. Lenny told the police that he was in a drugged state most of the time, but he heard Drake on the phone telling someone that he had the money and setting up a meeting to split it. His partner, someone on the inside, had plane tickets, and they were going to go their separate ways."

"Why do you think the Stillmans were the ones on the inside?" Mac asked.

"Carson's widow told friends and the police that she thought her husband was away on location for an acting gig," Zachery said. "She was a model and actress. Of course, after the kidnapping, her career was over. Less than a year later, she went missing. Her body was found in an abandoned warehouse used for trendy drug parties by Hollywood brat-pack types. She had been tortured and killed. Detectives claimed she was killed by drug dealers who Drake used to work for."

"Did he owe them money?" Mac asked.

"It's all in the book."

"I'd rather you told me. That could be a strong motive for kidnapping Lenny Frost and holding him for ransom," Mac pointed out. "He kidnapped Lenny for ransom to pay off the drug dealers, but then, when he got all that cash in hand, he decided to take the money and run and left his wife to pay with her life."

Harris jerked up in his seat. "Carson Drake would never have abandoned his wife or his children. The only way he would have not come back was if he were dead. Someone killed him." The writer tapped the top of the conference table when he said, "Drake told his wife that after this job on location Janice Stillman had agreed to represent both of them. Why would he say that if he didn't have an in with her—like helping her commit a major crime? Then, once his usefulness was over, she had him killed. She took the money and ran."

Mac scratched his temple and shook his head in disbelief. "Why would Stillman have her star client abducted?"

"Janice Stillman had been in the business her whole adult life," Zachery said. "She knew the drill. These teen idols last two to three years and then the next generation of fans go to the new face. Lenny was two years in and heavy into the party scene, drugs, and women. He was starting to have trouble on the set. The producers were giving Stillman warnings that if Lenny didn't get his act together, he was going to be out. Stillman saw that Lenny wasn't going to move into bigger roles. He was too unpredictable and inconsistent. Once the show was canceled, his career would be over. Everyone could see the writing on the wall. While Lenny still had some star power, she decided to make a big splash and possibly get him some new publicity at the same time. She had him kidnapped to collect an added bonus from the studio."

"Good theory," Mac said. "Prove it."

"Read the book and you'll see that I prove it. When they found Lenny, he was taken to the hospital to get checked over," Zachery said. "I have statements from nurses and doctors at the hospital. Janice Stillman was raising Cain to have him released as soon as possible." He pounded the tabletop with his finger. "But when he was finally released, do you know where she took him?"

"Where?"

"Not home to his house where he lived with his parents," Zachery said with a shake of his head. "Her house. The Stillman house. Lenny's parents said that even though he was their kid, they didn't see him until three days after that." The corners of his lips curled. "They're both dead now, but they told more than one reporter that Janice Stillman brainwashed Lenny to turn him against them. She whisked him home to her house to drill him about what he may have seen and heard while Drake had him drugged…as though maybe he remembered her killing Drake. She only let him back out in public after she was sure it was safe."

"Do you have proof about any of this?" Mac asked. He had to admit that it all made for a very interesting story.

"A year and a half after the kidnapping," Zachery said, "the studio canceled the show. No big surprise for anyone there. Lenny's flame was going out. Janice dumped Lenny and moved east where she and her husband had the money for a big house in McLean, Virginia, a stone's throw from the Kennedys. Set her hubby up in business and bought herself a fancy club. Where did that money come from? They said she inherited it from a rich aunt." He scoffed. "Give me a break."

Shaking his head to comprehend what the writer was telling him, Mac scooted the chair in closer to the table and folded his hands on the tabletop. "That's pretty circumstantial. Why, after all these years, would Lenny suddenly kill her for revenge?"

With his fingertip, Zachery tapped the book resting at Mac's elbow. "Because in my book I laid out how she and her husband were the masterminds." He laughed. "The Stillmans filed a defamation of character suit against me, but they backed down when they saw all the evidence I had collected." With a smug grin, he folded his arms across his chest. "Then Lenny contacted me. We had a long talk. Things were starting to click together in his mind."

"What things?" Mac asked him.

"Like how this woman who was supposed to be like a second mother to him used him just like everyone else in his life…and he never even saw it coming."

Mac sat back in his seat to study Harris, who was peering back at him with a smirk on his lips. "When did this conversation take place?"

"One week ago."

There was a knock on the door.

"Give me a minute." Mac stood up from the table.

David had the door open for Mac to step into the hallway. "We found Lenny Frost. He's at a lakeside pub in McHenry, only four miles from the murder scene."

"Good," Mac replied.

"No, bad," David said. "He's holding a bunch of people hostage and wants to talk to Mickey Forsythe."

Chapter Four

The Blue Whale Pub, Deep Creek Lake
McHenry, Maryland

The Garrett County Sheriff Department and Maryland
State Police had the bar surrounded and the lakeshore road
blocked off from traffic and spectators by the time David
pulled his cruiser up to the Blue Whale Pub. The police chief
was directed to drive around the barricade.

The local bar was squeezed in between a ritzy restaurant
and lounge and a canoe and kayak rental shop that hadn't
opened yet for the summer season. The sheriff's deputies
were evacuating the lounge of customers and employees.

Mac glanced into the cruiser's back seat to see if the
excitement outside had served to wake up Gnarly from his
party weekend. The German shepherd lifted his head to look
out the window. His ears stood up tall and he cocked his
head as if to decipher the sounds. Then, with a sigh as if to
say, "Wake me up when you need me," he dropped back
down onto the seat.

"Hound," Mac said.

When David slid out of his cruiser, a sheriff's deputy directed him and Mac to a black van parked across the road from the pub. From inside the van, the sheriff and his officers where surveying the scene via audio and video equipment that had been placed at strategic angles around the building where Lenny Frost had taken hostages.

A muscular middle-aged man with a military haircut, Sheriff Christopher Turow looked up from where he was conferring with one of his deputies who was monitoring the surveillance. A newly retired army officer, Turow had held the position for a total of three months.

"O'Callaghan..." The sheriff cast an annoyed glance at Mac. Assuming his slacks and sports coat were the uniform of a civilian, he responded with "Haven't you media vultures done enough damage?"

"This is Mickey Forsythe," David announced.

"Really?" the sheriff scoffed.

"Really?" Mac whispered to David.

"You're the closest thing we've got." David turned back to Sheriff Turow. "Mac Faraday is Robin Spencer's son."

"Mac Faraday." Turow looked Mac up and down. "My deputies have told me about you."

By the glare in the sheriff's eyes, Mac was unsure if he had heard good or bad things about him.

"You said Lenny Frost was asking for Mickey Forsythe—" David reminded the sheriff.

"Who is a fictional movie action hero," Sheriff Turow said. "He might as well be asking to talk to Iron Man."

"Actually," Mac said, "Mickey Forsythe is a literary character. He was a homicide detective until he came into a very large inheritance—"

"Like someone we know," David interjected.

"Mickey's hobby is solving murder cases," Mac said. "He runs into action along the way, but he's not really an action hero, which is what Iron Man is. So the comparison of Mickey Forsythe to Iron—"

"There are a lot of similarities between Mac and Mickey," David said. "It's spooky considering that Robin Spencer had given Mac up for adoption at—"

"We don't really have time for this," Turow cut him off. "Frost says he will only talk to Mickey Forsythe. The guy is looney."

"What about Diablo?" the deputy sitting at the console asked with a laugh.

"What's a Diablo, Parker?" Turow asked.

"He's sleeping off a wild night in the back of my cruiser," David said.

"Are you talking about Gnarly?" Sheriff Turow asked.

Mac swore he saw a hint of congeniality cross the lawman's face. *I guess Gnarly's reputation isn't all bad.*

"The one and only," David said.

"Leave him in the cruiser until we need the big guns." The smile that had come to the corners of his lips disappeared. Sheriff Turow thrust a finger in the police chief's direction as if to make his point. "You've screwed up things enough for one day, O'Callaghan."

"How did I screw this up?" David asked.

"If you had kept a lid on your witness instead of letting him blab all over the media about Lenny Frost killing the Stillmans, then your suspect wouldn't have been the wiser that we were looking for him and taken all those people hostage."

"Okay," David said, "I'll take responsibility for my people not keeping a closer eye on Stillman, but that's all I'm taking responsibility for. Right now, we have a situation and I'm here to offer my help."

"This isn't Spencer," Turow said. "You're out of your jurisdiction."

"That man is a suspect in the murder of two people in Spencer," David said. "That means we have a stake in the outcome here. This is your baby, but if you think we're going to walk away and wait for you to call us when it's over, you've got another think coming."

"Exactly what is the situation?" Mac interrupted to ask. "Do you know how this happened?"

"From what little we know," Turow said, "Lenny Frost went into the pub shortly after it opened at eleven thirty. The television was on. Lenny, along with everyone else in the bar, saw a newscast about him being a prime suspect in the murder of his agent and her husband. The bartender recognized Frost and reached for the phone, but Lenny was too fast for him. There was a fight during which the bartender went for the gun behind the bar. Lenny disarmed him and now he has the gun and is holding everyone hostage. The cook in the back got a call into nine one one before he caught her and called her into the bar area with the rest of the hostages. He took the cook's phone and told the emergency operator that he wants to talk to Mickey Forsythe."

"Do you know how many hostages he has?" David asked.

"One is a kid," Turow said. "Bartender's wife and little boy came in for lunch with Daddy."

"Great," David said with sarcasm.

"The operator said the cook was able to list the owner, two regular customers, and a woman who came in alone."

Mac counted off on his fingers. "So we have the bartender and his family, the bar owner, the cook, and three customers. Eight hostages."

"Have you ever met Lenny Frost?" the sheriff asked Mac. "Is that why he wants to talk to you?"

Mac shook his head. "Never met him. I saw him perform at his comedy club, but that was years ago—back when I was a detective. My ex-wife was a fan of his back when she was a teenager. If my talking to him can help…"

When Turow looked dubious, David said, "Mac was a detective in DC for over twenty years. He's trained and licensed in the state of Maryland. We're not talking about some civilian from off the street. Let him try."

Turow waved Mac over to the phone. "We got a direct line into the pub just before you got here."

Deputy Parker stood up to offer Mac his seat. The sheriff picked up the receiver and handed it to Mac. When Mac reached for it, the sheriff pulled it back. "Just talk to him and find out exactly what he wants. Try to get a sense of his state of mind—besides looney."

"I know what to do." Mac took the phone.

The sheriff pressed the button. Everyone in the van grew quiet and crowded in closer to listen and observe. The phone at the other end of the line was picked up on the fourth ring.

"Blue Whale Pub and Grill. We're closed for a police stand-off right now," the deep baritone voice answered.

Sheriff Turow rolled his eyes in David's direction. "Told you," he mouthed. He moved his finger in a circled at his temple.

"Lenny?" Mac asked. "This is Mickey Forsythe, Lenny. I understand you wanted to talk to me."

"Mickey?" The voice's octave rose with excitement. "Is this really you, Mickey?"

"Yes it is, Lenny," Mac said. "I want to help you."

"Hey, man, I really need your help, Mickey. Remember when you told me that if I never needed your help, no matter what, that you'd be there for me. Did you mean it, Mickey?"

"Of course I meant it, Lenny."

"I really need you now, man." His voice shot up into a squeak.

"And I'm here to help, Lenny," Mac said. "Tell me what you need for me to do."

"Someone is trying to frame me for murder, Mickey," he said. "They killed Janice and Austin, just to frame me. I need you to prove that I didn't do it, man. Will you help me, Mickey? Can you do that for me…your old buddy and pal?"

"Of course, I can, Lenny," Mac said in a smooth tone before plunging on. "But first, I need for you to do something for me. I need you to release the bartender and his family. If you let them go, I'll come in and talk to you about what's going on and we'll get everything straightened out. Can you do that for me, Lenny?"

There was a moment of silence, while Sheriff Turow's face turned red. Mac was surprised to see David's eyes narrow and his face twist into a grimace.

"Okay," Lenny said. "You come in so I can tell you my side of the story and I'll let the bartender, his wife, and the little boy go. I'll meet you at the front door in five minutes."

Click!

"What did you just do?" Sheriff Turow asked.

Mac hung up the phone. "I got him to agree to let the bartender and his family out. We're going from eight hostages down to five."

"Six counting you," the sheriff said. "Do you honestly think he's going to let you go once you go in? Now he's got the great Mac Faraday in there."

"Yes, I'll be in there," Mac said. "I'll know what to do to keep Lenny calm and the hostages safe." Seeing David shaking his head, he added, "I know what I'm doing."

"No you don't," David said.

"This was your idea." The sheriff poked the police chief in the chest. "You said he could help."

David told Mac, "You didn't see Lenny's rap sheet."

"DUIs and assaults," Mac said.

"After the kidnapping, after Lenny sobered up the first time, he started training in martial arts," David explained. "He's got a black belt in karate and a very high degree of training in kickboxing, jujitsu, and a couple of other fighting sports. Not only is he completely unhinged, but he's a trained, highly skilled fighter."

"Which makes him extremely dangerous even if you are able to disarm him," the sheriff agreed.

"He broke a man's arm in two places during a bar fight," David said, "He plead out and got community service and agreed to go into rehab…again. He was in this bar—"

"And already downed two beers since taking everyone hostage," the sheriff said.

"That means he's off the wagon again."

"So he's under the influence, a highly trained fighting machine, and completely off his rocker," Mac said with a shrug. "Sounds like another day of fighting crime in the big city."

"Fact is," David said, "this bad guy can kill you with his bare hands."

"Then I guess my best weapon of defense against Lenny Frost is my quick wit," Mac said while taking his gun out of his holster.

"I'd take Gnarly in there with you if I were you," Sheriff Turow said.

ఴ ఇ ఴ ఇ

They had five minutes to get Mac suited up to go inside the bar. It went without saying that he was not going inside without protection, even if he was unarmed. Bogie retrieved a ballistics vest from the back of his cruiser while David gathered other equipment for Mac to take inside.

Seeing Mac getting suited up, Gnarly abruptly woke up and jumped to his feet. Yelping, he scratched at the back door of the cruiser.

"I guess you've finally recovered from the afterglow," David said while studying the screen of his computer tablet. Satisfied, he slipped out of the cruiser and opened the back door to let Gnarly outside.

The German shepherd galloped over to where Mac was taking instructions from the sheriff. As soon as he laid his eyes on the sheriff, Gnarly stopped.

Sheriff Turow stopped in mid-sentence to look at the German shepherd who cocked his head at the lawman. Then, with his tail wagging, he ran up to the sheriff. Jumping up, Gnarly planted his front paws on the sheriff's shoulders and licked his face.

"Gnarly, mind your manners." Mac grabbed the dog by the collar and lowered his feet to the ground. "I'm sorry, he doesn't do that to people he's never met." When Gnarly made another attempt to greet the lawman, Mac pulled him back.

Sheriff Turow wiped the dog drool from his lips with the back of his hand. "That's okay. I like dogs. He must have sensed that." Once again, his tough exterior melted to reveal a smile. "He's a beautiful dog, and smart, too...based on what I've heard from my deputies."

"Smartest dog I've ever seen." David handed a tiny round instrument to Mac. "He used to be in the army. Wonder why they kicked him out?"

Gnarly sat down in front of the sheriff. The two of them locked eyes.

"Maybe because he was smarter than his CO," Sheriff Turow muttered in a low voice. He flashed Gnarly a quick smile.

Suddenly, the German shepherd went around to Mac's side where he brushed his snout against his master's thigh.

Spotting Mac attaching something to the top of his shirt above the ballistic vest, Turow asked, "What's that?"

"It's a button cam." David held out the tablet for the sheriff to see. "We'll be able to see, hear, and record everything that goes on inside the pub." The device that Mac pinned to the top of his shirt was identical to a button.

"You have a button cam? Our department doesn't have a button cam."

"*I* have a button cam," Mac said. "It was a gift from my daughter. She's a senior studying forensic psychology at William and Mary in Williamsburg."

David handed Mac another small device. "This is a bug. Just in case you need to leave and Frost allows you to come out, then we can still keep tabs of what is going on inside. When you get a chance, attach it to something in the center of the pub, like the underside of a table."

Mac turned to the sheriff. "Any toys you want me to take in for you?"

"All I have is this." Sheriff Turow gave him a hand-held radio. "Channel nine. Before you do anything for Frost, get the names of each of the hostages and make sure they're all okay. Call it in here so that we can check them out in case friends or family are looking for them. We need a signal from you that you want us to move in—that you're in trouble. A code word. Pick a word that isn't likely to slip out in normal conversation but easy to remember."

Mac glanced down at where Gnarly was gnawing at the toe of his shoe like it was a chew toy. "Beast."

"Beast it is." Turow nodded to Deputy Parker to take note of the code word.

"Are we ready?" Mac asked David who was checking the reception on the tablet.

David gave him a thumbs up sign.

Taking in a deep, cleansing breath, Mac made his way around the barricade to cross the parking lot toward the small bar perched along the shore of Deep Creek Lake. The expansive, glitzy restaurant and lounge located on the other side of their parking lot made the pub look even drearier.

Why did Lenny Frost stop here? If he had committed two murders, he should have been getting out of town. He had over twelve hours to escape. He could have been in two other states within less than an hour. Why did he stick around? Why did he come to this dive?

The cold wet touch on his hand made Mac aware that he was not alone. Abruptly, he realized Gnarly was keeping in step with him and by his side. Mac stopped and pointed back to where David and the sheriff were watching from the other side of the barricade. "Gnarly, go back."

"Gnarly, come!" David called to him.

His ears standing at attention, Gnarly turned to Mac and sat down.

Mac pointed across the parking lot to where a line of officers, with their weapons aimed at the pub, were waiting. "Go!"

His eyes not leaving Mac's face, Gnarly stared up at him.

"You're not going in there." Mac reached for his collar to lead him back, but Gnarly dodged his hand and ran for the front door of the pub.

Aware of laughter behind him, Mac raced up behind Gnarly. As soon as they got to the door, it opened. Gnarly slipped inside so quickly that Lenny Frost, focused on Mac, didn't notice. His hands up, Mac stopped. With both hands on the grip, Lenny was aiming a 45-caliber Ruger semi-automatic in his face.

"Lenny," Mac gasped out. "It's me…Mickey…Mickey Forsythe…" He tried to sound upbeat in spite of the gun inches from the space between his eyes. "It's been a long time, buddy."

"I know," Lenny said. "Turn around."

Praying that Lenny didn't intend to shoot the impostor in the back, Mac slowly turned his back on the man with the gun.

"Good," Lenny said. "I see you're unarmed. I guess they didn't get to you. Turn back around and come on in." He explained while Mac stepped inside, "Can't be too careful. They've gotten to everyone I've ever trusted. You're the last friend I have."

The door opened to the bar that was small, musty, and dark. There were only twelve tables in the room with doors on the other side that opened up to the outdoor bar and dock where boaters could come in from the lake for a drink.

On the television over the bar, the news was on with the latest update about a BOLO being out for Lenny Frost, former child star and teen idol.

I hope David gets those news stations to cut off soon. We can't have Lenny knowing what we're doing out there. The news reports will take away any element of surprise.

The hostages were lined up in chairs against the wall with the photo gallery of the bar's history and dartboard. At the end of the row of hostages, a young man who looked barely old enough to be drinking was prying a small boy from Gnarly, who the boy had in a bear hug. The large dog's ears were folded back and his eyes wide at the unexpected and enthusiastic display of affection. "Doggie!" the boy squealed with delight into Gnarly's ears.

"Let go!" the father ordered and pleaded at the same time.

"He loves dogs," the bartender's young wife said in a nervous and tearful voice.

"I love him!" the preschooler shrieked while clinging tightly to Gnarly.

"I see Diablo still has fans wherever he goes," Lenny said to Mac.

"Oh yeah." Mac reminded him, "We agreed. The bartender and his family get to leave. You need to let them go."

Lenny waved his gun at the family. "Okay! Out of here. Bartender, wife, and kid. Leave! Now!"

In the melee over Gnarly, the wife was the only one who noticed that they were free to go. Slapping her husband's back to get his attention, she yelled, "We can go, honey. Grab Timmy and let's get out of here."

"Come along, Timmy!" With his arms around the child's waist, the bartender stood up.

"I don't want to go!" Timmy objected.

When the father lifted the boy, who still had his arms and legs wrapped around Gnarly's mid-section, he lifted the dog up, too. Gnarly's weight took them all back down onto the floor.

"I said to go," Lenny said.

"We're trying!" the wife sobbed.

"Timmy!" the father ordered.

"I want to stay!" Timmy cried out. "I love him!"

"I'll buy you your own puppy!" the father offered in desperation.

"No!" the wife yelled in horror.

"Today?" the boy squealed. "Promise?"

"Promise!" the bartender said in desperation. "Now! Let's go!"

"Okay!" Timmy released Gnarly and ran screaming with delight past Mac and Lenny and out the door. "Puppy! I'm getting a puppy!"

The bartender turned to the wife, whose face was filled with fury. "A puppy!" she yelled. "You promised him a puppy?"

"I had to," he responded with a shrug.

She turned to Lenny. "Shoot me now and put me out of my misery."

Mac grabbed the hand with the gun. "Don't." He gestured to the couple. "Get out now while the getting is good."

The bartender grabbed his wife by the arm and dragged her out the door. Enraged about the promise of a puppy, she cursed the whole way.

Gnarly shook to smooth his fur back into place and took a position in front of the remaining hostages who sat along the wall.

While Lenny studied him, Mac took the opportunity to size up the man with the gun as well. He didn't miss the smell of cigarettes and booze on him.

For an alcoholic, Lenny Frost was surprisingly fit and much taller than Mac expected. His table was in the back when he had seen him perform years before at the comedy club, so he had not noticed how much larger he was than he had appeared to be years before as a teenager on television. While Lenny's body was firm and muscular, his face resembled a tattered roadmap with lines formed from a hard life of drinking and emotional hardship. His hair, which had once been brilliant red, was now the color of rust mixed with gray.

Mac reminded himself that Lenny was the same age as David, who, Mac knew, had no gray. Even if he did, it would be hard to spot with his fair features. David had done two tours with the Marine Special Forces in both Iraq and Afghanistan and he had seen a lot of death and inhumanity. Still, he did not have the hardened, war-torn appearance that Lenny Frost had.

"Man, you haven't aged a bit, Mickey," Lenny said with a laugh.

"I guess I'm living right." Thinking that Lenny was somehow trapped in the time of making the Mickey Forsythe movie that had won him an Oscar, the golden achievement in his young life, Mac said, "You've certainly grown up, Lenny."

"Oh, yeah! And it's been quite a ride."

"I need to check on the hostages." Without waiting for Lenny's consent, Mac went over to the group lined up against the wall in hard-backed chairs. He had to step around Gnarly, who had taken a position between the hostages and the man with the gun.

The cook and bar owner were easy to pick out. They were an older man and a middle-aged, skinny woman with straight brown hair tied back in a ponytail. She wore small, round wire-framed glasses and had a pointy nose. The woman's faded white apron was covered with a large grease stain in the front. She was still wearing the plastic gloves worn for sanitary reasons while handling food. Wearing a clean white apron, the bar owner was a pot-bellied man with a sour expression on his face.

Of the three hostages left, two were elderly men dressed in old sweaters over baggy blue jeans. They both clutched ball caps in their laps. One was for the Pittsburgh Pirates. The other was for the Baltimore Orioles.

The last hostage, a slender redhead with long wavy hair that fell down past her shoulders, was even more out of place than Lenny Frost. Her face and figure were flawless. She wore a spring sweater that hugged every curve in her body and tight jeans with high heel shoes.

The thought that she was a prostitute crossed Mac's mind, but when he got closer, he observed that she didn't have the used-up look that comes with a hooker who has been working for any length of time.

"Is anyone hurt?" Mac asked the group. "Are you all okay?"

"Of course we're not okay," the bar owner blurted. "That lunatic is holding a gun on us. That's not okay!" Shaking his head, he cursed. "Idiot!"

"Shut up, Carl," the cook said before telling Mac, "We're fine."

"You may be fine, Edith," Carl replied, "but I'm not."

"We're not hurt," Edith told Mac.

"I need your names." Mac turned to ensure his button cam projected a clear picture of each of them to those in the command center outside.

"Names, shnames," Carl grumbled. "We've got a mad man pointing a gun at us threatening to kill us, and what do the police do? They send in a dog to entertain the kid and an idiot to take names."

"Shut up, Carl, or I'm going to shoot you myself," Edith said before turning her attention back Mac. "You have to forgive Carl. He hasn't had a bowel movement in two days, and now all this…well, everyone has their limits."

Mac backed up a full step. "Can you give me just the facts, Ma'am?"

"I'm Edith Collins. This grumpy old man is Carl Kincaid."

"This is my restaurant," Carl said.

"Is that what this is?" one of the old men scoffed. "I thought it was the local dump."

"And your name…" Mac asked.

"Bernie," the old man said. "Bernie Stein—like the beer mug." He jerked at thumb at the old man sitting next to him. "This is Hap Goldman. Everyone calls him Hap because he's always happy."

Hap shot Mac a wide toothless grin.

"Nice to meet you, Hap," Mac said.

Bernie grasped Mac's hand. "Do you think you could convince the nut with the gun to let us have a pitcher of beer and watch the game?"

"No one is drinking any beer unless they're paying for it," Carl said.

"As long as we're being held hostage, we might as well make the best of it," Bernie said. "It isn't like we're going anywhere. So why not watch the game? It's Tampa Bay against the Pirates. It's the first game of a doubleheader, and Hap and I want to see it. Then later it's the Chicago Cubs against Arizona."

"No one is drinking my beer!" Carl said.

"Let's see what the man with the gun has to say about that," Bernie said. "Hey, Lenny! The game is about to start. Can we watch it? Carl says we can have beers all the way around! On the house! You can have some, too!"

"I did not say that!" Carl objected.

"Sounds like a party." Lenny pulled out a bar stool and the two elderly man galloped up to the bar. With the excitement of two little boys raiding the ice cream shop, the two men licked their lips when Edith came around behind the bar to pour their beers.

Holding a gun on all of them, Lenny slid a used empty mug that he had been imbibing from since arriving down to the end of the bar for her to refill.

Keeping himself between the hostages and the gunman, Gnarly moved across the bar and lay down on the floor. While he was in the reclining position, his eyes never left Lenny Frost and the gun in his hand.

Carl stood up to confront Mac. "You're the police. Do something! They're stealing my beer!"

"Actually, I'm not the police," Mac told him.

Flabbergasted, Carl sputtered before asking, "Then what are you?"

"A rich man trying to help."

Scoffing, Carl hurried over to the bar where Bernie, Hap, Edith, and Lenny were changing the channel to the baseball game. Their preoccupation was a good thing. Lenny was now watching the game instead of himself on the news.

Mac turned his attention to the last hostage and found that the redhead was watching him with her piercing blue eyes. Her arms were folded under her bosom.

"I didn't catch your name," Mac said.

"That's because I didn't tell you," she replied.

The two of them eyed each other. Once again, Mac was struck with how polished and attractive she was. She did not fit in with the Blue Whale Pub clientele at all.

"LeClair DuBois," she said.

"Where are you from, LeClair?"

"Georgetown, Maryland," she said. "I came out here this weekend with my boyfriend. We were staying at the Wisp when we had a fight and he left. I was stuck here all by myself. I never even heard of Deep Creek Lake until this week. I decided to come have a drink to think and decide what I was going to do next." She cast an eye over in Lenny's direction. "Then he walked in and pulled a gun on all of us." With a hollow laugh, she unfolded her arms and looked down at the toe of her high heel shoe. "Some romantic weekend getaway, huh?" With her head bowed, she gazed up at him through her long eyelashes.

"Yeah, some romantic weekend," Mac said while thinking about Archie, who was waiting for him at home with twelve dozen white roses. He wondered if they had been delivered yet.

Need to get this wrapped up.

A cheer drew Mac's attention back to Lenny, who was leaning on the bar and cheering with Bernie and Hap. They were all downing mugs of beer—even Edith.

"This is the weirdest hostage situation I've ever been in," Mac muttered for those watching in the van.

On his way over to where Lenny was drinking his beer and clutching the gun, Mac casually ran his fingers under the edge of a table to attach the listening device.

Lenny was startled when he clasped him on the shoulder. His eyes widened before he seemed to recall who Mac was and why he was there.

"We have to talk," Mac told him. "I need to know what's going on. The police think you killed your agent—"

"I didn't kill her or Austin," Lenny said.

"Can you prove it? Where were you last night between six and ten o'clock?"

Mac was accustomed to seeing one of two reactions to the question about an alibi from prime murder suspects: either despair over not having one, or delight over having a solid alibi and being cleared of the crime.

In Lenny's case, the reaction was one of anger. He bit off each word when he spoke to Mac. "I was at the Wisp alone in my suite, drinking myself into oblivion until I passed out and woke up all alone. How's that for an alibi?"

"Not good."

"They knew it. They set me up."

"Who, Lenny? Who brought you here? Why are you here in Deep Creek Lake? Who is behind this?"

"I don't know," Lenny said. "That's why I sent for you. All my life, people have been using me, lying about me—chewing me up and spitting me out. Hell, I've actually gotten used to it. But killing Janice and Austin and framing me? That's new."

"You must have some idea—"

"None."

"Come on, Lenny," Mac said. "People don't go framing other people for no reason at all."

"Someone set me up, Mickey!" Lenny yelled. "First they turned my fans against me with lies about how many drugs I was doing and setting me up for DUIs and all that stuff.

Then they kidnapped me and canceled my show, and then Hollywood blackballed me. Then, just as I was going to make a comeback—just when the door opened again—this happened."

"What door opened, Lenny?"

A smile crossed Lenny's face. "Ronald Cunningham."

"The movie producer?" By the grin on Lenny's face, Mac sensed that he had the right man. Ronald Cunningham was the biggest action-adventure moviemaker in Hollywood.

"I don't have to tell you about it, Mickey," Lenny said. "Cunningham is making three movies about you and he wants me to reprise my role from the first one—the role that won me the Academy Award. This is it. This will be my comeback. No longer will I be a has been. With that role—they'll see that I still have it."

Unsure of what to say, afraid that the wrong thing would send Lenny over the edge, Mac refrained from shaking his head to show doubt.

"That's why I came to Deep Creek Lake," Lenny said. "I was meeting Cunningham and Janice here to talk about my contract."

"Ronald Cunningham was coming here?" Mac gestured to the dive where they were. A multi-millionaire movie producer holding a power meeting at the Blue Whale Pub? No way.

Lenny nodded.

"Who set up the meeting?" Mac asked. "Your agent?"

"Actually, Cunningham's assistant did," Lenny said. "They put me up in the penthouse suite at the Wisp last night. Five-star treatment the whole way."

"You call *this* place five star?"

"She must have picked the wrong place," Lenny replied.

"Why didn't you stay at your agent's house?"

"Janice's hubby, Austin, was a bastard," Lenny swore. "He blamed me for everything. He was the one who convinced Janice to abandon me. Ever since she brought me out here, Austin was riding her ass to dump me again. Last year, he banned me from their house after I tripped and landed on top of their dining room table in the middle of their fancy dinner party."

Recalling that the passcode for the Stillman's security system had been changed in the last month, Mac asked him, "Could Janice or Derrick have given you the security passcode for their home here on Deep Creek Lake?"

Lenny scoffed. "Why would they? Austin flat out said that I am not allowed to set foot on their property. Besides, that paranoid old man changes the code after every trip out here."

Thinking over this information, Mac scratched behind his ear. "If that was the case, then why would Janice have arranged for you to meet with Ronald Cunningham here? Why not in the city?"

With an expression of exaggerated ignorance, Lenny made a broad gesture of shrugging his shoulders.

Mac took his cell phone from his pocket and hit a button on the screen.

"Who are you calling?" Lenny held up the gun.

"Ronald Cunningham." Mac spoke into the phone. "Alexis…how are you this fine Saturday? Is he there?"

"You have Ronald Cunningham on speed dial?" Lenny asked.

"He can't make those movies about my life without my permission, can he?" Mac replied before turning back to the phone. "Ronald? No I haven't signed them yet. Hey, are you negotiating to sign Lenny Frost for a role in the Forsythe films?" Not wanting Lenny to see the answer in his face, Mac turned away. "Could any of your people have been talking to his people? That's what I thought. I'll have my business manager call you next week. Thanks. I've got to go."

When Mac turned back around, Lenny's face was as red as his hair used to be.

"Lenny, I'm sorry," Mac said in a soft voice while raising his hands up in a sign of defense. "Ronald Cunningham has no intention of reprising your role from the first film. He doesn't even have the rights to make the movies because we've been unable to reach an agreement. Why would he have signed you up when he still doesn't have the rights to make the movies?"

"They set me up."

"Yes, someone did," Mac said. "Someone lured you to Deep Creek Lake so that you would be in the vicinity when they killed your agent and her husband, and had you come here to…" Not having an answer, Mac glanced around.

"They're out to get me!" Abruptly, Lenny raised the gun and aimed it at Mac's face.

Barking, Gnarly jumped up to his feet.

"Halt!" Mac held his hand straight up while ordering Gnarly to stand down.

Abruptly, the joy of the ballgame and the beers was over. Edith backed as far away from the bar as she could get. Keeping his eye on the gun, Carl slid in behind the bar and ushered her behind him.

"They've *always* been jealous of me," Lenny said.

"Who, Lenny?"

"Them!"

"Who are they, Lenny? Tell me so that I can help you," Mac said. "Who would want to frame you for killing Janice and Austin Stillman? Who would want to kill them and why?"

"I don't know!" Lenny grasped the side of his head with one hand while waving the gun in Mac's direction with the other. "I loved Janice! She was the only one—even my parents thought I was a loser—but Janice believed in me. I'd live with them for weeks. They were like my family. They even took me on vacation with them. She was good to me, man! Why would I have killed her?"

He picked up his beer mug and flung it across the room. "I know why! To get to me! They have been working to ruin me ever since—jealous! They're all envious of me and my talent and they have been trying to take me down and they've managed to succeed and this—this is the final straw to break me—killing the only people who have been loyal to me my whole life and framing me for it!"

As if struck with a sudden thought, he grasped the gun with both hands. His red-rimmed eyes were wide as he held the gun steady, with it pointed at Mac's chest. "You want to help me?"

Still clutching his cell phone, Mac held his hands up. "Yes I do, Lenny. I do want to help you. Tell me what you want me to do."

"Find out who it is," Lenny said. "Find out who killed Janice and who is framing me."

Mac looked around at the hostages gathered in the bar. Gnarly was staring at the gun, while waiting for his signal to disarm the gunman.

Too risky right now. If the gun went off when Gnarly's jaws clamped down on his hand, a bullet could ricochet and hit any of them.

Lenny's eyes went to the clock above the bar.

12:21 in the afternoon.

"Midnight," Lenny said. "You have until midnight."

"Midnight to do what?" Mac asked.

"Midnight to prove I didn't kill them and find out who has been behind this conspiracy to ruin me my whole life."

"That's a tall order," Mac said.

"If anyone can do it, Mickey, you can."

"And if I don't?"

"You have twelve hours to murder," Lenny said in a low, steady tone. "At midnight, I'm going to kill everyone in this bar—you last, so that you can see everyone die before you—because you failed. Then I'll shoot myself."

CHAPTER FIVE

Garrett County Sheriff's Command Center

David bent over the computer tablet that was picking up the feed from the button cam. With a few touches of his fingers on the screen, he captured the image and sent it to his cell phone.

"What are you doing?" Sheriff Turow asked. "O'Callaghan, need I remind you that this is not your case? My department is handling this situation."

"That's right." David stood up. "You're handling the hostage situation and I'm investigating a double homicide in my jurisdiction. You heard Frost. He's giving Mac until midnight to solve these murders and then he's going to kill everyone in there, including my man. I'm not going to let that happen."

Turning around in the tight confines of the van, David found Bogie blocking his way out. "Bogie, you stay here. I want to know everything that they're doing. Keep me informed about everything that happens inside that pub."

"Where are you going?" Bogie asked.

"Back to the station to question Derrick Stillman," David said while climbing out of the van. "He's got the most to gain from his parents' deaths, and he was close to Frost. Seems to me he's the best place to start when looking for suspects."

David waited until he was outside before taking his smart phone out and forwarding the image he had sent to his phone to one of his favorite numbers. In the text message accompanying the photo he wrote, "Meet me @ station. I need U."

ଓ ଯ ଔ ଯ

"Okay, Lenny," Mac said in a calm tone while stepping toward the pub's small stage where Lenny had propped himself on a stool. He shifted to place himself between Lenny and the gun and the hostages, who had returned to watching the ballgame, at the bar. "You want me to prove that you didn't kill your agent and her husband. I can't do that unless you help me. Tell me who would have killed them to frame you. Give me a name."

"A name?" Lenny asked with a loud scoff. "There are so many."

"Seriously, Lenny." Mac lifted one foot onto the stage and leaned in to him. "Two people were murdered. You're being framed. That's more than just simple jealousy. Someone wants you out of the way. Who would want you out of the way enough to kill two people?"

"Sally Riggleman," Lenny said without hesitation.

"Who's Sally Riggleman?"

"No-talent comic wannabe at the club—always trying to upstage me," Lenny said. "Bitch has no talent. It was only her luck that Janice happened to be there when she auditioned and liked her. Said we needed a female comic to balance me out."

One of Mac's eyebrows arched. "So Janice went against you to hire this other comic?"

Lenny's temper flared. "I'd always had the say on what comics we hired and what ones we didn't. We agreed to that when Janice called me out from Hollywood."

"Where you were making a big splash," Mac noted in a tone heavy with sarcasm.

Lenny whipped up the gun and aimed it to Mac's forehead. Edith, the barmaid, screamed. With a growl, Gnarly jumped to his feet.

"Wait, Diablo!" Mac's eyes crossed to look at the barrel of the gun. "If you shoot me, Lenny, you'll have no one to help you. So I suggest you put that gun away and tell me about Sally Riggleman and why she'd want to kill Janice, the one who went to bat to get her a job at the club."

Lenny hesitated before lowering the gun. "We have an open mic on Wednesday night. Winners of open mic perform that weekend. A few weeks ago, Sally showed up and did this lame routine about women and how they think differently from men and crap like that. Janice happened to be there that night. I mean, like—she's never there!"

"But she owns the club," Mac said.

"Janice didn't get it," Lenny said. "She doesn't—like..." He threw up his hands with a laugh. "Get this. She thought Sally was hilarious. She was laughing so hard she was crying but—" With the barrel of the gun, he jabbed Mac in the chest while saying in a mocking tone, "Sally doesn't even use the F-word in her routine. She's that lame."

"The nerve," Mac breathed. "And people still laughed at her."

"She must have had a bunch of friends come in on Friday and Saturday," Lenny said, "because the whole audience was rolling on the floor laughing their fool heads off, and the next thing I know, Janice is ordering Derrick to sign her on for six months."

Mac shook his head. "If Janice did that to me, I'd be first in line to kill her. We need to go pick Sally Riggleman up right away."

"Point is," Lenny said in a low voice. "Sally got a big head over all that and has been nosing around the club trying to work her way into my gig as the headliner and host ever since. Last week, I caught her listening outside Derrick's office during a private meeting. She's looking for dirt on me, and I called her on it. I told her that the only way she was going to take my spotlight was to kill Janice because she would never replace me as headliner."

CS   &O   CS   &O

Spencer Police Station

"Is it true?" Tonya sprang up from behind her desk when David came into the station's reception area. "We have until midnight to find out who killed the Stillmans and we better pray to God that it isn't Lenny Frost or he's going to kill everyone in that bar—including Mac?"

"You've been talking to Bogie." David noticed two men in suits stand up from where they were waiting in the reception area. "Is their son still here?"

"In the observation room," Tonya said. "Fletcher finished taking his statement but told him to wait. The other guy, Zachery Harris, the writer—he hurried out of here like he had places to go right after you guys left."

She pointed to the men, who David was eying. "These two came in about a half an hour ago. They're insisting that they have something important to talk to you about."

The taller of the two men stepped forward and opened his federal agent badge for David to examine. "Police Chief O'Callaghan, I'm Special Agent Alex Fredericks, and this is Special Agent Richard Saunders. We're with the DEA—Drug Enforcement Administration—"

"I know what DEA stands for." David wished he could suck back the arrogance that had slipped into his tone.

Agent Fredericks slipped his badge back into the inside breast pocket of his suit. "We'd like to discuss the Stillman murder case with you."

Aware that they were standing in the open reception area, Agent Saunders gestured in the direction of David's office on the second floor. "Can we talk in private?"

Consenting, David hurried up the stairs to his corner office that had a view of the lake and docks behind the police station. He wasted no time in demanding answers after shutting the office door. "I hope you can excuse my bluntness," the police chief said, "but we have a serious situation right now. One of my men, and a very good friend of mine, is being held hostage by Lenny Frost over in McHenry. Frost has given us until midnight to find out who committed these murders." David clasped his hands on his hips. "So I'm not going to waste any time playing games with you two. If you have anything to help me get those people out, you better give it to me right now."

"That's why we're here," Agent Fredericks said. "There's something you need to know and keep in mind about this case."

"What is that? Out with it."

"Lenny's Comedy Café has been under investigation by the DEA for several months," Fredericks said. "It came to our attention that the manager had become a major dealer with one of the most influential drug operators in the DC area and he was working with some major uptown players—all out of the club."

"Are you telling me that Janice Stillman and her husband were killed because they were involved in drug dealing?" David suppressed the groan that wanted to escape from his lips.

"She wasn't involved, and neither was her husband," Agent Saunders said. "We managed to clear them of involvement. They owned the club, but they left the day-to-day operation to their son, Derrick."

"We needed someone we could trust on the inside," Agent Frederick said. "So a month ago, we confronted Janice Stillman and her husband with the evidence that we had collected."

"What was their reaction?" David asked.

"Outrage," Saunders said. "They agreed to go along with everything we asked, even to help our undercover agent get inside—anything—just so that would help their son get some leniency when it was all over."

"Is Derrick Stillman involved in the drug operation?"

Agent Fredericks nodded his head. "The comedy club is nothing more than a front for him. When the Stillmans learned that at our last meeting, they confided in us that they were changing their wills. Derrick was going to be disinherited and the comedy club was going to go to Lenny Frost."

David let out a breath. "Did Derrick know that?"

"That we don't know," Saunders said. "They were keeping the information a secret until after we made our arrest."

"You say the club is under investigation," David said. "Does that mean you have Derrick under surveillance?" When the two agents exchanged glances and said nothing, the police chief took it as a yes. "Where was Derrick last night?"

"He was on a date with a young woman," Fredericks said. "He went to her apartment in Georgetown and didn't leave until shortly after three o'clock this morning. He came straight here."

"Which means he has an alibi for the murder," David said. "Yet…he could have paid one of his drug dealer friends to do it." He held up his hand in a signal for them to wait when his cell phone vibrated on his hip. Seeing that the call was from Bogie, he tapped the screen to put him on speaker phone. "Yeah, Bogie."

"Lenny gave Mac the name of a potential suspect who he believes had motive to kill Janice Stillman."

David grabbed a notepad and pen from his desk. "Give it to me."

"Sally Riggleman."

Glancing up from the paper, David saw a smirk cross the lips of Agent Fredericks while Agent Saunders's eyes widened into an expression of concern. "Who is she?" David asked Bogie while keeping his eyes on the agents.

Bogie said, "Lenny claims she's a regular ladder-climbing comic out to steal his spotlight in anyway possible."

"And killing the Stillmans accomplishes that how?"

"David," Bogie said in a low voice. "Lenny's light is on but no one is home. His mind is so twisted that he thinks this murder is only to get to him. The guy is downright paranoid. But he gave Mac that name. Do you want me to stay here or track her down?"

"I'll track her down," David said. "Thanks, Bogie. Keep up the good work." He still had his thumb on the disconnect button when he looked up from the desk to the agents. "This Sally Riggleman is your agent, isn't she?"

"We can't confirm or deny that," Agent Saunders said. "You have to understand that, O'Callaghan."

"Of course, I understand," David said. "I've worked undercover operations. But you heard my deputy chief. Lenny is crazy."

"We know that," Fredericks said. "We wouldn't be surprised if he flipped out and killed the Stillmans because he was afraid he would lose the spotlight to Riggleman."

"He'd inherit the club and be the headliner for the rest of his life," David said.

"Exactly," Fredericks said. "Between motive and being nuts—"

"You need to find out what Derrick Stillman knew about his parents' will and what was going on with Lenny Frost," David said. "People are going to die if we don't get this sorted out."

CHAPTER SIX

"Can everybody hear me?" Lenny said into the microphone on the stage.

Perturbed that the ballgame was being interrupted,
Bernie frowned into his beer. Even Hap's toothless grin fell
when he turned in his seat on the bar stool. From the stage,
Lenny grinned at his captive audience working on their
second pitcher of beer. With a groan, Gnarly dropped down
onto the floor and buried his snout in his front paws.

Mac tore his attention from LeClair DuBois, who was
watching him from out of the corner of her eyes while facing
the deck at the back of the pub. Unlike the other hostages, she
was sipping a glass of warm white wine that Edith had served
to her. When the cook walked by with the glass, Mac had
caught a sniff of the cheap wine, which turned his stomach.
He noticed LeClair grimace after taking the first sip.

Lenny waved his gun. "Now that I have your attention,
I'd like to take this time to thank you all for coming today. I
hope everyone is having a good time. A funny thing happened
to me on the way over here. After years of licking the curb, I'm
once again on top. I've finally made the top ten—yep, that's

right! I'm the most wanted man in the country right now—as in the FBI's ten most wanted. How many of you out there have ever made the ten most wanted listed?" He waved the gun around the pub. "Don't be shy. Let's have a show of hands. Who all here is wanted for a couple of murders?"

Hap's smile fell and he turned to Bernie, who asked Mac in a loud whisper, "Is he going to be doing that throughout the game?"

Mac went over to the stage.

"Oh, we have a volunteer, ladies and gentlemen," Lenny called out into the microphone. "Tell the audience your name." He held out the microphone for Mac to speak into.

"Lenny…"

"How about that? My name's Lenny, too. What did you do to get in the top ten?"

When Lenny held out the microphone to him, Mac snatched it out of his hand. "You gave me less than twelve hours to find the Stillmans' killer. Well that isn't going to happen without you pulling yourself together and helping me."

"I told you," Lenny replied. "Sally Riggleman. Pick her up, grill her, and she'll confess. Either that or pin it on her somehow…if you want everyone here to survive the bar's last call."

"And you don't? Have you that little compassion?"

"Listen," Lenny replied in a low voice. "No one gives a shit about me—never did. Did you ever call me even once after the movie wrapped? No! You just moved on to the next case and left me behind—just like everyone else. So why should I give a shit about you, Diablo—" He waved the gun in the direction to the group at the bar. "Or them?"

Unsteady on his feet, he turned in the direction of the one hostage who had not bellied up to the bar.

"How about if I prove to you and everyone else how serious I am by shooting her?" Lenny aimed the gun at LeClair.

She whirled in her seat. Oddly, instead of screaming and ducking out of the line of fire, she glared at the threat.

Mac grabbed for Lenny's wrist, but Lenny was too fast for him. Pulling back, he thrust the gun into Mac's face. "Back away, Sport, or I'll make you my first victim."

Mac's hands shot up. "Okay, okay. Calm down, big guy." His tone was as calm as possible in the face of Lenny, his eyes crazed, waving the gun around. "You've already proven to me and everyone outside how serious you are. Killing hostages won't prove your claim that you are not a murderer."

"You were the only one who treated me like I mattered. How was I supposed to know you were acting?" He laughed. "Of course, you were acting. That's what everyone around me has done my whole life. I should have known better, but hey! What was I supposed to think? I was a kid. How was I supposed to know that the drug—all that fame and wealth and success, everyone telling me that I was 'it'—was only temporary?"

"No one knows that, Lenny."

A snarl came to Lenny's lips when he thrust the gun in Mac's direction. "It wasn't temporary for you, Mickey."

Gnarly was on his feet. Mac held out his hand in a signal for the dog to stop.

"What would you do if someone took all of it away from you, Mickey?" Lenny asked. "Only then would you find out that you, too, are an addict."

"I'm fortunate not to be addicted to anything, Lenny."

"Everyone who tastes it is addicted to it."

"Tastes what?"

"Success. Fame. Stardom. Once you taste it, you never want it to stop. You give that to a kid, like I was, then of course he'll do anything to get his toys back when you take them away."

"Which led to your other addictions," Mac said.

"It's worse than heroin." Lenny's eyes were glazed over. "Even people who get close to it, but can't quite grasp it, will risk everything—"

Mac saw the hand holding the gun go limp as Lenny became lost in a memory—of what, Mac did not know.

"—even put his life in the line of fire and get himself killed for that one chance at the brass ring—"

Flexing his fingers to make a grab for the weapon, Mac inched in closer.

"That's what got Drake killed," Lenny said in a loud whisper. "His addiction. Wasn't my fault."

Mac's eyes met Lenny's.

Startled to see Mac so close to him, Lenny leapt back out of his reach and aimed the gun at him. "What are you doing?"

"I want to help you, Lenny."

"Then have your people pick up Sally Riggleman and pin these murders on her." Keeping his eyes on Mac, Lenny lowered himself down to pick up the beer mug next to his floor. He drained what was left in the glass.

Scratching his neck, Mac shook his head. "Do you seriously think that she set up this phony meeting here? That she lured you here? That she killed two people to maneuver herself into the headline act? How could she ensure that after all that she would end up being the headliner? It doesn't make sense, Lenny. Is there anyone else you can give me?"

"Like who?"

Mac propped his foot up on the stage. Peering into Lenny's bloodshot eyes, he asked, "Did you recently have a conversation with Zachery Harris about your kidnapping?"

Lenny's chest expanded with the deep breath that he sucked in. "Yeah, what about it?"

"He wrote a book about it," Mac said. "About your kidnapping, and he named Janice Stillman as the mastermind behind it."

"She wouldn't do that to me."

"Seems he made quite a case for it," Mac said.

"Not really," Lenny said with a chuckle. "Yeah, I talked to him. He called me because he wanted me to tell him what happened. Of course, I wouldn't help him. Last I heard, Janice sued his butt."

"His butt, but not the rest of him?" Mac replied.

It took a full moment for Lenny to catch onto Mac's quip. Laughing, he grasped him by the shoulder. "I like you. You have a weird sense of humor." His breath was so foul that Mac had to turn his head to cough.

"Hey, Edith!" Lenny released his grip on Mac's shoulder. "My beer mug is empty. Can you help me out?"

"Coming up!" Edith was in the midst of refilling the pitcher from which she, Carl, Bernie, and Hap were drinking.

A crash came from behind Mac.

Instinctively grabbing for the gun that he usually wore on his hip, he turned around to find the table where LeClair DuBois had been sitting was now overturned. She lay sprawled on the floor. Her legs were twitching.

"Oh, dear!" Edith hurried around from behind the bar to help the fallen girl.

Mac grabbed the hand-held radio and pressed the button to call the sheriff in the command center on the other side of the parking lot. "We need some help in here."

CHAPTER SEVEN

Spencer Police Department

Archie was at work on her laptop at an empty desk in the squad room when David escorted the two federal agents downstairs and out the door. "Took you long enough," she called to him through the open doorway.

"They're feds and were willing to talk," David replied while on his way into the squad room. "I don't get that very often. I assume Tonya filled you in." He went over to her desk to look at the laptop's monitor. The screen was filled with a montage of websites and databases that made no sense to him. Only Archie would be able to decipher it.

"I've been running a full background check on Lenny Frost," she said.

"So is everyone else right now."

"He's been blackballed from Hollywood for years," she reported.

"Due to his drug problems," David said with a nod of his head. "Tell—"

"Not just drugs," she interjected. "He's got some real emotional problems."

"Paranoia," David said. "We picked that up from the audio feed."

"Symptoms of manic depression as well," she said. "He was diagnosed years ago during rehab at the Recovery Center in Hollywood. He's supposed to be on meds. Whether he stays on them or not is up for debate."

"He shouldn't be drinking while on those meds. He's been drinking one beer after another since taking those hostages." David cracked a smile. "So have the hostages."

"Are you serious?"

"It's a very unusual collection of hostages."

"I'll say," she replied. "If I was taken hostage by a man with a gun, I would want to be cold-stone sober in order to keep my wits about me."

"If we get lucky, they'll all pass out drunk and we can just go in, wake them up, and send them home," David said.

"Or Lenny could go completely off the deep end and shoot everyone before midnight," she replied.

"I thought you were the optimist."

"I was until I got a look at Lenny's history," she said. "He's also got a host of assault charges against him. Black belt in martial arts." Her emerald green eyes were ablaze when she turned to him. "Why did you let Mac go in there?"

"Does Mac listen to you when you tell him not to do something?"

"You're the chief of police," she argued.

"Like my orders mean something to him," he said with scoff. "What did you expect me to do?"

"You have a gun," she said. "Why don't you use it?"

"I can't shoot Mac." David stood up straight. "That's illegal."

Tears came to her eyes. "What if Lenny kills him?"

Draping an arm across her shoulders, he gave her a hug. "Mac's going to be fine. Gnarly's with him."

She pulled away and rose up from her chair so fast that David stumbled. He had to catch himself on the next desk to keep from landing on the floor. "You let Gnarly go, too? How could you? What if that maniac shoots him?"

David became aware of another pair of eyes glaring at him from Tonya's desk in the reception area. "You let that poor innocent dog go in there with that lunatic?"

"Gnarly is about as innocent as the serpent in the Garden of Eden," David said. "If you don't believe me, ask every shop owner whose inventory he has regularly pilfered. Gnarly's picture is actually up in most businesses around Deep Creek with a red circle and a slash through it."

"So he's got sticky paws," Tonya said with a shrug. "That's still no excuse to send him into the line of fire."

Their eyes, filled with fury, were locked on David from both sides.

"Archie, you can help," David said.

Her eyes narrowed.

"I'm suspicious about one of the hostages in the pub." David brought up the image on his cell phone to show Archie. "She doesn't seem to fit with the rest of the customers. I'm wondering if she's part of the set up to lure Lenny Frost to the pub." He held up the phone for her to see. "The name she gave Mac was LeClair DuBois. I sent this picture to you. Can you run a facial recognition on her to see if she has any other identities or background that we should know about?"

Still, Archie did not move.

Tonya's glare broke when the phone rang.

"Archie, I'm sorry," he said. "I hate it when you get mad at me. Will you accept my apology?"

"After this is over, you won't let Mac and Gnarly do something stupid like this again?"

"Next time I'll shoot them before I let them go into another hostage situation."

"You promise?" she asked.

"Promise."

She plopped down at her laptop and went to work bringing up the image he had sent her.

"It's Bogie, Chief." Tonya hit the mute button on the phone. "One of the hostages has collapsed. The EMTs are going in to remove her."

"Lenny is letting her go?" David asked.

Tonya shrugged her shoulders. "I guess so."

"Which hostage is it?" David asked while the phone on his hip vibrated.

"I'll find out." Tonya reached to tap the mute button.

"If it's that DuBois woman," David said while bringing his phone to his ear, "send Fletcher to the hospital and tell him to stick to her like glue. I want to question her after Archie brings up what she can find on her."

David turned around to make his way down the hall to the interrogation room where Derrick Stillman was still waiting. He was surprised the victims' son hadn't started screaming for his lawyer yet. "O'Callaghan here," he said into the phone.

"Chief O'Callaghan," the police officer from Maryland replied, "I hope you haven't released that suspect whose alibi you asked us to check out for you?"

"No," David said. "Why?"

"Because it looks like it's worthless," the officer said. "From what we've been able to find out, Madelyn Preston doesn't exist. She doesn't have a driver's license. We finally got the cell phone number for the woman whose name is on the lease for that apartment and managed to get in touch with her on an aircraft carrier in the Pacific. She didn't sublet her apartment. She has no idea who Madelyn Preston is."

David halted in front of the interrogation room door. "His alibi is a lie?"

"That's what we think. You still got him?"

"You bet." David disconnected the call and placed his hand on the door knob. He was a hair's breath away from throwing open the door and barging in to demand the truth before he remembered his conversation minutes before with the two DEA agents.

Derrick Stillman was under surveillance. He has an alibi. The DEA confirmed that he had gone into the apartment building for a date with a woman. Then why lie about who he had spent the night with? Unless he's not the one lying? Only one way to find out.

David threw open the door to the interrogation room. Derrick Stillman jumped in his seat when the police chief slammed the door shut. He couldn't move fast enough to escape when David smashed his hand down flat on the tabletop.

"You've got some serious problems, Derrick."

The young man regrouped to return his glare. "Yeah! Number one, my parents have been murdered and you've had me cooped up in here. Have you guys picked up Lenny Frost yet?"

"Oh, we have Lenny all right," David said. "He's holding several people, including a very good friend of mine, hostage. But right now, that's the least of your problems. Your alibi is junk."

"What do you mean?"

"It's a lie!" David pounded the tabletop and leaned across at him. "Lying to me is a big mistake, Stillman. You know why? Because it wastes my time. I hate to have my time wasted—especially when I don't have it to waste. Not only that, but the only thing worse than a liar is a stupid liar." He rose his voice an octave. "Did you really think we weren't going to check it out, Stillman? Did you really think that we weren't going to look for Madelyn Preston to confirm your alibi?"

Derrick's glare was transformed to bewilderment followed by fear. "I gave your people her cell phone number. Call her."

"There's no answer," David said. "Her cell phone is turned off."

"She must be—"

"She doesn't exist, Derrick!" David leaned in closer. "Madelyn Preston is a lie—just like your alibi!"

"Hey!" Derrick thrust his chin out in defiance. "Who I spent the night with last night was no lie!"

David cocked an eyebrow. The corner of his lip curled. "Are you telling me that you slept with her? You were with her all night? In her bed?"

Derrick opened his mouth to speak, but no words came out. David could see his mind working. The standoff broke up when Derrick averted his gaze.

Slipping into the chair across from him, David softened his tone. "How long have you known this woman?"

Derrick took a couple of beats to answer with a shrug. "A week?"

"How did you meet her?"

Again, Derrick hesitated before replying. "She asked to borrow my phone to make a call. Her cell battery was dead and she needed to call her agent to tell him that her car had broken down."

"Where did this happen?"

"The coffee shop where I eat breakfast every morning."

"Every morning?" David asked. "Same time every morning?"

Derrick's face was blank.

"What type of agent was she needing to call?" David asked. "Real estate?"

"Talent," Derrick said. "She's a model, a cheerleader for the Washington Redskins."

"Did you ever see her perform at the games?" David's tone was filled with doubt. He tried not to smile at what appeared to be the oldest con in the book. *Guy's lucky she didn't roll him and take his wallet.*

Derrick covered his face with his hands.

No, this is worse. She set him up to take the fall for his parents' murders. David's amusement evaporated. "Tell me about last night."

"Last thing I remember is showing up at her apartment. We were supposed to have dinner. The table was set. I smelled food in the kitchen." He shook his head. "She claimed I got drunk and passed out on the sofa, but…"

"You woke up on the sofa?"

"She woke me up," Derrick said with a snarl. "She told me that I had too much to drink and passed out. Thing is, I don't drink. I've been sober for nine years. I didn't ask her for a drink. But she said I was drinking and I can't remember. I thought I had a relapse, but now—" He sucked in a deep breath. "She set me up!"

David could see by his flushed cheeks and deep breaths that Derrick's efforts to control his anger were failing as he was beginning to realize what may have happened to him. "What time did you get there?"

"Six o'clock."

"Even if she had slipped you a mickey right after you got there," David said, "she wouldn't have had time to get out here to Deep Creek Lake."

"Mom wrote Lenny's name in her blood," Derrick pointed out.

"Why would Lenny have killed your parents?"

"He's crazy," Derrick said. "Ever since Hollywood spit him out when he stopped being cute. I know it's not fair, but hey—you adapt. Lenny couldn't."

"Does he blame your mother for getting him blacklisted?"

"He thinks everyone is out to get him," Derrick said, "or if they aren't out to get him, that they have screwed him somehow, someway. Even Mom, who bent over backwards after she retired to try to help him out after his career went to pot." He sucked in a deep breath. "That's the type of person she was. She wasn't anything like the Hollywood agent stereotype. She cared, and most of her clients were kid actors like Lenny."

He sat up in his seat and leaned across the table to David. "Do you want to know why we moved out here? Mom was at the top of her career. She had big-name clients, but she retired and gave it all up to move us out here and set Dad up in business, which did great—don't get me wrong."

"Why did she give it up, Derrick?"

"Because of me." Derrick blinked away the tears in his eyes. "Lenny had no home life. He was a star, but both of his folks were up to their eyeballs in sex, drugs, and rock and roll. So Mom would bring him home to give him a taste of a stable environment. He even had his own room at our house. When he got kidnapped and they released him from the hospital, he wanted to come stay with us—not his folks—us! He considered our family his and our house his home."

Derrick uttered a hollow laugh. "Mom expected me to be a good influence on him." His smile fell. "Unfortunately, it was the other way around. Lenny had all these women and drugs of every kind that you could want and he shared it with me. The studio actually hired a man, his assistant, to keep Lenny happy. But when Lenny started being too happy and it affected his work, they turned off his faucet, which shut it off for me, too. Mom and Dad sent me to rehab, and by the time I got out, we were living in a new house and I was going to school back here in the east."

Thinking about the DEA investigation, David asked, "Have you been clean ever since?"

"I wish it was that simple," Derrick said. "It would have saved my folks a lot of heartache." He shrugged his shoulders. "I partied all through college. Somehow I managed to graduate. Then I ended up in rehab again. This time, I wanted to get off the stuff. Dad was ready to throw me to the wolves, but Mom..." He swallowed. "She had a heart of gold. She bought me the club." He laughed. "I had graduated with a degree in business, but literally, everything I know about running that club I learned the hard way."

"Have you been clean since then?" David asked again.

"Ever since." His voice shook when he added, "Mom and Dad were really proud of me."

Believing him, David studied the man sitting across from him. Derrick was fighting to regain control of his emotions long enough to help them capture his parents' killer. *Are you playing me? Do you know the DEA is investigating you? Are you playing the innocent to get me on your side? If so, you're good. You're very good.*

"I am very sorry for your loss, Derrick." David then added in a casual tone, "It must be hard running a comedy club with the Hollywood types coming in carrying their little recreational drugs when you're a recovering addict."

"Struggle every day," Derrick said. "Once I got over being an idiot, it became easier."

"Excuse me?"

"I used to be a real idiot," Derrick said. "Don't get me wrong. I still am an idiot, but not the type I used to be. I always had to be the player—the big shot. Drugs made me feel like I really was the coolest player. Once I got sober and my brain dried out, I saw that it was the big shots who were the real idiots. Now that I see them all for what they really are—idiots—then it isn't so important for me to be one of them. Now, I'm able to walk away—which I do every night when the club closes. That's why I couldn't believe Madelyn when she said I got drunk. I don't remember even having one drink, but she said I was drunk when I got there."

Something is not right here. I'm believing this guy.

Derrick chuckled. "I'm not Superman. I'll admit it's a struggle every day. As a matter of fact, I don't work the club on the weekends because of all the drugs and booze flowing around."

"Aren't the weekends your biggest nights?" David asked. *It's probably when the major drug deals are going down.*

"I'll work during the day," Derrick said, "but being on hand when the club is open—I leave that to my assistant. It's just too much temptation." He shrugged. "It's my handicap and I've learned to live with it. That's why I have such a great assistant. We wouldn't be the success that we are if it wasn't for her."

"What's your assistant's name?" David had his pen poised.

"Zoe Reese."

After making note of the name and the spelling, David sat forward in his seat. "Tell me about Lenny. If your mother moved you from the West Coast to get away from Lenny, how did he end up here?"

"Easy," Derrick said, "He's a great actor. Remember, he's won an Academy Award. He had the talent. If he could have cleaned himself up and stayed clean, then he could have gotten any agent he wanted to represent him. But every single time he got clean, within thirty days he was right back where he started and it was all Mom's fault for abandoning him." He rubbed his chin with his hand. His eyes filled with tears. "Lenny played the poor little abandoned one-time child star card a lot. So much that after his last stint in rehab a few years ago—*Star Rehab*—Mom brought him out here and foisted him on me with a permanent gig at the club. Once again, she hoped that I could be a good influence on him."

"But you weren't best friends anymore?" Unsure whether to believe him or not, David cocked his head. *A reformed drug addict playing drug dealer? That doesn't make sense. Either he's lying or the DEA has it wrong.*

Derrick stared across the table at him. His eyes widened. Holding out his hands, palms up, he asked, "If you don't believe me that Lenny's nuts, then I can prove it to you."

"How?"

"YouTube," Derrick said. "Two weeks ago, this new headliner, a whale of a talent, Sally Riggleman—remember that name, she's going to be big—started doing our main show on the weekends. She came in during one of the open mic nights and Mom happened to be there. Mom insisted that we hire her. She was right. This lady has talent with a capital T. Well, Lenny threw a fit. He decided she was out to get him. So, a couple of weeks ago, Lenny starts heckling her from the audience. Very bad form. Well, he heckled the wrong lady because Sally buried him." With a shrug of his shoulders, Derrick finished. "I'm surprised it wasn't Sally who ended up dead."

"That video is on YouTube?"

"Went viral." Derrick thumbed the screen on his smart phone. "I'll send it to you. I'm sure he's convinced that Mom insisted on hiring Sally as part of some conspiracy. That's why he killed her."

"Well if this woman drugged you, then it most likely would have something to do with the murder," David said. "Will you agree to a blood test to see what she may have slipped you last night?"

Derrick nodded his head. "You bet. A blood test should also show whether I did get drunk like she said. I'd want to know that. I'm only a couple of months from my ten-year pin."

"We should be able to find that out for you." David stood up to leave when, struck with a thought, he turned back to Derrick. "What did Madelyn Preston look like?"

"Gorgeous," Derrick said with a grin.

"I don't suppose you have her picture?"

"You bet." With a cocky grin, Derrick turned his cell phone around to show David the screen. "I snapped this picture of her while she was mixing what was supposed to be a Virgin Mary last night." He held up the phone to show David the image of the stunning redhead, her back to him, mixing a drink at the bar. Her lovely face and blue eyes framed in long lashes were reflected in the mirror behind the bar.

"That's Madelyn Preston?"

"Yep." In response to David's chuckle, he asked, "What's wrong?"

"I know why she's not answering her phone." After handing the phone back to him, the police chief jotted down a phone number on the notepad and slid it across the table for Derrick to read. "Send the picture and video to this phone number."

David's cell vibrated on his hip when he rose from the table. With one hand he opened the door while bringing the phone to his ear with the other. "O'Callaghan here."

"A couple of my deputies are searching Frost's suite at the Wisp," Sheriff Turow told him. "They found something that you should see for your murder investigation."

"I'll be right there," David said while making his way into the reception area. "How's things on your end?"

"Frost is still waiting for Forsythe, a.k.a. Faraday, to work his magic. He's definitely unstable. But we have had a break, if that is what you want to call it."

"What's that?" David asked.

"One of the hostages was smart enough to fake an epileptic seizure. Frost is letting the EMTs remove her from the scene. I sent in one of my guys in an EMT uniform to scope out the place. Faraday slipped him a note."

"What does the note say?"

"Don't let this woman out of your sight," Turow said. "Whatever that means."

CHAPTER EIGHT

Mac was not thrilled. If anyone was going to get out of the hostage situation early, he would have preferred that it was one of the drunken hostages enthralled with the game.

Not LeClair DuBois.

His gut told him that she was faking the seizure, which was followed by unconsciousness. If her plan was to get carried out of the bar on a stretcher, it worked.

The few times in his career that Mac had run into someone faking, he had learned how to test for lack of consciousness. A flick of his finger on the upper cheek would cause the person to flinch and open his or her eyes.

Not LeClair DuBois. She was that good. The twitch of her eyes was fleeting. Her hand tensed where he was holding it.

Mac's first instinct was to call her on it. *Not here. Not now. Not in front of Frost and all these innocent victims.* Instead, he went behind the bar and wrote a note to slip to the deputy he spotted coming in with the EMT. Then, while they were tending to LeClair, Mac used her phony unconscious state to his own advantage. He searched the purse that had fallen to the floor when she launched her performance.

Mac's gut was also telling him that she would be in the wind as soon as she got to the hospital, taking along with her the answers to most of his questions. That meant he had to gather as much information on her when he had the chance.

During the commotion of the EMTs checking out the fallen woman, Mac ducked behind the bar to search her purse. He had her wallet in his hand, and when he became aware that someone was watching him, he looked up to see a pair of brown eyes following his every move.

On a bar stool, Gnarly was sitting between Bernie and Hap. He had paused his snack of a big bowl of stale popcorn to eye his master. The two old men were torn between their ballgame and the woman being treated by the EMT.

"Is it legal for dogs to sit at the bar?" Mac asked Bernie.

"How old is he in human years?" Bernie replied.

"He's three—"

"Which makes him twenty-one." Bernie held out his empty beer mug to Mac. "As long as you're back there, can you give me a refill?"

Mac shot a glance in the direction of Carl, who seemed to sense instantly what was happening. He hurried over from where he was watching the excitement. "You're drinking all my inventory."

"The man with the gun said we could," Bernie said, "and he's in charge." He shook his mug to get Mac's attention. "We don't want to get the boss mad, do we?"

Not wanting to draw more attention in his direction, Mac snatched the mug from Bernie's hand and refilled it. When he handed the mug back to Bernie, he found two more mugs and an empty pitcher lined up on the bar in front of him. Seeing that one of the glasses belonged to the bar owner, Mac turned to him.

"It's my beer," Carl said.

Once the hostages' drinks were taken care of, Mac returned to searching the purse. He was running out of time. The EMT would be asking for her identification to take to the hospital.

Her wallet showed her identification as Sela Wallace with a California address. *LeClair DuBois is a phony name. I was right.*

Spying her smart phone, he touched the screen to take him to the call list. Then he whipped out his own phone to snap a picture of the calls she had recently made. *Someone on this list has to have a clue about what she's doing here.* Since he had his camera on, he snapped a picture of her driver's license, too.

The EMTs had the woman loaded on the stretcher. Mac was stuffing her wallet and cell phone back into her purse when his fingers came in contact with a small plastic bag. He pulled it out to see that it was a clear ziplock bag containing two to three tablespoons of white powder.

Cocaine? Maybe that's why she gave me a phony name and wants out of here. Mac glanced across the pub in Lenny's direction. She could be Lenny's hook-up for a fix.

"Has anyone seen her purse?" Edith asked anyone who might be paying attention.

Shoving the baggie into his pants pocket, Mac held up the purse. "It's over here. I moved it to get it out of the way." He handed the purse across the bar to Edith, who had hurried over with a serving tray containing the wine glass that had fallen over when the woman collapsed.

Edith trotted over to give one of the EMTs the purse, and he placed it on top of the motionless woman on the gurney. The cook waited to watch them go out the door and then close it on their freedom before she returned behind the bar.

During the whole ordeal, Lenny sat on the bar stool in the center of the stage. Clutching the gun that rested on his thigh, he watched all the goings-on with a hate-filled expression on his face.

Mac put on a pair of disposable latex gloves from a box on the counter. When Edith came back behind the bar, he asked her, "Do you have any cocoa powder?"

She paused to regard him while he picked up the wine glass and held it under the counter light used to help read labels and drink mix instructions in the darkened pub. "Sweetened or unsweetened?"

"Unsweetened."

Eying the detective studying the glass, she hurried back into the kitchen.

"I think Diablo wants another bowl of popcorn," Bernie said.

"Of course he does," Carl said. "He's as big of a mooch as you two."

Gnarly responded with a snarl.

"Figure it out yet, Mickey?" Lenny suddenly called out from his seat on center stage.

"I need to call my people." Mac took the cocoa powder from Edith.

Curious to see what he intended to do with the powder, she crowded in close to him to watch while he dipped a basting brush into the powder and gently dusted it across the glass in search of a fingerprint.

"Go ahead," Lenny said. "Tell them they need to get moving. You have less than ten hours to find out who set me up, or people are going to start dying."

"What are you doing?" Edith whispered.

"Dusting for fingerprints," he whispered before raising it to respond to Lenny. "Are you sure you haven't met anyone here in this pub before, Lenny?"

"Positive."

"Well, someone lured you here for some reason." He turned to Edith. "Get me some tape and a white recipe card."

"You're dusting for fingerprints with cocoa powder?" She yanked open a drawer and extracted both.

"You'd be surprised what you can do with common everyday objects." Mac tore off a piece of tape. "I once arrested a man for attempted rape and murder. He attacked his victim in the kitchen. She blinded him by throwing black pepper in his eyes. Then, while he was on his knees wiping the tears from his eyes, she clocked him over the head with a cast iron frying pan. He was still unconscious when I got there."

"I like that." Edith grinned. "Do you think that woman is behind all this?"

"Have you ever seen her in here before?" Mac asked.

"Never," she answered. "We don't get many of the big city crowd—just locals looking for a place to escape life."

"I could be wrong, but I think she was coming in for more than the game."

Bernie leaned across the bar to where Mac was easing the tape across the two fingerprints he found on the globe of the wine glass. Carefully, he lifted the prints to transfer them to the blank recipe card. "Hey, Mr. Forsythe, what happens if the second game in the doubleheader goes into extra innings? Do you think Lenny'll wait until the game is over before he starts shooting? I really don't want to die not knowing who won."

"I'll do my best to make sure he doesn't shoot you until after the game is over, Bernie."

"I'd appreciate that, Mr. Forsythe," Bernie said with a grin. "I could tell you were an upright guy." Signaling Mac with a thumbs up, he nodded to Hap. "Ain't he a good guy, Hap?"

With a wide toothless grin, Hap nodded his head so fast that he resembled a bobble doll while duplicating his buddy's approval with two thumbs up.

"Hey, Carl, Diablo wants some Buffalo wings," Bernie yelled down to the end of the bar.

"Why don't you just shoot me and put me out of my misery all ready?" Carl said to Lenny.

While their attention turned to Gnarly's need for Buffalo wings, Mac snapped a picture of the fingerprints and sent it to David O'Callaghan.

Folding the recipe card in half, Mac slipped it into his pocket and stepped out from behind the bar. "Well, then, I guess we need to get this show on the road." He tapped the screen to dial David O'Callaghan's phone number.

After three rings, David picked up on his end. "Hey, Mac, how's it going?"

Mac was aware of Lenny watching him from his seat on center stage. "The EMTs just took out one of the hostages."

"Bogie told me. It was the hostage who made me ask what's wrong with this picture. Is that her call log and driver's license you sent?"

"Along with a recipe card," Mac said.

"I forwarded them to the crime lab and Archie."

"She's in on this?"

"She's faster than waiting in line at the crime lab," David said, "and we don't have a lot of time, even if they have expedited our case. I just now got the call that Doc is emailing over the autopsy report on the bodies. Ballistics on the slugs says the murder weapon is a twenty-two caliber assault rifle—an AR-15."

"Not your average handgun," Mac said.

"Nope."

"I think our suspect may be a drug dealer. I found something in her purse."

"Drugs?" David asked.

"That's right."

"And Lenny has a recurring drug habit," David noted.

"Exactly."

"Which would explain why she was so anxious to get out of there when the police showed up," David said. "She may not have anything to do with the murders or any of this."

"Still…"

"I've already sent Fletcher to the hospital to keep an eye on her until I can get there to question her."

"Good." Nodding his head, Mac flashed a reassuring grin in Lenny's direction.

"I've just pulled into the Wisp," David said. "The sheriff deputies found something that they believe will help us in our case."

"What's happening, Sherlock?" Lenny snapped from behind him.

"Checking my messages for results from the ME," Mac lied while turning around and tucking the phone into his pocket. "She has finally finished the autopsy on the Stillmans. The police chief is on his way over to talk to her. How have you been doing with your sobriety?"

Lenny laughed. "I'll tell you what I told the doctors at my last rehab. I know I'm an alcoholic. I know I'm a drug addict. I know it and admit to it willingly. The thing is, I'm a *functional* alcoholic and drug addict. The operative word being functional. When I'm sober, I can't perform. I need the stuff in order to perform at my peak."

Thinking of the woman who was now on her way to the hospital after pretending to be unconscious, Mac asked, "Who do you buy your stuff from?"

"My addiction has nothing to do with this." Lenny's eyes narrowed down to tiny bloodshot slits. "I really thought you were brighter than that, Mickey. First time someone gets killed and you guys immediately pin the blame on the addict. Why is that? Is it because it's so easy?"

"More like it's often so very true," Mac said.

"That reminds me of a joke," Lenny said with a giggle.

"A joke?"

Carl groaned. "Oh, damn, the man with the gun has a joke."

"I suggest you laugh," Edith told Carl in a stage whisper from the other side of the bar.

"A guy walks into the bar." Lenny laughed loudly. "Okay, he didn't walk in, he was already there. One guy says, 'I slept with my wife before we were married, did you?' The other guy says, 'I don't know, what was her maiden name?'"

Carl and Edith laughed loudly, at which Bernie, Hap, and Gnarly, wrapped up in the game, shot glares of annoyance over their shoulders.

In response to Mac's expressionless face, Lenny said, "Think about it, Mickey." He leaned over to add in a whisper, "Maybe you're not as smart as I originally gave you credit for being."

"Actually, I am."

03 80 03 80

A Garrett County sheriff's deputy was waiting for David in the parking lot at the Wisp. Once again, his phone vibrated to signal a call. The ID read that it was from Agent Fredericks of the DEA. The deputy waited at the door while David took the call.

"We trust that you didn't blow our operation while talking to Stillman," Fredericks said when David accepted the call.

"No, even though I'm a small town police chief, do give me some credit," David replied. "I'm wondering if you're barking up the wrong tree."

The agent scoffed. "Why would you think that? You don't know anything about our investigation or the evidence that we've collected."

"Do you have any evidence directly connecting Stillman to the drug dealers?"

There was silence on the other end of the line.

"You have nothing," David said.

"What do you have?"

"My gut," David said. "This guy wants nothing to do with drugs. He's so determined to stay clean that he doesn't work at the club on Fridays and Saturdays. When do most of the deals inside the club go down?" The silence from the other end of the line answered his question. "I think someone is using Derrick Stillman for their cover."

"Like who?"

"I don't know," David said. "His assistant, Zoe, would be a good place to start. He said she runs the club when he's not there. I have another question."

"What's that?"

"Were your men watching the woman that Derrick Stillman met last night?"

"Of course," Fredericks answered. "We needed to find out if she was connected to the drug dealers. Found nothing to suggest that."

David asked, "Did she leave the apartment building during his date with her?"

"No," Fredericks said. "They were both in until Stillman left around three in the morning. Why?"

"Right now, she's here in Deep Creek Lake. She was one of Lenny Frost's hostages until just a little while ago when she faked a seizure to get taken out. She's on her way to the hospital by ambulance."

"That's weird."

"You're telling me," David said, "Listen, I have a double homicide to investigate. I'd like to suggest that you ask your undercover cop to dig deeper and take a look at Zoe Reese, Stillman's assistant, before you go arresting him and ruining his life and reputation. He's already lost enough."

"We'll have a talk with our agent," Fredericks said. "Just don't be blowing our operation. Got that?"

"Got it."

The sheriff's deputy escorted him up to the suite that Lenny Frost had booked on the top floor. "Frost has the suite reserved through the whole weekend," he reported. "He checked in yesterday afternoon." He held the elevator door open for the police chief. "He was scheduled to check out Tuesday morning."

"Did you find any firearms that could have been the murder weapon used to kill the Stillmans?" David asked.

"No firearms, but still something interesting," the sheriff's deputy answered while leading David down the long hallway to the corner suite. Making sure no one went into the room, his partner was waiting in the hallway.

The three men stepped inside the suite. The deputy who had been waiting in the hallway went into the bedroom off to the left and held open the door for the police chief to enter.

"We found it in the closet." The senior deputy told David while his partner slid open the glass doors of the closet to reveal a large canvas suitcase on wheels. He wheeled it out, lifted it, and placed it on the bed.

"Don't tell me that there's a dead body in there," David said.

"Not yet," the other deputy said. "Take a look and tell us what you think."

The deputy who had taken the suitcase out of the closet unzipped it to open it. David stepped over to peer inside. As they had said, there was no dead body. The suitcase was empty except for a stack of heavy-duty oversized garbage bags, a roll of duct tape, and a pair of disposable plastic gloves still in the factory wrapper.

David glanced over to the luggage stand against the wall. There was an open suitcase on the stand with a pile of disheveled clothes. No clothes were hanging in the closet. He peered inside the bathroom to see a toiletry bag.

"Lenny obviously brought his clothes in that suitcase," David murmured. "Who checks into a hotel with one big empty suitcase? Unless he's planning to take something out with him that he hadn't brought in."

"Whatever it is," the senior deputy said, "it needs a heavy-duty garbage bag and duct tape."

David picked up the disposable gloves. "What does a stand-up comic need with latex gloves?"

"Pretty suspicious stuff if you ask me," the deputy said.

"This suitcase isn't big enough for both of the Stillmans, and no effort was made to conceal the bodies," David said. "What, or who, was meant to leave this hotel in this suitcase?"

CHAPTER NINE

Downstairs, David found that the Wisp's lounge was open. There were a few parties of hotel guests at various tables near the windows taking advantage of the mountain and lake view. Upon his entrance, the lively conversation stopped and heads turned to take in the uniformed police chief with a gold police shield pinned to the breast of his stark white shirt.

When David stepped up to the bar, the bartender, a young woman, hurried over. "I guess you're here about the hostage situation down at the lake," she asked him breathlessly.

"Actually, I'm investigating the murders that caused the hostage situation," David said while thumbing through the pictures on his phone until he found the one of LeClair Dubois. "Did you work here yesterday?"

"I worked last night," she replied with a quick nod of her head. "I served Lenny Frost about a dozen drinks, double scotch, straight up, until close to eleven o'clock, then the manager asked him to leave."

"Last night?" One of David's eyebrows arched. "Do you remember what time he came in?"

The young woman looked almost up to the ceiling to think before she answered. "I came on duty at six o'clock. I was here about an hour when Lenny Frost came in. We were starting to get busy. The reason he stands out is because I didn't recognize him and he was flirting with me. The drunker he got, the more offended he was that I didn't have any idea who he was. Then he got loud and nasty. He's one of those mean drunks. You need to look out for them. They're the ones that pull out a gun and shoot you for looking at them wrong, not that we get many of them in here—but the last place I worked…" She shook her head. "One of the guys at the bar told him to leave me alone. Then Lenny started picking a fight with him. I signaled for the manager, and he told Lenny to leave or he would be calling the police."

"And you're positive about the time?" David asked.

Again, she nodded her head. "If you want to be sure, you can check the security tapes."

"Security tapes?"

"We have them all over the hotel." She pointed up to the ceiling.

David recognized the small, shiny black half ball above his head that housed a hidden security camera.

"I'm sure the security video caught it all and it will have a time stamp," she said. "Do you want me to get the manager so that you can see it?"

"You betcha."

She turned to walk away before David stopped her. He held out his cell phone for her to see the image of LeClaire Dubois and asked if she recalled seeing the woman in the hotel before.

The bartender checked the image for a long moment before shaking her head. "I could be wrong. A lot of people come through here. Unless they're a regular or threaten to wreck the place like Lenny Frost did, I don't really remember them."

"Really?" David said with a grin and a wink. "I guess it's a lucky thing for Lenny that he got drunk and picked a fight. Otherwise, he wouldn't have you to alibi him."

❦ ❦ ❦ ❦

"Oh, dear," Archie gasped from behind her laptop at the desk in the squad room.

Tonya sat up in her seat. "What's wrong?"

"I got a hit on the fingerprints Mac sent, plus the name on the driver's license and facial recognition. I know who that woman in the bar is."

"Who is she?" Tonya hurried over to read what Archie had uncovered. "She's not in the bar anymore. She went to the hospital in an ambulance. Fletcher is there to keep an eye on her." She peered over Archie's shoulder.

"Sela Wallace, Burbank, California," Archie read. "Thirty years old. She's a stunt woman and an expert marksman. She specializes in stunts for fight scenes and participates in firearms competition."

"I guess that means she would know how to use an assault rifle." Tonya went back to her desk and picked up the radio.

"I wonder if she ever does any contract work," Archie said.

"I need to warn Fletcher and the chief to be careful when they try to question her."

❦ ❦ ❦ ❦

David was walking through the emergency room entrance of the hospital in Oakland, Maryland, when Tonya called him with the news.

"That certainly makes her a person of interest," David said. "Mac thinks he found cocaine in her purse. Lenny likes cocaine. Now we find out that she's into firearms. No wonder she was so anxious to get out of that pub."

"Well, according to what Archie has found out, this Wallace woman is a black belt in martial arts."

David turned the corner for the corridor where the examination rooms were located. Fletcher and the sheriff's deputy were waiting outside the door of the room where Sela Wallace was being examined by the doctor. "Martial arts?"

"She specializes in fight scenes in movies," Tonya said.

"Lenny Frost has a black belt in martial arts," David said. "Find out where she got her training. Tell Archie to dig deeper."

"Will do, Chief," Tonya said. "Be careful. And tell Fletcher to be careful, too."

David thumbed off the call and stepped up his pace down the corridor. "Is Sela Wallace ready for us to interview her yet?'

"Nurse is still with her," the deputy answered. "The doctor went to take care of another patient and the nurse said she would come get—"

"She's been in there for an awfully long time," Fletcher interjected.

"Well, we don't have a lot of time." David pressed through the door. Inside the examination room, he found the privacy screen pulled around the bed. With one arm, David swept the curtain aside to reveal the nurse strapped down onto the bed and struggling to scream through the makeshift gag made up of gauze bandage.

Before rushing to her aid, David whirled around to his officer and the deputy. "She's escaped! Go find her!"

Cʒ ꝏ Cʒ ꝏ

"Hey! Since we're hostages, don't we get food?" Bernie called across the bar to where Lenny was pacing on the stage.

It was the seventh inning stretch and Bernie was making plans to eat before the second game. "I mean, aren't you allowed to call the police and make demands for food?"

"You've been doing nothing but eating and drinking ever since we got taken hostage." Carl tried to stand up but, discovering that he had lost the feeling in his feet, decided better of it.

"Yeah, but nothing good," Bernie said.

"You wouldn't know it wasn't good by the way you've been wolfing it down," Carl argued.

"I think we're running out of the draft beer," Edith said. "After this last pitcher, we're going to have to start on the expensive stuff."

"You mean we've been drinking the cheap stuff all this time?" Bernie turned around on his bar stool to call over to Lenny. "What type of hostage situation is this? They've been holding out on us!"

"What do you guys want?" Edith asked in a polite tone to calm down the increasingly agitated hostages.

"Steak!" Bernie said. "And wine. Good wine. Not that stuff that comes in a box, either."

With a wide toothless grin, Hap nodded his head.

"From the Spencer Inn!" Bernie wiped the drool from his mouth with the back of his hand.

Hap increased the speed of the nod of his head.

As if to voice his agreement, Gnarly sat up on the stool where he was seated, placed his paws on the counter, and barked.

"Steaks sound good to me, too." Lenny waved a hand at Mac. "Make it happen. Call your people and tell them we want steak dinners from the Spencer Inn all the way around and some of their expensive wine, too."

"And don't forget dessert," Bernie said.

"The police aren't going to just send in steak dinners." Mac turned to Lenny. "You need to give them something in return as a show of good will."

"Like what?"

"One of your hostages."

"Send out Carl," Bernie volunteered.

"It's up to the guy with the gun to decide," Carl said.

"Well, it should be you," Bernie said. "You're the pain in the butt who's been serving us cheap stuff during this whole hostage thing."

"Well it being cheap didn't slow you down in drinking all of it," Carl objected.

"Now everyone just calm down," Edith said. "Let Lenny decide who has to leave now that the good stuff is showing up." She gestured across the bar to Lenny on the stage. "You decide who you want to kick out, Lenny."

"Call me a chauvinist," Mac said, "but I believe it would be best to let the woman go."

"Why me?" Edith blurted out with her hands on her hips. "What did I do?" She looked mad enough to want to slap Mac.

"Don't you want to go home to your family?"

"The only family I have is Carl!" She jerked a thumb in the direction of the bar owner.

"I'm not your family," Carl objected.

"I know, you old coot," she said, "but you're the closest thing that I have to a family and family sticks together through thick and thin, even if you are constipated and cranky."

"If I'm the only family you have, then I sure feel sorry for you."

"You should," she replied. "Because I've been in love with you for twenty-five years."

Sputtering and hissing, Carl covered up his face and rubbed his ears. "What has gotten into you, woman? Have you lost your mind?"

"Damn right I lost my mind!" she yelled while advancing on him. "I can't believe it either."

"Are you saying…" Carl wiped the heavy sweat from his brow and bald head. "All these years that we have been fussing and fighting with each other… it's been—" His voice dropped to a whisper. "—sexual tension?"

"What did you think it was?"

"I thought we just plain hated each other."

"I wish," Edith said. "How do you think I feel? Of all the handsome, decent, polite gentlemen that I have met in my life, I had to fall in love with a cheap, nasty, smelly old coot like you. Life sure can be cruel, can't it?"

"I could say a few things about you, woman."

She was now standing toe to toe with him. "Well, you better say it, because he's shooting us at midnight. So I suggest you get it off your chest now."

"I love you, too, you old biddy."

She threw her arms around him and kissed him full on the mouth. Refusing to let go after all their years of bickering, she pushed Carl back against the bar, letting him go only when they both needed air.

"I guess the woman isn't going," Lenny told Mac.

"Then send them both out," Mac said.

"I'm not leaving," Carl gasped. "Someone has to keep track of the inventory these drunks are eating and drinking."

"Then let's send out the drunks," Mac said.

"We'll miss the game!" Bernie wailed. "You can't make us go!"

"Send out the dog," Carl said.

"I like the dog," Edith said.

120

"So do I," Bernie said. "Don't you like the dog, Hap?" When Hap nodded his head, Bernie added, "The dog stays."

"I guess that leaves you," Lenny said to Mac.

"Me?" Mac clutched his chest. "I came in here to protect all of you."

"Yeah," Bernie said, "and you've been doing nothing but yapping all throughout the game. I vote that you leave."

Hap nodded his head in agreement.

Lenny turned to Edith and Carl, who both nodded their heads.

"Sorry, Mac," Edith said. "You just don't fit in with us."

"Sorry, Mac," Lenny said, "You've been voted off the island." He pointed to the exit. "Take your torch and leave."

Mac didn't think he would ever see the day that he was kicked out of a hostage situation. Sure, he didn't want to be there. The last thing he wanted was to spend the rest of the day with an unstable man with a gun threatening to shoot everyone at the stroke of twelve, but he had to stay. He was the best hope these bunch of drunken lunatics had. They needed him to protect them. How could they not see that? He had to argue sense into their minds. "But—"

"Hey, who served that dog chili?" Carl bellowed when he saw that Gnarly was standing with his front paws on the bar licking the last remnants of what had once been a very spicy chili.

"I'm taking my ticking gas bomb and going home." Mac scurried to the exit with Gnarly on his heels.

ଓ ଅ ଓ ଅ

In the hostage command center, Bogie, the sheriff's deputy, and Sheriff Turow stared out the window in stunned disbelief when Mac and Gnarly, their heads hanging in shame, came out of the bar.

Bogie was the first to find his voice. "Did that really happen? Did our hostage negotiator get voted out by the hostages?"

"Yep," Deputy Parker said. "Maybe it's Stockholm syndrome."

"Only four hours in?" Bogie replied. "They just tossed Mac and Gnarly out for steak. I don't think we should wait until midnight for Lenny Frost to shoot them. I think we should end this now and go in and shoot all of them for being nuts."

Parker turned to Sheriff Turow. "Have you ever seen anything like this, sir?"

"Nope." Sheriff Turow shook his head. "I've never seen anything like it—not in all my three months as sheriff."

CHAPTER TEN

"What happened?" David demanded to know when he stepped into the police command center to find Mac and Gnarly sitting in the corner, not unlike two naughty children.

"They got voted out," Bogie said.

With a groan, Gnarly dropped down to bury his snout under his front paws.

Catching a whiff of a foul odor, David covered his nose. "What—"

"Twiddle-Dee and Twiddle-Dum gave Gnarly a bowl of chili before voting us out," Mac said.

"And you let them?"

"He's been eating nonstop for the last four hours and those bunch of drunks, also known as our victims—they've been drinking one beer after another along with our suspect." Mac hitched his chin in the direction of the pub. "This hostage situation and stand-off has turned into a wild party. I've never seen anything like it. They voted Gnarly and me out for steak dinners."

"Actually, you were the only one they voted out," Sheriff Turow said. "They wanted Gnarly to stay."

"I think it's time we put an end to this," David said.

"I agree." Sheriff Turow nodded his head.

"No way they'll agree to that before they get their steak dinners," Mac predicted.

"Lenny wants us to prove he's innocent," David said. "Well, I found proof. He's got an airtight alibi. He was making a scene and picking a fight in the lounge at the Wisp all last evening."

"Good," Sheriff Turow said. "You can tell him that he's in the clear and can release his hostages. My men and I will eat the steaks."

Mac held up his hand and turned back to David. "Wait a minute." Slowly, he rose out of his seat. "Are you sure Lenny's alibi is airtight?" he asked through gritted teeth.

"The Wisp has a security camera in their lounge," David said. "He's on a security tape with a time stamp."

"Then why did he do all this?" Mac waved his arm while asking. "If he's got an airtight alibi, then why didn't he just come in when he found out that we were looking for him and tell us? Why take hostages and cause a police stand-off?"

"Lenny Frost is crazy," David said. "He's made a career of acting out without thinking anything through. You can see it in his record. Drug possession. DUI. Bar fights. Assault. If he didn't have advocacy groups holding him up as the poster boy for laws regulating child actors, he would have spent more than a day in jail."

"More like five to seven years," Bogie said in agreement.

"He's never grown up," David said.

In his mind, Mac recalled the hours he had spent in the pub with Lenny Frost and had to agree that his thought process was not like most adults.

"After we talk Frost into releasing his hostages," the sheriff said, "then you can ask him why he didn't simply come forward with his alibi. Right now, let's concentrate on getting him to put his gun down and come out." He turned to Deputy Parker. "Get Frost on the phone."

Mac asked David, "What did you find out about Sela Wallace or whatever her name is?"

"She overpowered a nurse at the hospital and escaped," David said. "According to what Archie was able to uncover about her background, Sela Wallace is a stunt woman and a firearms expert. She's definitely involved. How, I don't know. She's not the shooter. She's got an alibi, too."

"Maybe it's just a matter of her being in the wrong place at the wrong time." Mac took the baggy containing the white powder from his pocket. "We need to have this analyzed. It could be cocaine and she was afraid of getting caught with it. Either way, she wanted out of there." He handed the bag to the sheriff's deputy who checked it into evidence.

"Frost…" the sheriff said into the phone.

"Where's Forsythe?" Lenny asked. "I want to talk to Mickey."

The sheriff handed the phone to Mac.

"Hey, Lenny," Mac said in an upbeat tone. "How's it going in there?"

"The first game has ended," Lenny said.

"Pirates won!" Mac heard Bernie yell into the phone.

"Hey," Lenny said, "we forgot to give you our dinner orders before kicking you off the island."

An uproar of laughter erupted in the background.

"Lenny," Mac said with gritted teeth, "about the investigation—"

"What investigation?"

"The Stillmans—"

"Oh, yeah," Lenny said. "That's right. Have you got them yet?"

"We're getting closer," Mac said. "Why didn't you tell me that you had an alibi for last night?"

"Huh?"

"I asked you about your alibi and you told me that you were in your suite alone last night," Mac said. "In fact, you were in the Wisp's lounge picking a fight. We have witnesses and a security recording. You lied to me about your alibi."

"Oh, yeah," Lenny said without emotion. "That's right. I was in the lounge and some—"

"None of this was necessary." Mac fought to keep the frustration out of his tone.

"They're still going to find a way of blaming me for it. They'll say I hired someone to kill the Stillmans for me."

"Fact is, you were in the Wisp while they were being murdered," Mac said. "You don't have to do this."

"Do you have the person behind this?"

"Not yet, but we've got a suspect."

"When you have her under arrest, then we can talk." Lenny's tone was cold. "You have until midnight. Now, Mickey, are you ready to take our dinner orders?"

ଓ ଃ ଓ ଃ

"You have to pull over." Mac grasped the door handle in the passenger seat to David's cruiser. "You have to pull over *now.*"

Mac and David were on their way to the police station on the Spencer side of the lake to compare notes and try to make sense of the Stillman murders and Lenny Frost's role in it all. However, Mac and David had driven less than two miles before Gnarly started making all-too-familiar noises in the back seat.

Recognizing the sound uttered from deep in Gnarly's throat, Mac didn't have to repeat himself before David threw the steering wheel to get the cruiser off the road and hit the brake pedal. Mac jumped out and threw open the back door. Like a cannonball, Gnarly flew out and hit the ground running to go down over the hillside toward the lakeshore where he stopped and threw up an odious mixture of stomach acid, buffalo chicken strips, nachos, pizza, and chili.

The odor drifted back up to the cruiser. Unable to look at or smell it, Mac and David turned their backs, went around to the front of the cruiser, and waited for Gnarly's stomach to stop churning.

"I guess Gnarly's weekend is worse than mine," Mac said.

Chuckling, David checked his phone. "Hmmm."

"What?" Mac asked.

"Derrick Stillman also has an alibi for the time of the murders," David said. "He's been under surveillance by the DEA ,who has been investigating his club for being part of a major drug operation. He took a picture of the woman he was with." He gave Mac a sidelong glance. "Sela Wallace."

"Who was in the Blue Whale when Lenny took the place hostage," Mac said.

"The feds swear she did not leave the apartment during the night," he said. "So she has an alibi for the time of the murders, too. Now, here is where it gets interesting."

"As if it's not already interesting."

"Derrick passed out," David said. "He claims he doesn't drink, but last night…he consented to a blood test." He handed the phone to Mac. "Results are in. Zero alcohol. However, he was slipped a roofie."

"A roofie?" The corners of Mac's lips curled when he read the text. "She slipped him a date rape drug?"

"Here's what I think happened," David said. "Roofies remove a person's inhibitions—making her, or, in this case, him open to suggestions."

Mac was nodding his head. "Derrick knew the passcode to his parents' security system. Once he's properly drugged, she simply asks him for the code. He gives it to her."

"And then she calls her accomplice here in Deep Creek Lake," David said.

"Gretchen heard the killer's phone ringing at seven thirty," Mac said.

"Derrick's date started at six," David said. "Plenty of time for her to drug him and get the code. The phone call was Sela Wallace giving the shooter the passcode." Seeing the frown in Mac's face, he asked, "What's wrong?"

"Why?" Mac asked. "What's the motive? Nothing was stolen that we could see."

"Lenny inherits the club," David said. "His alibi is awfully convenient, if you ask me."

"If Derrick is involved in drug dealing, his parents could have been killed as some sort of warning to him not to say anything to the feds," Mac suggested. "Or, he could have drugged himself to look like the innocent victim. How about that whole thing of blabbing to the media about the killer being Lenny Frost? He could have had the shooter write Lenny's name in his mother's blood to point the finger away from him to Lenny. That certainly took the spotlight off him."

David turned to go around the cruiser and climb inside. "We need to apprehend Sela to find out what connection she has in all this."

Mac went to the edge of the hillside to call down to Gnarly. "Are you through?"

Slowly, Gnarly staggered up the hill to him.

"Have you learned your lesson?" Mac chastised him. "That will teach you to make a pig of yourself." He opened the rear door.

Looking up at the seat that now appeared too far above him, Gnarly sat down with a sigh.

"Jump in." Mac gestured for him to hop up into the back seat.

Gnarly looked from the seat to his master and back again.

"Seriously?" Mac asked.

With his ears folded back flat on his head, the sick dog groaned. His big brown eyes pleaded for help.

"The things I do for you," Mac said with a sigh before squatting down and lifting Gnarly up to place him in the back seat.

CHAPTER ELEVEN

Spencer Police Station

Archie did not hesitate to run across the reception area to throw her arms around Mac's shoulders and hug him when she saw him come through the front door. "Oh, I was so worried," she breathed into his ear.

He wrapped his arms around her to hold her close. "I love you so much."

Abruptly, she pulled away. Catching sight of something behind him, she uttered a gasp.

"What—" She shot a glare at him. "What did you do to Gnarly?"

On unsteady legs, Gnarly made his way to the sofa and crawled up. With a pain-filled sigh, he plopped down and dropped his head over the edge of the cushion. His usually tall and grand ears drooped.

"How could you let—" Archie sputtered.

"I was busy." Mac pointed at the sick dog. "He's got no self-control whatsoever. Lady Tala's mother dumped him here this morning because he was…and then, at the pub, he proceeded to eat Carl out of house and home—including chili."

"Chili!" Tonya jumped out of her chair as if she considered making a run for it.

"You let them feed chili to Gnarly?" Archie asked in horror.

"I was trying to save lives," Mac argued.

"I think the worst of it is over," David said.

"How long ago did he eat the chili?" Tonya asked.

"A little over an hour ago," Mac said.

Shaking her head, the desk sergeant went around to the other side of her chair to place it between her and the dog. "It's not over yet. The worst is yet to come."

David pointed up the stairs to his office. "Mac and I are going upstairs to go over the case. We need to compare notes."

Archie scooped up her laptop. "I'm coming with you. I've been digging deeper into Sela Wallace's background."

"What about me?" Tonya called to them while eying Gnarly like he was a ticking time bomb.

"We have gas masks in supply," David said before going into his office and closing the door.

Up in the police chief's office, Archie set up her laptop on the conference table while David briefed Mac about his interview with Derrick Stillman and the DEA investigation. "The feds are checking with their undercover agent to determine if Derrick knew about his parents disinheriting him."

"Can you imagine how awful it would be if Derrick was wrongly disinherited because of bad information from the feds?" Archie said with a shake of her head. "And his parents dying thinking that he was a drug dealer when he wasn't."

"Derrick could have been playing you," Mac told David.

"I don't think so," David said. "He looked me straight in the eye and was completely frank about his history of addiction. Besides, it will be easy enough to check out whether he works Fridays and Saturdays, which are big nights for drug dealing."

"The smart drug dealers make sure they're not on site when business is going down," Mac pointed out.

"My instinct tells me that he's straight up," David said. "What does yours tell you about Lenny Frost since you were face to face with him?"

"He's crazy…" Mac said, "and brilliant. That's a lethal combination that I haven't run into very often. When you're lucky, the craziness outweighs the brilliance to trip the killer up. Things go bad when the brilliance outweighs the insanity. Then, bad things happen, but the killer is so smart that only God can stop him."

"Which is the case with Lenny Frost?" David asked.

"Jury's still out."

"He's got an alibi for the kill window in the Stillman murders," David said. "If he shoots his hostages just because we don't have a suspect in custody—how crazy would that be?"

"That tells me there's something else going on here," Mac said.

"Oh, yeah, I can confirm that." David folded his arms across his chest. "Yesterday, he checked into the Wisp with two suitcases. He had his clothes in one. The second suitcase, an oversized bag on wheels, was empty except for heavy-duty garbage bags, duct tape, and disposable gloves. Now, I know I'm assuming something, but I think he was planning to leave with something extra—like a dead body."

"Can't be the Stillmans," Mac said. "Their bodies were left at the scene."

"Come look at this." Archie waved for them to join her at David's conference table. She had brought up the YouTube website on her laptop and had a video queued to play.

Taking the chair next to her, Mac moved in close enough to pick up the rosy scent of her hair. David sat on the other side of her.

Archie explained, "Derrick Stillman said that all we needed to do was go to YouTube for proof that Lenny Frost's porch light is out. Take a look at this video that was uploaded to YouTube a couple of weeks ago after he went head to head against one of the comics at the club. Her name is Sally Riggleman." She tapped the "PLAY" button.

To loud applause, a tiny blonde in a tight leather skirt and high heels stepped out onto the stage. With a cloud of platinum curls, she reminded Mac of a 1920s silent film movie actress. Grinning broadly, Sally greeted the audience and announced she was happy to be there.

"It is so much better being up here and working," she said. "I'm hoping that I do better at this job than my last one, which didn't go well. I was a narrator for bad mimes."

Archie giggled. "She's funny. You should see how she cuts Lenny down to size. It's embarrassing. She's got a very quick wit."

Sally went on to discuss her bad luck. "It all started four years ago when I broke a mirror. I've been sentenced to seven years, but my lawyer says he can get me off in five for good behavior."

Over the laughter of the audience, Lenny yelled, "Do we get any time off from your bad jokes?"

There was stunned silence in the audience.

The camera switched over to where Lenny was standing at the bar. He had a wicked grin across his face as he handed something off to a robust looking woman in a dark suit. When the spotlight swooped over to them, she ducked to avoid the light and hurried away in the direction of the backstage area.

A stunning redhead was at Lenny's arm.

"Pause the video." Mac slapped his hand down on the keyboard to halt the video.

"It's just starting to get good," Archie said.

In the next sequence, Lenny, enjoying his own joke, turned to the redhead who returned his laughter.

"It's already good," Mac said. "That's her."

"Her who?" Archie asked.

"Sela Wallace," David said. "The woman whose background I have you digging into."

Narrowing her eyes, Archie peered at the woman one step behind, yet next to, Lenny Frost. "I didn't see her. I was so focused on Lenny that I didn't—but she's right there with him."

Mac noted the date the video was posted. "This was uploaded fifteen days ago."

"Derrick stated that he had only met Sela Wallace, who had given him another name, a week ago," David said.

"Lenny acted like he didn't know her in the Blue Whale." Mac sat up straight. "He said something…" His voice trailed off while he went deep into thought.

"What did he say?" David asked.

"It hit me as weird at the time…" Mac studied the image of Lenny Frost and Sela Wallace on the computer monitor. "He said 'when you arrest her.' Not when you arrest him, but her. Why would he say her unless he knew the killer was a woman?"

"Murder for hire?" David asked. "She has an alibi, but maybe she contracted the shooter and she was meeting Lenny at the Blue Whale to settle up."

"They clearly know each other well," Archie said. "Look at her body language. She's turned toward him. Her body is open. Usually when a woman is in close proximity with someone, in particular a man she doesn't know, she'll have an arm or her purse or something in front of her to block him off. It's subconscious. But look at her. She doesn't have her arms crossed. She knows and is open to him. I wouldn't be surprised if they were intimate."

"All I care about is that they know each other," Mac said. "Now I want to know when and how well they know each other. Well enough for her to kill for him?" He grasped Archie's elbow. "I want to know everything you can find out about Sela Wallace."

"I'm on it," she said. "But can I finish watching this video first?"

Mac checked the time on the laptop. It was 4:51 p.m. "You have seven hours and nine minutes before Lenny commits murder."

CHAPTER TWELVE

Physically, Mac was sitting behind a vacant desk in the squad room while staring at the wall across from him without even seeing it. Mentally, he was replaying the whole day to analyze Lenny Frost, his relationship to Sela Wallace, and her role in the Stillman murders.

What prompted Lenny to grab the gun and take everyone hostage when he had an airtight alibi for the murders? Why didn't he just come into the station and give his statement to clear his name? If he had, we probably would never have taken a second look at him. Is he crazy? Has paranoia pushed him over the edge even when he didn't need it to go over?

"Do you think he'll do it?"

David's question was in keeping with Mac's thoughts. Startled to hear the words voiced, Mac sat up in his seat to see David standing in front of him. "If we don't find Sela Wallace before midnight and charge her, do you think Lenny will kill everyone in that pub?"

"Or will they care?"

"Why would they not care if they get shot or not?" David asked.

"I swear," Mac said with a shake of his head. "This is the weirdest collection of characters I have ever run into. It's like…" His voice trailed off. "I don't know if it's because they can't see the reality of the situation or…"

David waited for him to continue. Finally, he changed the topic to what he had wanted to say in the first place. "A car was stolen from the hospital shortly after Wallace escaped. We believe she took it. It's an old green Ford sedan."

Instead of responding, Mac was staring straight ahead at the wall across the room.

"The sheriff has a BOLO out on the car," the police chief said.

"We're missing a vital piece of this puzzle," Mac muttered.

"But what?" David asked.

"If I knew that then the piece wouldn't be missing."

Behind David, Archie cleared her throat. "Are you guys ready for a break in this case?" Clutching her laptop to her chest like a book, she stepped around the police chief and took a seat on the corner of the desk.

"More than ready." Mac sat up in his seat and placed his elbows on the desktop. "Give it to me."

She set the laptop down and opened the lid. "Sela Wallace has a very interesting history. Did you know that three years ago she did a stint for steroid addiction at the Recovery Center in Hollywood?"

"No, I did not know that," Mac said.

"That's the same center where they shoot *Star Rehab*," Archie said. "And she was there during the same time period that Lenny Frost was appearing on that show."

"Derrick Stillman said his mother hired Lenny at the club after he left the center," David recalled.

"Based on how he's been guzzling the booze at the Blue Whale, I don't think the rehab took," Mac said.

"Do they let the regular patients mix with the celebrities?" David asked.

Archie shrugged her shoulders. "This facility has the celebrities right in there with the common folks—including during group therapy. Now here is something else to ponder." She tapped a key on her laptop. "Sela Wallace is not her original name."

"Another alias?" Mac replied.

"No, Sela Wallace is her legal name," she said. "She kept her married name after her divorce from her husband eight years ago. Her original name was Sela Drake."

"Drake?" Mac repeated the name with a gasp.

"Her father was Carson Drake, the actor who Lenny Frost claimed had kidnapped him and took off with a million dollars in ransom. Neither he nor the money was every recovered."

"I wonder if this is for revenge," Mac muttered. "She targeted Lenny—blames him…"

Grasping the phone ringing and vibrating on his hip, David turned away. "O'Callghan here."

"Maybe," Archie replied. "Sela has a brother who also legally changed his last name to Harris."

"Zachery Harris." Mac grasped her hand. "Is he a writer?"

"He took his mother's maiden name," Archie said. "Beginning of this year, his book about the Lenny Frost kidnapping, in which Harris claims Janice Stillman and her husband were the masterminds, was published. They duped Carson Drake into snatching Lenny with the promise of representing him and making him a star. Then, they killed Drake and let him take the blame. Of course, the Stillmans sued Harris—"

"And settled," Mac said. "Harris was in here this morning telling me about it."

Archie chuckled. "Oh, was he? What did he tell you? *They* settled?"

"That they backed off."

"Now that they're dead…" In response to Mac's raised eyebrows, she added, "Dead people can't sue. I called a friend of mine at Harris' publishing house. Stillmans did settle with the publisher for a very big amount, which the publisher is planning to collect from Harris. The Stillman suit against Harris was still going forward. Now that they're dead, they can't continue with the lawsuit and neither can Derrick on their behalf. You can't defame a dead person." She closed her laptop. "How's that for motive?"

"That's a whale of a motive."

"Here's something else," she said. "That phone log that you took a picture of from Sela's phone? A call made at around seven-thirty last night was to a phone registered in Zach Harris's name. She was using a burn phone, but not him. We can check the towers to see if he was in the area when he took the call, which will place him here at the time of the murders."

"Motive is revenge and ending the lawsuit," Mac said.

"That's not all."

"You've been a busy girl," Mac said.

"Zachery Harris got a call from that same phone just about ninety minutes ago," Archie said. "That call lasted a little over four minutes."

"She stole a car," Mac said. "They must be coordinating an escape or finishing off Lenny Frost."

Thumbing off his phone, David whirled around and pointed the phone at Mac. "That powder you took from Sela…"

"What about it? Was it cocaine?"

"And then some," David said. "It was a suicide cocktail of cocaine, heroin, tranquilizers, and sleeping pills all mixed together. It was potent enough to kill a horse."

"Kill the Stillmans, frame Lenny, and then kill him and make it look like a suicide," Archie said. "I wonder if she had a nice confession in that purse of hers."

"Works for me," David said. "We already have a BOLO out on Sela."

"You need to put one out on Harris and his vehicle for the shooting," Mac said. "The murder weapon is a semi-automatic assault rifle. If Harris is the shooter, then he probably still has the weapon."

"Do you want me to run a trace on his credit cards to see if I can turn up further proof that he was in the area last night?" Archie asked.

"My people should be doing that," David said.

"Then why did you call me in?"

"Because you're faster," he said with a grin. "Our red tape slows us down."

She cocked an eyebrow at him. "There are advantages to skirting the law."

"You said that, I didn't," David said. "Check security cams and credit cards to see if you can place Harris here during the time of the murder and keep monitoring his phone. Let's run this past Lenny and see if he'll release the hostages and let us take him into protective custody."

Archie jumped down from the desk to follow David. When they saw that Mac wasn't following, they stopped to turn around.

"Why didn't Lenny come to us?" Mac asked.

"He's crazy," David said. "He doesn't think."

"What about the suitcase in Lenny's room," Mac asked. "The one with the trash bags and duct tape?"

"We'll ask Lenny all of our questions after we get him to release the hostages," David said.

"If the Stillmans were in on the kidnapping, why did they sue?" Mac cocked his head at them. "Certainly, the suit put them under a microscope. If they were guilty, they would never have sued."

"Maybe they weren't involved," Archie picked up the copy of the book that Harris had given to him earlier. "My friend said Harris used a lot of circumstantial evidence and a confidential source who he refused to reveal." Placing the book in the center of the desk, she urged him to stand up and follow them.

Mac shook his head. "You guys go on." He picked up his cell phone and thumbed through the contact list. "I need to make a phone call. I'm going to go back to the beginning."

"The Stillman murders?" David asked.

"Lenny's abduction."

"Just the man I need to see." Tonya stepped into the doorway to block David and Archie's exit. She held out a clipboard to the police chief. "Signature on the time sheets for payroll."

David removed the pen from his breast pocket and took the clipboard. "I'm assuming that all these times are right." He smirked at her.

"If you've suddenly decided not to trust me, then you can take the clipboard up to your office and read the whole thing, along with everything else that I have you sign."

"No," David said, "you'll just go to jail with me."

With a wicked grin, Tonya looked him up and down. "Sounds cozy," she laughed before turning to Mac. "Oh, something happened in the break room." Capturing Mac's attention, she added, "and Gnarly loves you so very much."

"Poor Gnarly." Archie knelt to greet the German shepherd who turned the corner to come into the squad room. With his ears folded back, he hung his head and laid it across her lap.

Mac asked Tonya, "How much?"

"Based on the slime content and smell," Tonya said, "fifteen." Despite David being in mid-signature signing the papers on the clipboard, she snatched the pen out of his hand. "Here, you can use the chief's pen."

Mac took his checkbook from the inside breast pocket of his sports coat.

"Are you paying Tonya fifteen dollars to clean up Gnarly's mess?" Archie asked.

"No," Tonya replied with a glance over her shoulder while handing the pen to Mac. "He's paying me fifteen hundred dollars to clean up Gnarly's mess."

"Mac, how could you?" Archie chastised him.

"It's a mutually beneficial relationship." Mac ripped the check from his checkbook and handed it to the smiling desk sergeant. "The mess gets cleaned up, I don't have to touch it, and Tonya gets some extra income."

"How do you think I was able to give myself that snazzy classic fire-engine red T-Bird for Christmas?" With a wave of the check, Tonya clutched the clipboard to her chest and trotted out of the squad room.

"Did you notice what just happened here?" David asked.

"Yeah," Archie said. "Gnarly has been indirectly paying for Tonya's antique car."

"No," David said.

"Yes, he has," Mac said.

"I'm talking about my being the police chief and she—" David stepped out into the hallway. "Have you ever noticed how much authority Tonya has here? She orders things in my name. She does up the time sheets." He gasped. "She has my passwords! It would be so easy for her—"

"Tonya would never take advantage," Archie said. "I'm sure it was Mac who set up this whole arrangement of her cleaning up Gnarly's messes."

"What's the point of being rich if I don't get any perks for it?" Mac replied.

David wasn't paying any attention. Staring down the hall, he muttered under his breath. "I wonder how hard it would be for her to set up a drug dealing operation in my name."

"What?" Archie gasped.

"I need to go make a phone call." David hurried down the hallway and up the stairs to his office.

With a dance in her step and a cleaning mask covering her face, Tonya passed the chief on her way into the break room with a bucket and mop.

Stroking the top of Gnarly's head, Archie told the dog, "Well, you certainly made someone happy today."

Across the squad room, Mac brought his cell phone to his ear.

His call was picked up on the third ring. "Delaney here."

"Special Agent Sid Delaney," Mac said. "Do you know who this is?"

"Mac Faraday," the special agent with the FBI replied. "How could I forget? How's that lovely lady friend of yours? Still putting away bad guys with her pink handgun?"

"I got her a red one for Valentine's Day."

"How's my favorite badass German shepherd?" the agent chuckled.

"Recovering from a wild weekend, I'm afraid," Mac said. "Hey, I have a favor to ask."

"Of course."

"Lenny Frost."

"I've seen the news," Delaney interrupted him. "I figured you'd be messed up in that somehow. What can I do?"

"The kidnapping back in nineteen-ninety-eight," Mac said, "could you get me copies of the case files for that and the murder of Carson Drake's wife some time afterward?"

There was a pause on the other end of the line before Delaney mused, "I don't know."

"It's important," Mac said.

"What do you think you could find that agents over the last fifteen years have never been able to uncover?" Delaney asked. "Carson Drake and the money were never found. Drake's wife was killed by drug dealers."

"There have never been any arrests," Mac argued. "I'm sure the money was marked."

"And never turned up in circulation," Delany said. "Look, I'm sure in your career you have run into murder cases where you knew who did it, but you simply couldn't get enough evidence to make an arrest?"

"Did they suspect the Stillmans of masterminding the kidnapping?"

"Well, Derrick Stillman was certainly a suspect," Sid Delaney said. "The kidnapper ordered him to deliver the ransom in Janice Stillman's car. It was to be placed in a certain type of athletic bag with a specific brand, color—everything. Derrick drove over a bridge and tossed the bag, which our people had outfitted with a tracking device. The agents watched that bag for hours. After dark, they checked the bag and found the tracking device, but the money had been switched for cut up newspapers. The only one who could have made the switch was Derrick Stillman, who says to this day that he never had anything to do with it."

"That's why the finger has ended up being pointed at his mother, Janice Stillman," Mac said.

"Money never turned up and no one has ever found any proof that she was behind it," Delaney said.

"How about her leaving Hollywood and having all that money to set up her husband in business?"

"She inherited a fortune from some relative," Delaney said. "Believe me, the feds have watched the Stillmans' finances very closely. They've gotten no money or lived anywhere above their means without the feds knowing about it. If they have that million dollars stashed away, they've never gone near it."

"Can I see the case file?" Mac asked.

"I'll see what I can do," Delaney said."

After Mac hung up, he looked across the squad room to where Archie was sitting cross-legged on the floor with Gnarly's head still in her lap. Tenderly, she was stroking the sick dog while humming softly to him.

Sensing his gaze on her, she paused in the petting. "What?"

Mac shrugged with a grin. "I was just thinking about what a happy little family we are."

With a groan and a whine, Gnarly pressed his head against her hand to urge her to continue.

"Maybe not all of us are happy right now," Mac corrected himself. Recalling the roses he had ordered, he asked in a casual tone, "How long have you been here?"

"Since a little after noon," she replied.

"Any deliveries come to the house?" He stood up and went around the desk.

She shook her head. "Why? Are you expecting something?"

"No." He knelt next to her. With his finger under her chin, he lifted her head up to meet his eyes.

Not believing him, she arched an eyebrow in his direction. "Liar. Now you've made me curious."

He smiled at her. "You're beautiful when you're curious." He kissed her lips.

Begging for her to resume petting, Gnarly lifted his head so that his warm snout bumped the bottom of Mac's chin.

"Get your own girl," Mac told him.

Uttering a long whine mixed with a groan, Gnarly's ears fell to the side of his head and he plopped back down into Archie's lap.

CHAPTER THIRTEEN

The scent of spring snapped Mac out of his thoughts on his way to David's cruiser in the station parking lot. Low in the sky, the setting sun cast a golden glow across the lake up onto the shore.

Time does have a way of flying by.

In a flash, he recalled that it had been almost three years to the day since he had discovered that his birth mother was a world-famous mystery novelist and she had left him a fortune beyond his wildest dreams. It seemed like only the day before that he had driven his brand new red sports car around Deep Creek Lake for the first time to his new home on Spencer Point where he met his half-brother and…first laid eyes on Archie Monday, the love of his life.

In an instant, his life changed forever.

Yes, Archie Monday is the love of my life.

"Mac, are you coming or aren't you?" David snapped him back to the present.

Mac blinked. "Yeah."

"Then get in the car." David slammed the driver's side door shut.

Need to do something about that. Fix things with her. Today.
As soon as I get home.

With a sense of determination, Mac yanked open the
door and climbed into the front passenger seat. He took out
his phone and thumbed the button for the Spencer Inn.

"Who are you calling?"

"Jeff Ingles."

"Manager at the inn? Why?"

"To make a reservation."

Assuming Mac was making dinner reservations for that
night, David chuckled. "You're pretty optimistic."

ɷ   ઠ   ઝ   ઠ

Ten minutes later, David's radio cackled while he was
turning his cruiser around the barricade at the Blue Whale
Pub. The police dispatcher announced, "Suspect vehicle
spotted at overlook and picnic grounds on Lake Shore Drive
in Spencer, mile marker two."

"That's directly across the lake from here," David noted.

Mac's phone vibrated. The caller ID showed that it was
Archie. He tapped the screen to put her on speaker. "Mac,
David, Harris just got a call from that burner. They're talking
right now."

"Can you locate Harris with the GPS in his phone?"
David leaned across the seat to ask into Mac's phone.

"I'm—" She cursed. "Call has been disconnected. They
were talking for less than a minute."

"They're coordinating." Mac searched the faces of the
many bystanders lurking along the hillside leading up the
mountain. "Zachery Harris is in the area."

"Maybe she was telling Harris where she was so he could
pick her up." David gestured for Mac to get out of the cruiser.
"You go take care of Lenny Frost. Tell Bogie to get him into

custody." He picked up the radio. "I'll go hunt down Sela Wallace and Zachery Harris."

David was on the radio with two of his officers when Mac climbed out of the cruiser and went over to the van where the command center was housed.

Bogie met Mac at the door. "Where's the chief going?" He stepped aside to allow Mac to enter the van.

"The car Sela Wallace stole was spotted directly across the lake from here." Mac shrugged out of his sports coat and took the ballistics vest the deputy chief offered him. "He's meeting a couple of officers over there to see if they can catch her."

Sheriff Turow and Deputy Parker flashed Mac wide grins. "Thank you for the steaks," the deputy said.

"As long as the staff at the inn was whipping up dinners for the hostages and Lenny, why not throw a few more on the grill?" Mac replied while patting the deputy on the shoulder. "Glad you enjoyed it."

"Like I said, this is the weirdest hostage situation I've ever seen," Sheriff Turow said. "Hostages inside singing 'Take Me Out to the Ballgame' out of tune, steaks all around, booze flowing freely—it's time to end this and for all of us to go home. Problem is, I can already tell you that none of those people in there can drive. They're all over the legal limit." He picked up the phone and hit the number to call the Blue Whale Pub. It was still ringing when he handed the phone to Mac.

Sucking in a deep cleansing breath, Mac waited several rings before a timid voice answered. "Hell-o?" The slurred greeting was followed by a long, loud belch.

"Who's this?" Mac asked in a sharp tone.

"Bernie. Who's this? ...Is that you, Mr. Forsythe? How are you? Are you mad at us for voting you off our island?"

"I'm not mad, Bernie."

"That's good," the elderly man burped. "I'd hate for you to be mad at us. You were only trying to save our lives. It's just—you were such a party pooper doing it."

Mac shook his head to adjust to the unexpected step of a drunken hostage answering the phone and making small talk. "Where's Lenny?"

"He's right here," Bernie said.

"Why are you answering the phone?"

"Because he's asleep."

"Asleep?" Mac gasped before catching himself.

"Asleep?" Sheriff Turow asked Bogie. "Did he say our hostage taker is asleep? How long has he been sleeping?"

Mac was already asking the same question.

"Oh," Bernie mused, "I don't know." They heard the phone cackle and then the old man asking, "Hap, when did Lenny pass out? Do you remember? He was awake during the second inning, wasn't he? Remember he was laughing at that beer commercial with the big dog?" He came back to the phone. "He must have fallen asleep during the third inning. Do you want me to wake him up?"

"No!" Everyone in the van screamed in unison.

"Do you want me to take a message for him?" Bernie asked. "I'd have to get some paper. I don't know where they have any here. Edith and Carl are asleep, too. The only ones awake are Hap and me."

"Don't worry about it, Bernie," Mac said. "I'll give Lenny my message when I see him later—in person."

"Okay," Bernie said. "You know what, Mr. Forsythe?"

"What, Bernie?"

The old man belched before saying, "You really need to loosen up. Don't be so serious all the time."

"I'll try to do that." Mac attempted to disconnect the call but the elderly man called out to him from across the line.

"Life is short you know, Mr. Forsythe!"

"I am very aware of that, Bernie." Once again, Mac tried to hang up. Sheriff Turow and his deputies were already suiting up to rush into the pub before Lenny Frost woke up.

"I'm just saying…" Bernie said.

"Thank you, Bernie," Mac said through gritted teeth. "I—"

"Anything else I can do for you, Mr. Forsythe?"

"No, Bernie. Thank you."

"Can I go back to watching my game, Mr. Forsythe?"

"Sure. Go enjoy your game." In spite of his frustration, Mac chuckled when he hung up the phone.

Bogie was grumbling while checking his equipment. "The game is now in the top of the fifth inning. Lenny has been asleep for close to an hour and we didn't know."

Sheriff Turow looked at each of the officers and deputies surrounding him. "That information never leaves this van. Understood?"

"Understood," Bogie said while slapping the fasteners on his vest. "It's time for us to end this, dry out our hostages, and go home."

ꜯ ꜰ ꜯ ꜰ

This is easy—too easy.

David found the old green Ford Sedan parked in the first space next to the trail weaving through the trees and rocks down to the lake shore, which was directly across the narrow inlet from the Blue Whale Pub. The sun was setting behind the mountain. In a few minutes, it would be dark. With the lack of outdoor lights in the area, it would be nearly impossible for them to spot Wallace hiding in the brush.

Studying the layout, David picked up his radio mike. "Brewster, Fletcher, I'm at the overlook. What's your ETA?"

"Two minutes, chief," Fletcher replied. Brewster clicked in directly behind Fletcher with an ETA of three minutes.

Best to wait.

Even as he thought it, David climbed out of his cruiser and made his way to the top of the path. Craning his neck, he could make out the water lapping on the boulders that lined the shore…and the silhouette of a rifle barrel aimed at the pub across the water.

Grasping his gun with one hand, David tapped the button on his shoulder mic. "Dispatch, this is Chief O'Callaghan," he reported while making his way down the darkened path. "Female suspect spotted at the bottom of the path at the mile two overlook. Suspect is armed with weapon aimed at Blue Whale Pub. Will attempt to apprehend. Back-up requested. Notify sheriff and his team at Blue Whale. Repeat. Back up requested and notify Sheriff Turow ASAP."

Leading with his weapon, David eased his way down the path toward the water. Along the rocky path, he stumbled over a loose rock and twisted his ankle. Cursing at the pain, he told himself that it was a lucky thing it was he, and not Mac or one of his other officers, on the scene. Judging by how desperate Wallace was, he didn't want to risk giving himself away by using a flashlight to light the rocky path. Having grown up on the lake, David knew every path and tree like the back of his hand. Everybody else would have been forced to use a flashlight, which would have put them at a possibly fatal disadvantage.

At the water's edge, with the sun dipping behind the mountain, the lakeshore was bathed in almost total darkness.

Keeping his breathing slow, David peered in the direction of the water while letting his eyes adjust to the dark. Eventually, he was able to make out the outline of the redheaded woman who had managed to fake her way out of a hostage situation, overpower a nurse to escape the hospital, and steal a car to return to where she had started.

This is one desperate woman—the most dangerous kind.

With the black metal of the assault rifle and her dark clothing, he could only barely make her out laying on her tummy on the ground with the rifle aimed across the water. She was peering at her target through the night scope.

David stepped out of the shadows and pressed the muzzle of his gun against the top of her redhead. "It's over, Wallace. Take your finger off the trigger and put your hands up."

For a long moment, they both stood frozen in silence.

"Don't risk it, Wallace," David said. "You pull your trigger and I'll pull mine. From this distance, you may miss. I won't."

Slowly, she rose up onto her knees. David backed up a step to allow her room to stand up. Then, in an instant, she twirled the rifle around and swung it to hit David across the face.

� ꙮ ꙮ ꙮ

Mac, Bogie, Sheriff Turow, and three of his deputies were crowded around Lenny Frost, who was passed out in a chair in the center of the stage. After eight hours of continuously drinking an unbelievable amount of beer and wine and topping it all off with a bottle of scotch, Lenny Frost had none of the dignity that comes from being an award-winning actor and star. He was sprawled out with his legs and arms at all different angles. His head hung back with his mouth wide open to allow drool to drip out of the corner of his mouth. He smelled like a brewery.

They had found Carl and Edith entwined in each other's arms on a booth bench with an empty bottle of wine and two glasses on the table before them. The expressions on their faces resembled those of a couple of love-struck teenagers.

Bernie and Hap objected when they were told in the bottom of the seventh inning that the hostage situation was over. They only agreed to allow the EMTs to take them to the hospital to be checked over after being assured that they would have the game on in the emergency room.

Lenny slept through the entire evacuation.

"Who's going to wake him up?" Bogie asked.

Everyone looked at Mac.

"I guess it's me." Mac crept up to the sleeping man and slipped the gun out from under Lenny's hand where he had been holding it in his lap. Mac handed it off to one of the deputies. Lenny snorted, wiped his nose with the back of his hand, and continued sleeping.

"This is incredible," Sheriff Turow said.

"Just when I thought I'd seen it all," Bogie said.

Mac leaned over and nudged the hostage taker in the shoulder. "Hey, Lenny, wake up," he said in a loud whisper.

With a phlegm-filled cough, Lenny folded his arms across his chest and turned away from Mac.

"Lenny, it's Mickey," he said while nudging him harder. "We have proof that you didn't shoot the Stillmans."

"Tell them to leave a number and I'll text them in the morning," Lenny mumbled in a slurred voice.

Mac raised his voice and patted him on the cheek several times. "Lenny, wake up. We need to talk."

With a shriek from deep in his gut, Lenny opened his eyes, while at the same time throwing a punch at the man standing over him.

Seeing the fist flying toward him, Mac ducked back so that all it hit was air. However, Mac was not prepared for what came next. Lenny backed up his punch with a side kick that connected with his mid-section. Mac doubled over. While the officers came in to get control of the drunken man, Mac stumbled off the stage, took a deep breath, and stood up.

In front of him, Mac could hear the rage and terror in Lenny's voice while he cursed at the officers and deputies trying to calm him down. Later, he would wonder at how over all that, he heard the shatter of the glass in the patio door behind him. The sound of the glass breaking was immediately followed by the horrific impact of the bullet striking him in the middle of his back—one instant before everything around him went black.

CHAPTER FOURTEEN

On his hands and knees, David was still shaking the stars flashing inside his head when he felt her boot make contact with his side. The wind knocked out of him, he felt like he had been stabbed simultaneously with two knives.

"What's the matter? Your mommy always told you it wasn't polite to hit girls?"

No way! He sensed rather than saw her throw her leg back to kick him in the gut where he was lying on his side.

Mentally, he pushed past the pain to see the foot coming at him. He tightened his midsection to take the impact and grabbed the foot with both hands. With a twist, he knocked her down onto her back. She hit the ground with a grunt.

Before she could recover, he sprung up and pinned her down with his arm across her throat.

Only then was he aware of the blood in his mouth from where the butt of the rifle had made contact. While trying to concentrate on her, he quickly glanced around to locate the gun he had dropped and the rifle she had used to slug him. "You're under arrest," he told her in a low voice.

"I don't think so," she gasped out.

156

David's weight was shifted to the side to hold her down and his right forearm was against her throat—he was off balance. Throwing her weight to the side, she rolled to land him on his back so she could straddle him.

On the rocky shoreline, David let out a cry when he felt the sharp edge of a cold hard rock tear through the back of his shirt and stab him between his shoulder blades. While his bulletproof vest protected him from bullets, it couldn't protect him from the pain of landing on top of sharp rocks. Gasping deep breaths, he pushed through the pain.

"This is going to be more fun than I thought." She flashed him a wide, toothy grin while reaching for his throat with both hands.

"Not tonight." David threw his arms around her and tucked her into his chest before kicking up both legs and doing a back roll. Once more, he landed on top of her.

As soon as they stopped rolling, David spotted the dark familiar shape of his gun resting next to a rock. But he couldn't let down his guard long enough to release her in order to grab it.

Cursing, she rose even as he straddled her. At the same time, David landed a punch to her face. Her head snapped back and she fell limp under him.

He grabbed his weapon and sat up to aim it at her head. "Fun's over. You're under arrest, Wallace." He waited for her reaction—for her to fight him, argue, curse him. Instead, there was nothing.

She lay motionless under him.

"Wallace?"

When he heard the crash of feet running toward him, David twisted his aching body around with his finger on the trigger. The stabbing pain in his side told him that she had broken a couple of his ribs.

The beam of the flashlight blinded him. "Chief! You okay?"

Shading his eyes against the glare, David recognized Officer Brewster's voice. "Where have you two been?"

"We took a wrong turn on the path coming down," Officer Fletcher confessed, while they explored the scene with their flashlights, "but then heard a fight—oh, wow, Chief! What happened?"

David followed the flashlight beam to where Officer Fletcher was illuminating the woman on the ground between his legs. Only then was David able to see what had taken the fight out of his suspect.

In death, Sela Wallace's hardened face was pale, which made her red hair stand out like fire in the glare of the flashlight beam. Behind her, the bright red took on a dark glow that flowed like a river across the rock that crushed the back of her head after David's punch had ended their fight.

CB SO CB SO

Deputy Chief Arthur Bogart may have been the oldest police officer on Deep Creek Lake, but that didn't make him the least by any means. As soon as Mac hit the floor, Bogie charged through the broken door without pausing to open it and ran out onto the deck and patio. He caught sight of the inside light of a car on the hill that rested behind the rear of the pub. From the far corner of the parking lot next door, the shooter had been able to get an angle shot into the Blue Whale Pub toward the stage where Lenny Frost had been passed out.

Shooter has to know what he's doing.

Hearing the start of the car engine, Bogie took off running around the outside of the Blue Whale Pub to the road.

The shooter would have to race his car from one end of the parking lot up above him and around the ritzy restaurant next door to turn out onto the access road, get to the traffic light at the intersection, and make his getaway.

Bogie could hear the deputies behind him racing to catch the shooter speeding away, but he didn't have time to stop to explain any strategy.

He shot Ol' Pat's boy! No way am I letting him get away.

Bogie hurtled a police barricade and ran out into the road at the same time the car was turning onto the access road. In the driver's seat, a young man with shaggy dark hair flashed Bogie a cocky grin and an obscene gesture with one hand while turning the steering wheel with the other.

You're not getting away on my watch!

Bogie threw up his arm and fired three shots at the driver's side and rear window of the car. The shooter gunned the engine. The car weaved from the left side of the road to the right.

"Is that him?" Sheriff Turow gasped out when he caught up with Bogie. "Are you sure that's our shooter?"

The spinning wheels on the passenger side of the car hit the ditch. The speeding car went air born. It ended its flight top-side down in the middle of the intersection and spun like a turtle on its back. The sparks from the metal hitting pavement ignited the gasoline leaking from its tank and ended the chase with a grand explosion.

"Bogie, tell me that's our shooter and your killer," Sheriff Turow said in a pleading tone.

Turning to the sheriff, Bogie's expression was filled with offense at the suggestion. He answered in a matter of fact tone, "I wouldn't have shot him if he wasn't."

CHAPTER FIFTEEN

"Stay with me, Mac," Bogie's voice sounded like it was coming from the end of a tunnel. "Wake up. Don't you give up. No son of Pat's is a quitter."

Forcing his eyes open, Mac's head exploded in pain from the bright lights over him and the wail of the ambulance's sirens. He felt Bogie squeezing his shoulder. When Mac tried to ask what had happened, his jaw felt like it was locked in place.

Something was pressed against the side of his head. His head feeling too heavy to move, Mac rotated his eyes to the side and saw bright red on a white gauze bandage that the EMT removed from his forehead.

"Bleeding…head…" was all Mac could make out of the jumbled words floating above him.

Mac turned his head back to Bogie whose lips were moving, but he couldn't make out the words he was saying.

"Archie…" Mac tried to force her name out of his mouth to communicate to Bogie. "I need Archie."

ख ଛ ख ଛ

"What happened?" Archie pushed Bogie away when he tried to take her in his arms to comfort the frightened woman. In pulling away, she collided with Tonya, who had driven her to the hospital after dispatch had called to say that Mac was down.

All Archie could see was the blood on Bogie's hands—the blood of the man she loved. "Why wasn't Mac wearing a vest when he went inside?"

"He was," Bogie said.

"Then what happened?" Archie's voice went up several octaves. "Why was he brought here in an ambulance and unconscious...and bleeding?"

"He was shot in the back..." Seeing the hysteria coming to Archie's face, Bogie grabbed her by the shoulders and explained. "The vest protected him, but the impact from the shot knocked him down and he hit his head on the stage. He got a cut on his forehead—" He showed her his bloody hands. "That's where the blood came from. The doctors believe he has a hairline fracture and a concussion. They're running an MRI on him now."

"He's going to be all right?" Tonya asked.

"They think so," Bogie said. "They're doing the MRI to make sure he doesn't have any bleeding from the brain inside his skull. He was conscious by the time we got here to the hospital, but he was out for quite a while."

Tonya hugged Archie, who let out the breath she had been holding since the call at the station.

"What happened to you?" Bogie blurted out to startle the two women.

They turned around to see David, his face battered and his torn uniform covered in dirt and blood. Clutching his ribs with one arm and pressing an ice pack to his swollen eye with the other, he eased into the first chair he came to. "I got beaten up."

"By who?" Tonya asked.

"Sela Wallace," he said. "Turns out she actually knew martial arts and can do stunts." With a groan, he shifted in his seat and checked the ice pack, which had blood on it from a cut underneath his left eye. "I think she broke some of my ribs. Brewster drove me in to get x-rays. Fletcher is still at the scene dealing with the state police."

"Did she get away?" Archie asked.

"No, she's dead." David said in a quiet tone. "I killed her…I guess that means I won." He sat up and looked around at the patients and family in the waiting area. "Where's Mac?"

"He's getting an MRI," Bogie said. "You didn't hear?"

"No," David said. "I thought you came because dispatch called about Wallace, and me coming here. What happened to Mac?"

"Someone shot up the pub," Bogie said. "The car was registered to Zachery Harris. Mac caught a bullet in the back." He held up his hand to ease David's fears. "He was wearing his vest. He fell and cracked his head."

"Did Harris escape?"

"Not likely," Bogie said. "His car crashed and burned. They'll need dental records for ID of the driver, but I believe it was Harris."

"Why do we have so much trouble taking our suspects alive?" Tonya asked with a laugh in her voice.

"If they'd stop trying to kill us then we could." David rose out of his seat so abruptly that he startled Tonya and Archie when he brushed past them and went down the hall.

Watching the police chief rush down the corridor, Tonya asked Bogie, "Was it something I said?"

"No," Bogie replied before going down the hallway after him.

The deputy chief heard David before he saw him. From down the hall, he could hear the sound of an open palm repeatedly pounding a vending machine in the break room.

"Piece of junk!" David cursed the candy machine before slamming his fist against the door.

"Didn't your papa used to tell you that you get more bees with honey than vinegar?" There was an extra down-home tone to Bogie's drawl while he leaned in the doorway. He tucked his thumbs inside his utility belt.

"Forget it." David gave the machine one last kick before turning away and going over to the window to look out into the darkened parking lot. "'I'm not really hungry anyway."

"Did you eat dinner?" Bogie sauntered over to the machine to see that a chocolate candy bar had come off its coiled container but had gotten caught against the inside of the door.

"No, but that's all right."

"You always did get cranky when your blood sugar dropped after not eating." Bogie rested one hand against the side of the machine while pressing the other against the door. "Your dad used to tell me over and over again about how, in most situations, use of force only makes things worse."

David turned around to see Bogie pressing against the vending machine's door while gently rubbing his hand across the glass that rested between him and the candy bar.

"Took me thirty years to figure out what he meant." Bogie stepped back and turned to David. "Most times, things are more likely to go your way when you simply use some gentle persuasion." Like a donkey, Bogie delivered a back kick registering only a single notch above a tap. The candy bar dropped down. He took out the snack and went over to the window to hand it to David. "No excessive force necessary."

David refused the offer. "You take it."

With a shrug of his huge shoulders, Bogie tore off one end of the candy wrapper.

"And I did not use excessive force." David pointed to his swollen face. "She started it. I ended it."

"Who are you trying to convince?" Bogie took a bite of the candy bar.

Saying nothing, David turned back to the window. Bogie joined him in staring out the window. He was halfway through the candy bar before David broke the silence.

"Do you know how many people I've killed during my career...both here and overseas with the marines?"

"Between the places you were stationed and situations that you've been in, both over there and here," Bogie answered, "I can only imagine."

"Each time, every single time..." David blinked his eyes and turned his head.

Bogie could sense rather than see the tears that came to his eyes.

"It never gets any easier," David said in a tone that was barely above a whisper. "Every time I have taken a life, it was a kill or be killed situation. These animals are trying to kill me. They are the enemy, against my country or me or law and order in my town, but still, every single time that I have ended up having to kill them, I feel ..." He sucked in a deep breath and hung his head. "It never gets any easier."

"That's good," Bogie said.

David turned to him.

Bogie directed his attention to unwrapping the paper around his candy bar. "It's good that you feel bad, because you're one of the good guys. Good guys don't want to kill anyone. But, for the sake of our society and way of life, we need guys like you, and me, and Mac. Good guys who are able to step up to the plate and do what has to be done, even when we don't want to do it, to protect everyone else. If you didn't feel remorse for the life that you've taken, then that would make you no better than those bad guys that you've killed.

Feeling bad about killing a bad guy proves that you're one of the good guys." He pointed a finger at David. "And if you weren't, I'd probably end up having to take you out, which would make me feel real bad." Bogie popped the last of his candy bar into his mouth and chewed. He asked around the candy bar, "Understand?"

Slowly digesting the information, David nodded his head while shrugging his shoulders. The nod of his head turned into a shake. "Are you saying that if I didn't feel bad you'd have to kill me?"

"Yep."

"You're not very good at giving pep talks."

"No, I'm not." Bogie slipped his arm across David's shoulders. "Point is, you did what you had to do to protect everyone in that pub. She, just like every other bad guy that you've ever had to take out, left you no choice. It's not your fault."

"I know," David said. "But even though I know that, it doesn't make me feel any better."

Looking into David's blue eyes, which were filled with sadness, Bogie grinned. "Your dad was the same way. He said I was lousy at giving pep talks, too."

Reminded of his father, whose death still left an aching wound in his chest, David shook off an additional dosage of remorse that he felt coming over him. "We need to get back to find out how Mac is."

Agreeing, Bogie turned away to toss the candy wrapper in the trash container.

In a fleeting instant, David recalled the dozens of times that Bogie had been there for him while he was growing up. Bogie took his role as godfather extremely seriously. He was the man that David could go to when he felt too intimidated to go to his father. He was more than a friend and godfather. He was a confidante.

Struck with a thought, David grasped the elder man's arm by the elbow. "Hey, Bogie."

"Yeah, son." Bogie turned to him.

"About Dad…" David said and then stopped.

"What about him?"

The two men stared into each other's eyes.

"It's about Mac…" David stopped to swallow.

The ends of Bogie's mustache twitched as the corners of his lips curled. "I know, David."

"You mean…" David asked, "I mean…Robin Spencer had Mac back when she was a teenager. Mac's father was… Robin's first love—"

"Your father was her one true love," Bogie said.

"You know then?" David asked in a whisper. "Dad…Mac is…Dad was his…birth father. That makes him…"

"David," Bogie asked with a grin, "do I look stupid to you?"

"You are far from stupid."

Bogie chuckled. "I've known about Mac longer than you've been alive. Ol' Pat and I had no secrets from each other." His eyes misted up. "Every time I see the two of you working together, bonding like brothers, I can feel your father smiling down on you both." He sucked in a shuddering breath. "You've both made him very proud."

"Thank you, Bogie," David said in a husky voice.

One corner of Bogie's mustache kicked up when he tapped the blood stains on David's white shirt. "Until you went and got yourself beaten up by a girl."

David slumped while Bogie left the break room.

ც ჯი ცვ ჯ

"For a small town police force, you Spencer cops certainly know how to kick butt."

David returned to the waiting area to find Ben Fleming, Garrett County's prosecuting attorney, chuckling along with Tonya and Archie. Bogie arrived directly ahead of him.

The laughter halted when Chelsea Adams, Ben's paralegal, got a look at the police chief. "What happened to you?" She dropped her service dog's leash and rushed over to him to examine his swollen eye and torn uniform.

Chelsea's platinum blonde hair framed her face in wispy waves. Her ivory skin gave her an almost albino appearance, which was accentuated by her jade colored pantsuit that brought out her light blue eyes. Her slight build, combined with her fair features, gave her a fragile appearance not unlike a china doll that would crumble under the force of a strong bear hug.

Chelsea's hair was almost as white as her service dog, Molly, a German shepherd, who was dressed for work in her gray vest with "Service Dog" stenciled in red block letters on the sides. Suffering from epilepsy since a serious car accident years before, Chelsea had enlisted the aid of Molly, who was trained to pick up early signs of seizures, which allowed her mistress time to take medication to stop it.

Since Chelsea's arrival in Deep Creek Lake six months earlier, Molly and Gnarly had become fast friends.

"I'm okay." David accepted Chelsea's assistance to help him into the waiting room. "What are you two doing here?"

"My phone won't stop ringing with calls from the media asking about the Frost situation," Ben said. "When the sheriff told me about the Spencer police killing two suspects, I decided to come find out for myself what was happening. When I heard you and Mac were both here at the hospital, I offered to bring Chelsea to give you some TLC."

After sniffing David's clothes, Molly sat down and peered up at him.

"Who did this?" Chelsea asked.

"Sela Wallace." David eased down into a chair. "One of our suspects in the Stillman murders."

"Sela?" Taking a seat in the chair next to his, Chelsea peered closely at the bruises on David's face and his torn, bloody uniform.

Bogie leaned over to whisper to her. "Yes, he got his butt handed to him by a girl."

"A girl hyped up on steroids," David said. "At least I'm still standing."

"Yeah, but it looks like she tagged you pretty good," Bogie said with a laugh.

"Even so, after tonight, Spencer police will have the reputation of being the last small town cops that you would want to mess with," Ben said. "Two suspects, and both of them are dead. Do you have any others?"

"Lenny Frost did take everyone in that pub hostage," David said. "That makes him look really good to me, especially since he already had an airtight alibi for the Stillman murders."

"Maybe he forgot he had an alibi," Archie said.

A doubt-filled expression crossed David's face. With a smirk, he cocked his head at her.

"Seriously," she replied. "Lenny Frost is a card-carrying alcoholic and drug addict. He could have had a blackout and honestly not remember he had an alibi for the time of the murders. He may have even wondered if he did commit them."

"You know, she's right." Bogie slowly nodded his head. "It's not believable, but it can happen." He tapped David on the shoulder. "Kind of reminds me of a case your dad and Robin worked on years ago. You were just a little tyke then.

The killer was out with a couple of buddies. They had been driving and drinking all day. The driver of the car was in the midst of a really nasty divorce. So, drunk out of his gourd, he swung by her house and beat her to death with the tire iron from his car. Then, he got back in the car with his buddies and they resumed bar hopping. His two buddies had no memory whatsoever of their friend going by the house. They alibied him. But, when confronted with the bloody tire iron that was in the trunk of the car with the victim's blood, it was clear what had happened. They were both passed out drunk during the murder and had no memory of any of it."

"Maybe," David relented. "But I can't get over Lenny and Sela Wallace being together in that video. Plus, they were both in the same rehab center at the same time. They have to know each other."

"Just because they know each other doesn't prove they were conspiring to commit murder together," Chelsea said.

"Too bad both of your key suspects are dead," Ben said. "They could have straightened this out."

"Well, Ben," David said with a pained sigh while clutching his ribs, "it was a case of kill or be killed."

"Look on the bright side, Ben," Bogie said. "We saved you a bunch of work and the state money from having to prosecute them."

"On the dark side," Ben said, "There's going to be speculation from here to eternity about what happened."

"I know," David said. "This case isn't over yet."

"Well, I suggest you close it fast," Ben said. "Lenny Frost and his hostages are all drying out. Frost's lawyer has already swooped in and cornered me saying that we don't have much of a case for holding him."

"Wait a minute!" Bogie said. "He had a gun on all of them and said he was going to kill them at midnight. We have it on tape."

"Unfortunately," Ben said, "the blood-alcohol level and fun-loving attitude of the hostages makes them unreliable witnesses for the prosecution."

"What about Mac?" Bogie asked. "He was the hostage negotiator. He was sober. He can tell what happened."

"And he got that family released," David said.

"Are you talking about the family that had to carry their child kicking and screaming out of the bar because he didn't want to leave?" Ben asked.

"You're not going to prosecute Frost, are you?" David asked.

"If you were on the jury for this case, would you convict?" the prosecutor replied. "Now, Lenny's lawyer has agreed to have his client stay in the psych ward for three days to dry out and be observed, but after that…" He shrugged his shoulders.

"He'll be gone," Tonya said, "and telling every news journalist about how it was all a big misunderstanding."

"Playing the role of the victim," Archie agreed. "You have to admit he's good at it. He won an Academy Award for playing the victim."

"Translation," Ben said, "if you want to tie Lenny Frost to these murders, you have three days to do it.

CHAPTER SIXTEEN

The first thing Mac saw when he woke up were two lovely pools of emerald green floating in front of him. When his vision cleared, he could see that it was Archie peering at him from where she was resting her head on his chest.

He was home…in the comfort of his own bed. The night in the hospital was only a foggy memory.

A smile came to his face. "My favorite sight first thing in the morning," he said in a raspy voice while running his fingers through her short blonde hair.

Then he felt a calloused paw on his shoulder. He turned his head in time to see a black snout followed by a long pink tongue, which traveled the path from the tip of his nose to both of his eyes.

"Ugh!" He pushed Gnarly away from where he had crawled up to place his front half on the bed. With his ears folded back, the German shepherd whined and tried to give Mac another kiss.

"He was worried about you," Archie explained. "He let you sleep in and got me up this morning. He's been sitting here staring at you ever since he came back in."

With a tired sigh, Mac relented and patted Gnarly on the head. "I love you, too."

Seeing this as a license to resume, Gnarly bound up onto the bed, pinned Mac down by his shoulders, and licked his face.

Retreating back to her side of the bed, Archie opted to save herself.

The pain from the bruise in his back where Mac had been shot traveled down his spine to his hips. With a cry, he shoved Gnarly away, only to have the dog push back and continue planting kisses in his ears when Mac turned his head. The love fest ended when Archie jumped out of bed, grabbed Gnarly by the collar, and dragged him, pulling and fighting, out of the bedroom.

Dropping back onto the bed, Mac gasped to catch his breath. Only then did he notice the sweet scent of roses. He gazed at the vase containing a dozen long-stemmed white roses on the dresser. Then, he noticed another on the end table next to the window seat. It took a full moment for him to remember ordering twelve dozen long stemmed white roses for Archie.

Was that really only yesterday that I did that?

Archie was giggling when she came into the bedroom and closed the door. She announced that Gnarly had found someone else to shower with affection.

"Chelsea spent the night tending to David's wounds," she said while climbing into bed next to him. "Molly is outside. So the two of them are chasing each other around the point."

"Has he told her about Lady Tala yet?" Mac asked with an evil grin while thinking about Gnarly's "indiscretion."

"Don't tell me that you're capable of blackmail." She climbed back into the bed, pulled up the covers, and wrapped her arms around him.

"How much do you think it would be worth to keep silent about Gnarly's hounding ways? An extra hour or two of sleep in the morning?"

"Rather than pay up, Gnarly may decide to just kill you in your sleep."

He was laughing when she grasped his hand and kissed him on the lips. "Thank you for the roses."

"You are very welcome, pretty lady."

Her eyes searched his. "Do you have any idea how much you scared me last night?"

"I scared myself." He tucked the comforter up around her shoulders.

Glancing around the room, he barely recalled Archie bringing him home in the middle of the night after the hospital had released him. He had no actual memory of the shot that hit him in the back. However, the sharp pain in the back of his ribs was a firm reminder. He fingered the bandage that covered up the stitches above his left temple and tried to recall where he had hit his head.

Then, Lenny Frost came to his mind.

"Where's Lenny?"

"Drying out at the hospital and getting three days of psych evaluation." Archie rested her head on his chest while clutching him with both arms. "David has two broken ribs."

"David?" Mac tried to sit up. "What happened to him?"

"Sela Wallace." She went on to explain about David catching up with her and the fight that resulted in her death. "We think her brother is dead. The shooter at the pub wrecked a car registered to Zachery Harris while trying to escape."

"Then the only ones left who can tell us what was behind the Stillman murders are Derrick and Lenny," he said with a sigh.

"If they were involved," she said. "Don't you think it's possible that Sela Wallace and Zach Harris acted alone?"

"Hard to say," Mac said.

She grinned up at him. "You usually have such a good sense of these things. Could your concussion be slowing you down?"

"Not my concussion as much as Lenny Frost's talent."

"What do you mean?"

"He's a great actor," Mac said. "I'll give him that. The problem is figuring out what role he's been playing. He's brilliant. That makes it difficult."

Draping a leg across him, she wrapped her arms around his shoulders. "Maybe it will all be clearer to you if you take your mind off of it for awhile." She pressed her lips against his. When she pulled away, she searched his face.

He uttered a low pained moan.

She furrowed her eye brows. "What's wrong?" Her tone was filled with disappointment.

He sighed. "Don't take this the wrong way."

"What?" she asked with a whine.

"I'm sorry, dear," he chuckled, "but I have a headache."

Filled with sympathy and disappointment, but amused at the same time, Archie sat up and slid over to her side of the bed. "The doctor sent home some pain killers. Do you want some?" After Mac agreed, she climbed out of the bed to go to the bathroom.

As soon as she left the bedroom, what sounded like a war between members of a dog pack erupted from the hallway outside the room. The chorus of growls, barks, and yelps escalated to a crescendo on the other side of the bedroom door.

Mac recognized Gnarly's yelps. They were partnered with vigorous clawing.

Archie ran out of the bathroom. Before she could reach the door, it flew open. Gnarly had finally managed to pull down on the latch with his paw to open the door. With

174

Molly nipping at his heels and tail, Gnarly flew across the room and dove under the bed where he made his den. He was crawling on his belly into his sanctuary when she managed to take his tail into her mouth and clamp down. With a final yelp, Gnarly yanked it away.

Instead of following in after him, Molly dropped down to stick her head under the bed and let off a final round of snarl-filled barks. When she finished, Gnarly replied with some high-pitched barks of his own.

Molly finished off the argument with one bark before turning and galloping out of the bedroom.

Holding a glass of water in one hand and the pain-killer in the other, Archie stood in disbelief.

Gnarly whimpered under the bed.

With a chuckle, Mac shook his head. "I guess Molly knows." He held out his hand to Archie for the painkillers.

She dropped the pills into his palm and handed him the glass of water. "Women can sense these things."

After washing down the medication with the water, Mac peered over the edge of the bed while handing her back the glass. Sticking his snout out from under the bed, Gnarly seemed to be checking to see if the coast was clear. Again, he uttered a long mournful cry.

"Well, Gnarly, old boy," Mac said while reaching down to pat him on top of his head, "you and I are going to have to have a long talk about women, commitment, and fidelity."

ଓ ଯ ଔ ଯ

"Does it hurt as bad as it looks?" While Mac sympathized with David and how painful the bruise and cut across his cheek had to be, he couldn't help the smile that tugged at his lips when he sat down across from him at the kitchen table.

It was almost lunch time, but they were eating breakfast. Since it was Sunday, Chelsea had the day off to tend to David's wounds.

Mac had woke up a second time to the sweet scent of French toast and sausage cooking downstairs. It was liberally mixed with the smell of freshly brewed coffee. He threw on his bathrobe, hurried down the stairs and across the cool granite living room floor to the sunken dining room. From there, he had pushed through the swinging door into the kitchen where Archie and Chelsea were preparing breakfast.

Knife in hand, Archie was slicing through a loaf of bread to dip into the mixture of egg batter and orange liquor to make the French toast. When Mac barged through the doors, she stopped with the knife in mid-air. "I knew the smell of breakfast would wake him up." She flashed a grin at Chelsea, who was turning over the sausage links frying in a pan on the stove. "What did I tell you?"

Molly was curled up in the corner. Not seeing Gnarly anywhere, Mac assumed he was still hiding out after the argument with his canine companion.

That was when Mac noticed David, dressed in a fresh uniform, nursing a cup of coffee at the kitchen table. It hurt Mac's face to look at the multi-colored bruise traveling from above the police chief's eyebrow and down across his left cheekbone.

"It does hurt as bad as it looks," David answered Mac's question.

Chelsea delivered a mug of coffee to Mac and freshened David's cup. "I still can't believe a woman did all that damage to you," she chuckled.

"She had a black belt," David said.

"You're a marine in special forces and a chief of police," Chelsea argued with a good-natured tone. She winked across the table at Mac.

"That's why I'm here and she's in the morgue."

"Hey, it happens." With a chuckle, Mac took a sip of his hot coffee. "The first time I ever got hit on duty was by a woman who wasn't much bigger than Chelsea." He cocked a thumb in the direction of David's petite girlfriend, whose tiny frame was as thin as a rail. "I tell you, I did not see it coming at all."

Archie brought a hot plate with French toast and two sausage links over to the table and set it in front of David. "What happened? Was she a murderer?"

"Domestic dispute," Mac recalled. "I had just graduated from the academy and was on patrol with my supervising officer. It was my very first domestic dispute call. Now, I knew that it was extremely easy for those types of calls to turn violent. But still, we got there and here was this big muscular guy in a dirty white T-shirt, and he was getting the daylights beaten out of him by his five-foot-tall wife. I mean, this woman was wailing at him. It was plain to see that she was high on something—the husband claimed it was crack and ordered us to arrest her—for his protection. When she refused to back down, I grabbed her arm and she spun around and—splat!" He threw up his fist to illustrate a punch. "She landed one right between my eyes."

While they laughed, Mac added, "She couldn't have been more than a hundred pounds, and I swear every ounce was in that punch. It was all I could do to keep from landing flat on my butt."

"Then what happened?" Archie asked while delivering his plate to him.

David slid the bottle of syrup across the table for him to use.

Mac poured the syrup over his French toast. "I'm counting stars and trying to recall why I didn't want to go into engineering like my parents—my adoptive parents—

wanted me to do. Then, through the ringing in my ears, I heard my supervisor yelling, 'Faraday, get in the fight.' That was when I saw that he had tackled her from behind and the two of them were rolling on the floor. Between the three of us, including the woman's husband, I managed to get her cuffed and called for an ambulance. While getting her onto the gurney, she decked one of the EMTs. Since I was the rookie, I was given the duty of riding to the ER with her—laying on top of her on the gurney to pin her down in order to protect the EMTs."

"Ah, the life of a rookie." David's tone was heavy with sarcasm.

Mac continued. "We got to the ER, and the doctor wanted to know why she was cuffed and strapped down. I told him that she was a danger to anyone and everyone and flipping out on crack. She needed to be tranquilized before we could let her loose. He reminded me that I was only a lowly uniform and he was the doctor. He ordered me to climb off her, unstrap, and un-cuff her. I told him that I couldn't be responsible for what she did if I did that. He ordered me again. So," with a cocky grin, he concluded, "I gave him what he wanted. I let her go."

"What did she do?" Chelsea asked in a breathless tone.

"She broke the doctor's nose."

Chelsea and Archie joined them at the table. After some jovial small talk, Mac noted David's uniform. "You're not staying home to lick your wounds today?"

"Lenny Frost is only going to be held at the hospital for three days for observation," David explained. "That doesn't give me much time to figure this whole case out before he takes off."

Archie pointed out, "If he leaves the area and you uncover evidence that he was involved in the Stillman murders, you'll still be able to get a warrant for his arrest and bring him back."

Mac glanced over at Chelsea. "He took hostages. Why isn't Ben charging him with criminal contempt, brandishing a firearm, and menacing, plus endangering the welfare of a child? The bartender's kid was there."

"Look at it from Ben's point of view," Chelsea said. "The hostages, the very victims in this case, felt comfortable enough to watch two ballgames—"

"They didn't even notice when their captor fell asleep," Archie said with a giggle.

"Plus," Chelsea said, "they argued with the police when they interrupted the game to rescue them."

"Not to mention that they actually voted out the very man sent in to protect them from the man with the gun," David said, to which Mac groaned.

Chelsea continued, "When the jury hears that—"

"I get your point," Mac said.

"Lenny'll be charged with something, but most likely he'll plead down to a misdemeanor and Ben will accept the plea to avoid an embarrassing trial," Chelsea said.

David looked across the table at Mac. "You were the one who spent time with him. What do you think? If things had turned out differently, do you think Lenny would have shot those hostages at midnight?"

"He was unconscious way before midnight," Chelsea smiled while pouring syrup onto her French toast.

"It was a very weird situation," Mac agreed. "Lenny Frost is..." With a shake of his head, he returned to his lunch and took a bite from his French toast before asking David, "What's your opinion of Derrick Stillman? He was the closest to the murder victims. He knew the security passcode. Maybe he knew he was under surveillance and used that to his advantage. He could have hired Sela and Zachery to commit the murders for him."

"Maybe he drugged himself," Archie suggested, "to divert suspicion away from him."

David shook his head. "My gut is telling me that Derrick didn't do this."

"Maybe it's not your gut but your broken ribs," Archie said.

"Why does either Derrick or Lenny or anyone else have to be involved?" Chelsea asked. "Carson Drake's children killed the Stillmans and tried to frame Lenny, who they blamed for their criminal father deserting them, which led to their mother's murder. Sela was meeting Lenny at the pub to poison him and make it look like a suicide. When Lenny saw the newscast saying that he was the prime suspect and Janice Stillman had actually written his name in her blood, he freaked out and took hostages, which ruined Sela's plan."

Archie took up the story. "Sela got away by faking a seizure, and then coordinated with her brother for the both of them to try to finish the job by shooting Lenny at the pub before the police could protect him."

"Except we have Sela with Lenny on that video shot two weeks ago," David said.

"She was getting close to him so that he would meet with her, giving her the opportunity to kill him." Archie looked to Mac for his approval of their theory. Instead of nodding in agreement, Mac was staring down at his now empty plate while listening to them. His expression wasn't one of approval or rejection of their hypothesis.

"Archie, you said Sela must have met Lenny at the rehab center three years ago," David said.

"Maybe that was what planted the seed for their plan," she argued. "Most likely, he talked about his kidnapping in group therapy and blamed Carson Drake for setting him on the road to addiction. Only he didn't realize his kidnapper's daughter was right there."

"Sounds good to me," Chelsea said. "What do you think, Mac?"

"Yes, Mac," David replied. "What do you think?"

Mac answered slowly, "I think…Lenny is an exceptional actor." Staring at the wall behind David, he sipped his coffee.

Each of them falling deep into his and her own thoughts, silence fell over the kitchen while they ate until the living room erupted into loud barks as Gnarly signaled the arrival of visitors. Molly's paws dug into the granite floor until she caught traction and tore out of the kitchen. Judging by the tone in her bark, Mac was unsure if she was going after the visitors who had interrupted her nap or Gnarly.

By the time Mac reached the foyer, Molly was ambushing Gnarly from behind while he was in position at the front door to check out the visitors. She chomped on his tail and pulled him onto the floor. With a yelp, Gnarly whirled around to get an earful from the white German shepherd.

"Molly!" Chelsea yelled in a sharp tone from where she stood after following the ruckus. Instantly, Molly shut up and backed away, while glaring at Gnarly. "What's gotten into you? Come here!" Chelsea ordered.

His ears laying on the side of his head, Gnarly slumped and gazed with big brown eyes at the other dog who returned to the kitchen with her mistress.

"She'll forgive you." Mac patted the German shepherd on the head before peering through the glass door to see two men in suits waiting for him on the front porch. He recognized one as Sid Delaney, a special agent with the FBI. The other was an older man who appeared to be the same age as Bogie, though much smaller. His face and demeanor seemed to be much more war torn.

When Mac opened the door, Gnarly shot out to give both men a nasal pat down to determine if they were friends or foes. While Sid greeted Gnarly with a two-handed pat and rub behind the ears, the older man stepped back and threw his hands up in surrender.

"It's okay, Jeb," Sid laughed. "Gnarly is one of the good guys. He's chief of security here at Spencer Manor. Believe me, no one gets past this guy."

When his snout picked up something on Jeb's left ankle, Gnarly's ears stood at attention. With his eyes trained on the visitor's ankle, he sat down. Then he cocked his head and looked up at Jeb as if to ask, "Would you care to explain what it is you have strapped around your ankle?"

"I take it you're packing?" Sid asked Jeb.

"I'm never not packing."

Sid introduced his companion to Mac and Gnarly. "This is Jeb Winkler. He's retired FBI. You were asking about the Lenny Frost kidnapping case. Jeb here was the chief investigator on the case. When the news hit about Lenny yesterday, Jeb started making phone calls and, after I started making phone calls on your behalf, we connected."

Sid then turned to Jeb. "This is Mac Faraday, retired homicide detective, now millionaire playboy."

"But you still work homicide cases?" Jeb asked with a cocked eyebrow.

"I'm not good at golf." Mac gestured for them to come inside. He tapped the top of the dog's head. "He's clean, Gnarly."

Assured that the visitors were friends and not foes, Gnarly escorted the men inside. Still unsure, Jeb lowered his hands and follow Sid into the mansion's two-story foyer.

Special Agent Sid Delaney greeted Mac with a handshake and a chuckle. "I see you've really taken to this life of leisure since we last met." In response to the confusion that came to

Mac's face, Sid tapped the collar of the bathrobe that Mac had forgotten he was still wearing.

"Oh, geeze," Mac sighed. "I've been busy."

"So I can see." Sid tapped his own forehead to indicate that he noticed the bruise on Mac's. "Lenny Frost do that to you?"

"Inadvertently," Mac said. "Actually, this happened when Zachery Harris, formerly Drake, shot me in the back while trying to shoot Lenny."

Noticing David with his black eye coming in from the kitchen, Sid chuckled. "You Spencer police are real badasses. Who gave you that shiner, O'Callaghan?"

"A girl," David said with a chuckle while slipping his cell phone back into its case on his utility belt.

After Sid introduced Jeb to Spencer's police chief, the retired agent said, "Don't tell me," Jeb said, "a wife decided to defend her husband on a domestic dispute call."

"No," David replied, "an attempted murderer resisted arrest."

Inviting them to sit down in the living room, Mac explained, "She was Sela Wallace, formerly known as Sela Drake, Carson Drake's daughter."

Jeb and Sid exchanged glances.

"Then the rumors that I had been hearing while calling around are true," Jeb said. "Carson Drake's kids did kill the Stillmans in retaliation for duping their father into kidnapping Frost?"

"I was just coming in to tell Mac," David said with a nod of his head. "Ballistics got a match on the assault rifle they found in Zachery Harris, a.k.a. Drake's, car. The bullets from the murders, the pub, and Mac's back were fired from that rifle." He added, "They also found the remains of a wig with bright red hair in the burnt out car. That fits with the scenario of Harris committing the murders and wearing a red wig so that any possible witnesses would claim it was Lenny."

Shaking his head, Jeb rubbed his fingers across his forehead. "I knew Drake's kids were obsessed, but I didn't think it would come to this."

"What can you tell us about the Lenny Frost kidnapping?" Mac asked.

"Why do you want to know?" Jeb replied.

"Same reason you were making phone calls yesterday trying to find out what was going on with Lenny," Mac shot back. "The Frost kidnapping case was never officially closed."

"Carson Drake and the ransom never turned up," Jeb said. "Until that happens, the case is still open, which is why I was never able to answer any of the questions that the Drake kids had been asking me all these years."

"What questions were they asking?"

"Why didn't we investigate the Stillmans?" Jeb asked. "Truth is, we did. We investigated them very closely for years. For Pete's sake, the last one to have the ransom was their son, Derrick. But, we could never find anything concrete to tie them to Lenny Frost's kidnapping. And Lenny told us point blank that it was Carson Drake. Carson was the last one he remembered being with. He was the one whose voice he heard telling his accomplice on the phone that he had the money and that they were going to meet to split it before he took off. With that statement, we knew that Carson was in on it."

"And yet," Mac said, "Zachery Harris claimed Carson had been telling people directly before the kidnapping that Janice Stillman was going to represent him after this gig, which turned out to be the kidnapping."

"That points to her being his accomplice," Sid said.

"Have you found any real evidence to prove that she did dupe Carson Drake into kidnapping Lenny?" David asked.

"At this point," Jeb confessed, "after all of these years, I'm willing to believe anything. This is one of those cases that pretty much broke my career. Yeah, Lenny was found safe and sound after breaking lose from where he was handcuffed to the bed and calling the police. But the kidnappers got away with a million-dollar ransom and now two people, who may or may not have been involved, are dead."

"With or without evidence, what do you think happened?" Mac asked him. "Do you think Janice Stillman and her husband were in on it?"

Jeb looked from Mac to David to Sid in silence. He sucked in a deep breath and then let it out. "The situation had all of the ingredients for that to be the case. Carson Drake was a second-rate actor who wanted to be a star. He worked his way into the right circles by being a drug dealer. He supplied Lenny and Derrick. But he didn't want to be a dealer all his life."

The retired agent sat forward in his seat. Looking around as if to ensure no one was listening, he said, "Personally, I've always thought Carson Drake got something on Lenny that could have ruined his clean teeny-bopper image and tried to blackmail him. Some of my information did confirm that as a drug dealer, Carson did have access to that type of information and was not above using extortion to get his break." The corners of his lips curled. "Do you remember Kate Coleman?"

Mac glanced over to David, who was nodding his head. "What about her?" Mac asked. "How is she connected to this case?"

"The length of a pop star's fame is quite short," Jeb said. "Janice Stillman was Kate's agent. That was how she met

Lenny Frost. Nine months after Kate's show was canceled, her Porsche took a nose dive off an overlook in the Hollywood Hills."

"I remember when that happened," David said. "She was only nineteen years old."

"Six months after that, Lenny Frost was kidnapped," Jeb said.

Mac asked, "What does Kate's death have to do with Lenny's kidnapping?"

Jeb looked straight across to where Mac was peering at him. "After Lenny's kidnapping, and after it hit the media that he had identified his abductor as Carson Drake, we started getting information about him. Kate Coleman's sister called me."

Jeb sat forward and rested his elbows on his knees. "Kate, like Lenny, was into drugs. Carson was her supplier. According to Coleman's sister, Carson Drake and Kate would do drugs together. One night, she had gotten so wasted that they had sex and Drake recorded it. Then, he held it over Kate's head, threatening to send it to the media unless she got him a regular spot on her television show."

"Did she?" Mac asked.

"Yes," Jeb said. "But, as luck would have it, six months later the show was canceled. There was nothing she could do."

"And the recording?" Sid asked.

"Never surfaced," Jeb said.

"Did you see the tape?" Mac asked.

"No," Jeb said. "Kate's sister had seen Kate's copy. Carson Drake had the master. She said that after Kate's death, she destroyed the copy she had. Now here's the interesting thing."

"More interesting things?" Mac asked.

"I decided to look into Kate Coleman's accident," Jeb said, "and learned some things that had never been made public. The majority of the injuries that Kate Coleman suffered in that crash were postmortem."

Instantly picking up the meaning of the actress's injuries, David announced, "Kate Coleman was already dead when that car went off the road. Someone murdered her, put her dead body in the car and pushed it off that hill to make it look like an accident."

Jeb nodded his head. "Not only that, but the driver's seat in the car was positioned all the way back. Kate was five feet two inches tall. She wouldn't have been able to reach the gas pedal with the seat that far back."

Mac asked, "Could Carson have killed her because she threatened to ruin his career by exposing him as a blackmailer?"

"Coleman's body was thrown from the car," Jeb said. "At first it was assumed that she had been driving. The media had already been speculating about it being a suicide before the ME discovered that the injuries were consistent with her being dead before the crash. Her blood alcohol level was way above the legal limit," Jeb reported. "Plus, she had cocaine in her system as well."

"What was the cause of death?" Mac asked him.

"Blunt force trauma to the back of the head," Jeb said. "She was hit in the back of the head with something."

Mac noted, "You said Carson Drake was her supplier and they did drugs together. Did the police look at him for killing her for whatever reason?"

"Carson Drake's name did come up," Jeb said. "He had been seen with Kate earlier the night of the accident. But he had a solid alibi for during the kill window...Lenny Frost."

"Lenny and Kate used to be pretty hot," David said. "He was a couple of years younger than she was and talked about how crazy he was for her. He was broken hearted when she died—at least, he claimed he was."

"Then he wouldn't lie to give Kate's killer an alibi," Mac said.

"Unless Carson Drake was holding something over his head," Jeb suggested.

"So, when Kate fails to make Carson Drake a star, he finds something to use against Lenny Frost," Mac said. "Janice, who lost one client to this menace, Kate Coleman, decides to kill three birds with one stone. Get rid of Carson Drake, garnish publicity for her falling star, and make a nice profit to boot." He sat back in his seat.

"Unfortunately, we can't prove any of that," Jeb said.

"If Carson Drake was blackmailing Lenny, what would it have been with?" David asked.

Jeb answered with a shake of his head and a shrug of his shoulders. "Back then, a video of Lenny smoking pot would have been enough. But then, it was a known secret among his fans that he was heavy into drugs and was certainly no virgin."

"Then if Carson exposed any of that, it wouldn't have done much damage," Mac said.

"Unless it was bad enough to have voided Lenny's contract with the studio," Archie announced while coming in from the kitchen.

Chelsea and Molly were directly behind her. Spotting the white German shepherd, Gnarly, who had been lying under the coffee table, bumped his head on the underside while scurrying out in order to escape. He climbed up onto the sofa next to Mac.

After Mac introduced the ladies to Jeb, Archie slipped onto the arm of the sofa where Mac was sitting. Between Gnarly and Archie, he was pinned in. "Most studios do have morality clauses in their contracts with their stars, especially when those stars have squeaky-clean images. Anything that could tarnish that image reflects badly on the studio. With Lenny, we're talking about fifteen years ago when the show he was in was a clean sitcom. If all of those rumors about his hard partying had been made public, it would have sent his star crashing to the ground, which not only would have cost Lenny his career, but also would have cost the studio a lot of money."

"As well as Janice Stillman, who received ten percent of Lenny's bankroll," Jeb said.

"So she had motive," Mac said. "What else did you have?"

"If we had had anything, I would have arrested her," Jeb said. "Basically, we had nothing. Derrick, her son, was with Lenny the night that he disappeared. But then, those two were best friends and were out partying every night. Derrick stated that Carson Drake was partying with Lenny when he left Lenny's place that night. Lenny had a television interview the next morning. When he didn't show, they found out that he and his car were missing. The studio was in a full panic by the time Lenny called to say that he had been kidnapped and his abductors were demanding a million-dollar ransom."

"Lenny made the call?" Mac asked.

Jeb nodded his head. "They had left an envelope at the studio gate. It had a picture of Lenny tied up and with that day's newspaper as proof that he was alive." He asked them, "Have you read Zachery Harris's book about the kidnapping?"

"No," Mac said, "but he did give me a copy."

"Read it," Jeb said. "He tried to interview me for it, but I refused. I couldn't be interviewed because I was involved in the case and it was still open. But I did read it. I wondered if he was any relation to Carson because of the hard line he took against the Stillmans. It was very biased, but I have to admit, he did have some good insight, stuff I didn't know at the time." He shrugged. "Still can't make sense of what I'm missing. Must be because I'm getting old."

CHAPTER SEVENTEEN

Why do the best ideas always come to you in the shower?

Against Archie's objections, Mac accepted David's invitation to go interview Derrick Stillman at his suite at the Spencer Inn. That meant an aspirin, a shower, and getting dressed.

Sitting in the steam shower, waiting for the aspirin to take effect, Mac's thoughts turned to Archie and pushing past his fear of giving marriage another try. Funny—once he pushed beyond his fear of being left as devastated and humiliated as he had been with his first wife, he was anxious to make it official.

He had to do it right. Archie had been so patient with him for so long. She was the love of his life and it had to be perfect.

That means a ring. Not just any diamond. Archie deserves the best. It takes time to find the perfect ring, or to have one custom designed. I can't waste anymore time. She's waited long enough.

Like a lightning bolt shooting down from the heavens to strike Mac in his seat in the steam shower, it hit him.

Yes, that'll be perfect. He stood up and grabbed the handle to turn off the shower. *No need to buy a ring. I already have it. Right here in Spencer Manor.*

190

He threw open the door. Without taking the time to dry off, he shrugged into his bathrobe and ran into the master suite to search through the jewelry armoire that Robin Spencer had left him.

Constructed of oak, the aged armoire was the size of an end table and filled with antique pieces, priceless jewels that had been passed down through the Spencer family for several generations. Ed Willingham, the Spencer lawyer who had handled his mother's estate, estimated that Robin's jewelry collection was valued at over five million dollars. Mac had given some of the less ornate pieces to his grown daughter, Jessica. Eventually, he expected her, and his son Tristan's wife, whenever he married, to split the collection. But otherwise, the bulk of the extensive collection was gathering dust in the corner of Mac's bedroom.

There was one particular piece for which he was hunting. *Why didn't I think of it before? This ring has a history that's perfect for sealing Archie's and my commitment to each other.*

He had all the drawers open and jewelry hanging out when Archie walked in. "I thought you were getting dressed. David is waiting." Her voice shot through him and made him jump as if he had been struck by another bullet. "What are you looking for?"

Mac slammed the drawer shut and closed the doors. "I was looking for a pair of earrings for Jessica." Closing the bathrobe that had fallen open in his search, he turned around. "She's going to New York with a bunch of her friends and they're going to a huge fashion show. She had a dress made by some big designer and she wants the perfect earrings and necklace and I thought I had seen some in here that would look nice."

Archie's eyes narrowed. Then, she placed her hands on her hips and cocked her head at him. "Really?"

"Really." Mac saw Gnarly had come in with her. The German shepherd sat next to her and cocked his head at him. Obviously, Gnarly wasn't buying his lie either.

Best defense is a good offense.

"What?" Mac shot back at them.

"Since when have you become fan of fashion?" she asked with a laugh. "Like you would know what would go with a dress that you haven't even seen."

"She described—" To Mac's relief, David blew the car horn to urge him to hurry up. "I have to go." With a peck on her cheek, he hurried past her to go out the door.

Archie was still laughing. "Go ahead. I'll call Jessica to ask her—"

"No!" Throwing his hand up to stop himself at the door, Mac whirled around. "Don't call her."

She turned around. "Why not?"

He wasn't prepared for this question. Finally, he came up with, "I want them to be a surprise."

In an effort to take their current conversation off her mind, he grabbed her and kissed her forcibly on the lips. What had started as a distraction dissolved into a sensuous moment. He wrapped his arms around her and held her close to him. She reached up to take in the taste of his mouth.

David blew the horn again. This time he held it longer to signify his impatience.

Reluctantly, Mac pulled back and gazed down into her beautiful eyes, the color of emerald jewels.

"I guess your headache is gone." She was breathless.

"It's certainly better," he said. "I have to go."

"I'll be waiting for you."

"You do that." He went out the door.

Running her fingers through her hair, Archie sighed deeply. Her heart still fluttered and she still tingled when he kissed her.

Mentally, she was returning to earth when the bedroom door flew open and Mac, ripping off his bathrobe, ran back inside. "I forgot to get dressed."

☾ ☽ ☾ ☽

Standing next to Archie on the front porch of the Spencer Manor, Chelsea's expression was of concern for David, who was still nursing his broken ribs, which were tightly wrapped. Worry made her face paler.

Even Molly cocked her head with concern at the two men. Only Gnarly, who was too busy licking Molly's ears, didn't seem to care about their well-being. He was more concerned with getting back on Molly's good side.

After getting in the cruiser and closing the door, Mac noted David staring straight ahead through the windshield. He snapped his fingers in the police chief's face to capture his attention. "What are you thinking so hard about?"

"Want to trade my broken ribs for your headache?" David turned the key in the ignition to start the cruiser.

"I would if I could," Mac said.

"You are aware that Lenny's kidnapping is completely out of our jurisdiction?" David eased the cruiser around the circular driveway and pulled out onto the road toward the other end of Spencer Point to take them up the mountain to the five-star resort, another part of Mac's inheritance from his birth mother.

"Yes, I do know that," Mac said.

"Then why are you so interested in it?"

"Because the Stillman murders, which are very much in our jurisdiction, are very much connected," Mac replied. "Derrick Stillman was the last one known to have had possession of the ransom money. Maybe, with the passage of time and the shift of loyalties, he'll be ready to tell the truth about what happened to it."

"That tells me that you think he was working with the kidnappers."

"Not necessarily because he wanted to."

"Do you remember I told you that Derrick Stillman was suspected of operating a drug dealing operation in his club?" David asked.

"Vaguely." Mac didn't want to confess that most of the previous day was a blur.

"Well yesterday I realized how much power an assistant to the boss can have, especially if they have passwords to email accounts, and how easy it would be to set up an operation and make it appear to be someone else's."

"Identity theft," Mac said.

"Derrick Stillman is a former addict who seems to go out of his way to avoid the drug world," David said. "I think he's sincere about staying clean. If Drake's kids killed his parents in retaliation, he would have said something by now."

"If he's so clean, why does he own a club?" Mac said.

"His mother set him up in business," David said. "I called the federal agents running the investigation and told them to take another look. They called this morning. It looks like I was right. According to their undercover agent, the major deals go down when Derrick is not around—Friday and Saturday. But, you know who is around?"

"His assistant," Mac said.

"Zoe Reese." David nodded his head. "They wouldn't give me any details, but something is going down this week— coincidentally while Derrick is taking time off to deal with his parents' deaths."

"Could the dealers have arranged for this time off to get Derrick out of the way? Maybe struck a deal with the Drakes?"

"Interesting question." David pulled the cruiser off the mountain road to park in Mac's reserved parking space next to the main door. "The sad thing is that according to the feds, the Stillmans disinherited Derrick, who most likely did nothing wrong. Now Lenny gets the club."

"But we don't know if Lenny knows that."

"No, we don't," David said while unclasping his seatbelt. "Nor do we know if Derrick was aware of being disinherited. He could have arranged his parents' murders for revenge."

"But you don't think he did it." Mac opened the door to climb out.

"No, I don't."

ೞ ಏ ೞ ಏ

On the top floor of the Spencer Inn, Derrick Stillman's attorney, a short bald-headed man, answered the door to the penthouse in response to David's knock. "Chief O'Callaghan. I'm Boris Ambrose." The lawyer peered up at David from over the top of his glasses while pumping his hand. "I was going to come see you this afternoon. Thank you for stopping by." When David introduced Mac to him, the lawyer released his hand to pump his. "Mr. Faraday, what a pleasure to meet you. Lovely resort you have here."

After thanking him, Mac extracted his hand and flexed it.

Boris waved them into the sitting area where Derrick was reading over a stack of papers. "I had stopped in to give my condolences to Derrick, and to go over his parents' wills. There are a lot of details to go over. Unfortunately, during such a terrible time as this, there are decisions to be made."

David and Mac exchanged glances. While Derrick's expression was one of grief, he did not look like he had recently received news of being disinherited from a multi-million dollar fortune.

Mac took the lead by asking, "I guess since Derrick was their only son, the Stillmans left him well taken care of."

"Austin Stillman was a savvy businessman," Boris said. "Janice had received a very large inheritance from an aunt, which she used to set her husband up in business, plus she bought the comedy club as an investment for Derrick. Both have done very well, and now it all goes to Derrick." He gestured at the distraught looking young man.

Obviously, the disinheritance didn't happen, Mac thought. He could see by the arch of David's eyebrow that he was thinking the same thing. *What happened here? Did the lawyer lose the new will or what? Maybe a pay off? Or did the feds get their information about the change in the wills wrong?*

"I saw in the news that Lenny was arrested last night," Derrick said. "Are you charging him with murder?"

"We found the murder weapon," David said. "It was in Zachery Harris' possession when he took a shot at Lenny. Harris was killed in a car crash while trying to escape the police."

"Harris?" Derrick repeated the name. "That writer who accused my folks of being behind Lenny's kidnapping and taking off with the million-dollar ransom?"

"He was Carson Drake's son," Mac said.

"Madelyn Preston," David said, "the woman you had spent Friday night with…she was really Carson Drake's daughter, Sela. She drugged you to get the security passcode, and then she called her brother here in Deep Creek Lake so that he could get into the house to kill your parents as revenge for making their father the fall guy in Lenny's kidnapping."

Mac told him, "We found evidence to place Harris in Deep Creek Lake at the time of your parents' murders. He used his credit card to purchase gas in McHenry."

"My parents weren't behind Lenny's kidnapping!" Tears came to Derrick's eyes. "No wonder he wrote that pack of lies he called a book. Harris had no proof that they did it. He spouted all this stuff based on circumstances—all because he—and now his sister?—refused to believe that their father was a second-rate actor who thought he could schmooze his way into the movies by getting big-name actors hooked on drugs."

"Is that what Carson Drake was?" Mac eased down into the chair across from him. "A small-time actor and drug dealer?"

"Exactly," Derrick said. "Do you want to know the worst part?"

"Tell me."

"Carson was on the studio payroll," Derrick said. "While Lenny was big, the studio wanted to keep him happy. Carson was Lenny's assistant. He *assisted* Lenny by getting him girls, booze, and drugs. Since I was his best friend, Lenny'd give me his leftovers. We both got hooked."

He gritted his teeth. "Then, when our habit got to be a problem—with Lenny losing it, coming in late or not at all, and getting bad publicity for behaving like an idiot— the studio started putting a limit on what we could have. Carson would stay in our good graces by giving us more—as long as we paid for it. Lenny did. At the end of the third season of Lenny's show, when his ratings started to drop, the studio fired Carson because Lenny wasn't worth the expense to them. Our party was over and Carson was out of a job. That's why he kidnapped Lenny."

"Was Lenny still buying from him?"

"Yeah, of course," Derrick said with a shrug of his shoulders. "Carson was Lenny's drug connection. But it wasn't that easy."

"Why wasn't it that easy?" David asked.

Chuckling, Derrick shook his head. "Everyone thinks these child stars, teenaged stars, have it easy. Money is flowing everywhere. But the stars really don't get that much of it. Lenny's folks had control over his money because he was a minor. *They* gave him a hot car to drive, and he had a generous allowance compared to other kids his age—including me. But the rest of the money went to his parents. They set up the financing so that they got paid big salaries, which they put up their noses. When Lenny turned eighteen, at which point he was a has-been, he got the money that they had put into a trust fund for him. He got a total of fifty thousand dollars. He'd been working since he was six years old. His parents had blown every penny. They claimed that it went to supporting Lenny and their family—he was the breadwinner, but he got nothing."

"So when Lenny had to start buying his drugs, he didn't have the cash to keep him in the lifestyle to which he was accustomed," David said.

"Carson gave us a lot free of charge," Derrick said, "on account that we lied to him. We kept promising him that my mom would represent him—be his agent—as long as he kept us happy."

David tapped Mac's hand. "That's why Drake was telling people that Janice was going to represent him. She didn't promise him that. It was Lenny and Derrick."

Mac asked Derrick, "Did your mother ever consider representing Drake?"

"She considered him a low-life drug dealer and hanger-on," Derrick said. "Kate Coleman—do you remember her?"

Mac and David nodded their heads.

With tears in his eyes, Derrick took in a shuddering breath. "I loved…" He cleared his throat. "Mom represented her and blamed Carson Drake for her death. He had gotten her hooked on drugs and she died in a car accident. The police said she was under the influence when it happened." Derrick stared down at his hands. "Mom never forgave Drake for getting her hooked."

When Mac reached out to touch his hand, he startled Derrick out of his thoughts. "You cared about Kate, didn't you?"

"Is it that obvious?" Derrick asked.

"Yes," Mac said in a soft voice. "I thought she and Lenny were a hot item."

"Only for the media," Derrick chuckled. "They were the hottest pop stars. Fans wanted the two of them to be an item. So they were—for all the cameras. When the cameras weren't around, it was me and Kate."

David said, "But when Kate died, Lenny Frost made a big deal—"

"Lenny Frost knows his way around the media machine very well," Boris interjected.

"Lenny's feelings for Kate went from hot to cold depending on what role he was playing," Derrick said. "She always thought he was a sleazy, manipulative, spoiled brat. Sometimes, I'd think he was trying to steal her from me. Other times, he told me that he hated her guts. To this day, I don't know which way he went with her."

"Where were things when she died?" Mac asked. "Were they hot or cold?"

Derrick lifted his eyes to look at Mac. "Kate and I had a fight. It was one of those dumb things." He rubbed his eyes and let out a gasp. "I just remembered this. Our fight was over Lenny. She wanted me to stay away from him. He had said something to her or—I don't know. I told her that she couldn't tell me what to do. One thing led to another. We had a big fight." Once again, a sob came to his voice. Tears came to his eyes. "And that was how it was the last time I saw Kate."

They sat in silence.

"I'm sorry," David said in a soft voice.

"So am I." Wiping the tears from his eyes with the back of his hand, Derrick stood up and retrieved a tissue from a box on an end table to blow his nose.

Boris told Mac and David, "If you've spent any time with Lenny Frost, you can see that sometimes he has a problem staying in touch with reality."

"How did Carson Drake fit into all this at the time of the kidnapping?" Mac asked.

"Lenny and I were lying to Drake about my mother representing him," Derrick explained. "Eventually, he figured it out and ordered Lenny to pay him for all of the drugs he had given us. Lenny didn't, so Carson kidnapped him." He looked at each one of them. "That's the truth. My parents had nothing to do with any of it."

Deep in thought, Mac rubbed his fingers across his lips. "Tell me about the kidnapping."

Derrick returned to his seat on the sofa. "I told—"

"I believe you that your folks weren't involved," Mac interjected. "But…a big hurdle in clearing them is the fact that it was *you*—," he pointed across the table at him, "—who the kidnapper insisted deliver the ransom in your mother's Mercedes. The bag was outfitted with a tracking device. Somehow, the bags got switched and the tracking device put into a decoy bag. It only could have happened while it was in your possession. Now, your parents are dead and a whole family is dead—the Drakes. Carson Drake's wife was murdered a year after the kidnapping. His two children were killed avenging his reputation. It's time for you to come clean with everything you know."

Derrick stared at Mac in silence. When he was unable to look at him anymore, he looked up at the police chief, and then to his lawyer.

"Your parents are dead, Derrick," Boris said. "If there's something that you haven't told us about that kidnapping, you need to tell us now."

"Carson Drake did it," Derrick said in a firm voice. "Yes, I switched the bags, because Carson Drake ordered me to or he was going to kill Lenny."

"When did you switch the bags?" David asked him.

"Before the drop," Derrick said with a sigh that sounded like relief at finally getting the truth out. "Lenny called me on my cell phone."

Recalling that the kidnapping happened in 1998, Mac asked, "Cell phone? This was—"

With a wave of his hand, Derrick explained, "This happened long before the police were tracking and monitoring cell phones and that sort of stuff. Lenny and I had cell phones back when all the other kids had pagers."

"So, Carson Drake called you on your cell…" Mac said.

"No, Lenny did," Derrick said.

"Lenny?" Mac replied with a furrowed brow.

"Because Carson Drake made him call me," Derrick said.

"When was this?"

"After he was kidnapped, after Carson had called the studio demanding the ransom and gave them the instructions for the drop—that I was to deliver it in my mom's Mercedes."

"But at that time," Mac recalled from what he had read of the case, "they did not know Carson Drake was the kidnapper. They didn't know that until after Lenny was found and said it was him."

"Exactly."

David tried to lean forward in his seat, but the sharp pain in his ribs forced him to sit forward on the edge of his seat to ask, "When did this call come in to you on your cell phone?"

"The same day as the ransom call," Derrick said. "Lenny sounded scared out of his mind. He said that Carson Drake had kidnapped him and that he was standing there with a gun to his head. He then told me what to do."

"Which was?" Mac asked.

Boris cleared his throat to remind them of his presence. "You do realize that my client is not admitting to being a party to any of this—the kidnapping—"

"We're not interested in arresting your client for anything unless he did something wrong," David said. "Right now, we just want to figure out the truth before more people end up dead."

"Go on," Mac told Derrick. "Lenny calls you on your cell phone—am I correct in assuming that he was calling on his cell phone?"

Derrick nodded his head.

"Exactly what did Lenny say?" Mac asked.

"I told you," Derrick sounded frustrated. "Carson Drake had a gun to his head and he was listening to every word Lenny said. The FBI was going to have me deliver the ransom. I was going to use a particular type of bag, a workout bag like the type that I used to carry my track clothes in. I was to get my track bag and stuff it full of newspapers and put it in my bathroom. There's an access door in the back of the linen closet, behind the towels, for the plumber to get to the pipes. I was to stash my bag there. Then, when the FBI gave me the ransom to deliver, right before I left, while I had the bag, I was to suddenly say I had to go to the bathroom, run up to my room, and switch the bags—making sure I found the tracking device to put in my bag and then deliver my bag with the newspapers."

Shrugging his shoulders, Derrick said, "Lenny asked if I got that. I said I did. He said to do it or Carson was going to kill him and it would be my fault."

"What were you supposed to do with the real ransom?" Boris asked.

"Nothing," Derrick said. "Oh, Lenny said that, too. He said to completely forget about the ransom and not to go near it. Carson had an inside guy—one of the FBI agents. So, if I told them about Lenny calling, the inside guy would know, tell Drake, and they would kill Lenny. So I told no one. I never went near the real ransom."

"How did Carson Drake get the ransom then?" Boris asked.

"The inside guy," Derrick said. "When the FBI realized they had been tricked, they interrogated me to death and searched the house. They said they never found it. But then, when Lenny called the police after Carson took off, he said he heard Carson tell someone on the phone that he had the ransom. So the inside guy must have gotten it. When Lenny got out of the hospital, we looked in the closet, behind the access door, and, sure enough, the money was gone. This FBI agent must have been on the take with the drug dealers Carson worked for." Derrick looked across the room at Mac who was studying him closely. "It wasn't my mother or father."

"Did you share your bathroom with anyone?" Mac asked.

"No," Derrick said. "It was my private bath that was attached to my bedroom. No one used it except me."

"Did you ever talk to Zachery Harris, the writer who wrote that book?" Mac asked him.

"No," Derrick said. "He asked for an interview, but I refused to ever talk about the kidnapping to anyone."

"According to his book, he had an anonymous source who knew the inside details of the kidnapping."

"Well, now that we know who his father was, it must have been Carson Drake," Derrick said. "Maybe he finally tracked him down."

Mac asked, "Do you think Carson Drake is alive?"

"Either he is, or the inside man who worked for the FBI has the money," Derrick said. "The money disappeared. Someone took it, and it wasn't me or my folks. I knew Carson Drake, so if he had come in to take that money from my bathroom, I would have known it."

"So the only ones who had access to that bathroom to get the money was one of the federal agents working the case, or someone you knew and trusted," David said.

"Exactly."

A slow grin crossed Mac's face when he sat back in his seat. "Someone above suspicion."

CHAPTER EIGHTEEN

After thanking Derrick for his time and offering their condolences once again, Mac and David stood to leave. Boris had opened the door for them to step out when Mac turned around so fast that he startled David, who was directly behind him. Stepping around the police chief, Mac called over to where Derrick was staring in grief at the paperwork spread out before him. "How tall are you, Derrick?"

Both Boris and David looked questioningly from Mac to Derrick, who was equally perplexed by the unexpected question. "Huh?"

"How tall?" Mac repeated his question. "How tall are you?"

"Five feet, eleven inches," Derrick said. "I'm considered average height. Just short of six feet. Why?"

"I noticed when we shook hands that you were a little shorter than I am," Mac explained, "I'm six foot one."

"Good for you," Derrick said with a shrug.

"Yesterday," Mac went on, "when I was in the pub with Lenny, I noticed that he was the tallest guy in the place. Of course, everyone who was in there was on the short side. I

205

guess that's part of Lenny's star presence. He stands out not just because of his personality, but also because he's so tall."

"He tells the media that he's six foot four," Derrick said. "Really, he's six two. He wears heels to seem taller."

"Not the only lie Lenny told," Boris grumbled. When David turned to him, he said, "Addicts are the best liars in the world."

"That's very true," Derrick said.

On their way out the door, David asked Boris to speak to them alone in the hallway—out of Derrick's earshot. "About the Stillmans' wills…" the police chief broached the subject.

"What about them?" Boris asked. "Rather standard stuff. Derrick gets everything. They had no other children or relatives."

Not wanting to give away details about the DEA investigation into the comedy club, David said, "A source told me that Derrick had been disinherited very recently, as in only weeks ago."

Surprisingly, Boris nodded his head. "Janice did come to me to disinherit him and leave everything to Lenny." Frowning, he swallowed. "It was the last time I saw them. Austin came in with her, and it ended up being a long and emotional meeting."

"Was the will changed?" Mac asked him.

Boris nodded his head. "But not in the way Janice intended it to be when she walked into my office." He folded his arms across his chest. "Our meeting turned into an intervention where Austin and I made Janice see how Lenny Frost had been playing her for years and how it had affected her relationship with her own son."

"How is that?" Mac wanted to know.

"As you have probably guessed, I am not a Lenny Frost fan," Boris said. "Neither was Austin. Janice was not your average talent agent. She represented child actors because she loved children and wanted someone on their side. Both of Lenny's parents were second-rate actors who ended up being a couple of drunks and addicts. His mother died of Hepatitis B. When his father wrapped his car around a telephone pole, he was three times over the legal limit."

"What does this have to do with the Stillmans' wills?" David asked him to move on to the heart of the matter.

"Talent agents have the reputation of being manipulative of their clients," Boris said. "That may have been how it started with Janice and Lenny, but it was not how it ended. Lenny turned the tables on her. After she ended their business relationship and moved her family back here—to get away from Hollywood and Lenny—he ended up following her and preying on her guilt. Everyone but her, including Derrick, could see it. When she came in to disinherit Derrick with some cock and bull story about him running a drug operation out of the club that she had set up for him, the first thing I thought about was Lenny, who—guess what—is working at the club as a headliner. Austin thought the same thing."

"Then you think Lenny was behind the drug dealing and framing Derrick for it?" Mac asked.

"Not necessarily the ringleader, but if you take a look at Lenny's history, you will see that trouble follows him around like a puppy," Boris said. "At that meeting, we finally managed to get Janice to see it." He turned to David. "So, to answer your question, yes, they changed their wills—to disinherit Lenny."

"Does he get anything?" Mac asked.

"Janice had set up a trust fund for him three years ago. Again, out of guilt. Lenny has been getting a monthly allowance from it. Something to provide for him when he can't get work, which is usually the case."

"How much is in this trust fund?" David asked him.

"One million dollars, which is a lot of money for Lenny. He's flat broke. The only money he has coming in is the salary from the Comedy Café and that allowance. He also gets the deed to the condo that he has been living in. Janice had bought it for him when he moved to the East Coast. Now that the Stillmans are dead, Derrick is going to sell the club, which means Lenny will be out of a job. With Janice gone, Lenny isn't protected anymore."

"Then Lenny had motive to want Janice alive," David said.

"Unless he didn't know that the Stillmans had changed their wills to disinherit him," Mac said. "What was he going to get before they had made the changes?"

Boris replied, "The trust fund, condo, and either guaranteed employment as the headliner at the club until his death or a percentage of the profit from the club, plus a gift of one million dollars. I guarantee Derrick won't keep Lenny on since he doesn't have to."

"The best friends are no more," Mac said.

"That ended for good when Derrick grew up and got clean. Then he saw Lenny for who he really was. Janice's perception was clouded by guilt."

Mac glanced up and down the corridor and lowered his voice to ask, "Is there any possibility that Janice could have told Lenny about her plans to make him the beneficiary before that meeting?"

"No," Boris said with certainty, "she was afraid of Derrick finding out."

"Afraid?" David asked.

"Of devastating him to the point of a major relapse," the lawyer explained.

"Let me get this straight," Mac said. "Due to the changes in the Stillmans' will, Lenny is out of a job, but he has ownership of the condo where he's living—"

"At current market value," Boris said, "it's worth three quarters of a million dollars."

"—and a trust fund worth one million dollars," Mac concluded, "but he's out of a gift of one million dollars, and what is possibly his last entertainment gig."

"Unless he can get the new club owners to hire him," Boris said. "I guarantee they won't put up with his shenanigans. Most people aren't as patient as Janice was with him."

 ෬ ෨ ෬ ෨

"What was that about?" David asked Mac once the elevator doors had closed.

With no one else in the car going down from the penthouse floor to the lobby, they had privacy and David could grill Mac about the strange line of questioning he had embarked on. "Why did you want to know how tall Derrick Stillman is?"

"Because he didn't look that big to me," Mac asked. "What do you think? Do you think he has to put his car seat all the way back?"

"You are now looking at Kate Coleman's death?" David chuckled. "*Our* case is the Stillman murders. We got their killers. Sela Wallace and Zachery Harris in retaliation for their father deserting them."

Crossing his arms, Mac leaned back against the wall of the elevator. "Are you satisfied with that conclusion?" With a cocked eyebrow, he waited for David's reaction. "Out with it. Something isn't sitting right in this case."

"Why did Lenny pretend not to know Sela Wallace and take those hostages when he had an airtight alibi?" David muttered. "I don't believe for one second that he forgot he had one. And who was he planning to put in that suitcase?"

The elevator doors opened. Holding the door open, Mac stood back and gestured for David to step out into the lobby ahead of him.

When Mac stepped out, he came face to face with Jeff Ingles, Spencer Inn's manager. "Mac, do you have a minute?

"I could give you two," Mac joked.

"This is not funny." The always nervous hotel manager took out his handkerchief and wiped his sweaty brow. "About that reservation you made yesterday…"

Mac grinned. "What about it?"

"Did you have to pick *that* night?"

"*That's* the night I want."

"But…" The whine in Jeff's voice made him sound almost like an alto. "Why can't you pick *another* night?"

"What's the point of owning a hotel if I can't use it when I want?"

"Do you have any idea what you're doing?" Jeff turned to David for help. "Did he tell you what he's doing to me?"

Answering with a shake of his head, David asked, "What's Mac doing to you, Jeff?"

"He's trying to kill me, that's what." Jeff's voice was filled with despair when he explained, "I about had a stroke when I read your message yesterday."

Amused by the manager's drama, David asked, "Do you want me to arrest him for attempted murder?"

"Like that's going to help," Jeff said with sarcasm.

"As long as I don't have an issue with the inn being closed to guests that night, why should you?" Mac asked.

"That's the biggest night of the year in the hotel business. We already have reservations from guests who made them months ago—some years ago. I can't go back and tell them—"

"But it's my hotel," Mac reminded him.

Jeff grabbed Mac by the arms. "Do you know what will happen if I tell all those guests that the inn is closed?"

Mac was surprised by the tight grip Jeff had on his arms. "What?"

"They'll go someplace else," Jeff said. "Another resort. Someplace else. Maybe even the Wisp. Do you know what that means?"

"What?"

"They're going to go *someplace else!*" Jeff shrieked.

Sympathy flooded over Mac. "How about—"

"What am I going to do?" Jeff wrapped both arms around Mac into a hug and collapsed against him.

Not wanting the hotel's manager to slump down to the floor, Mac held him up by his armpits. "Okay, I'm sure we can work something out."

A glimmer of hope came to Jeff's beady eyes. "What?" He looked up at Mac from where his head was resting on his chest.

"We don't have to cancel reservations for those who already have them," Mac said. "They can still come."

Jeff let out a deep sigh of relief. A wide smile crossed his face. He stood up straight and tidied up his clothes to regain his composure.

"On that night, the night I want," Mac continued, "they can enjoy the whole inn, dinner and open bar, as my guests. Everything will be on the house."

The smile fell. Jeff's face and body were instantly drenched in sweat. He was still fighting to find his voice when Mac ushered David toward the lounge.

Cℬ ℬ Cℬ ℬ

Mac was gesturing for two beers when the police chief's phone vibrated on his hip. While the bartender served up their drinks, David took the call.

"You should note this date on your calendar," Special Agent Alex Fredericks opened his conversation with David.

"Why?"

"Because I'm about to tell you something that I don't say too freely," the agent said.

"Gee, thanks, Fredericks," David said, "but I'm already committed to someone else."

"Don't be a smart-aleck," Fredericks replied. "You were right."

"Of course, I was." David grinned.

"Our agent focused on Zoe Reese, Stillman's assistant. Within hours, she made contact with the dealers we were looking for. We got a warrant to tap Reese's phone, put a tail on her, and she led us right into a beehive. They're planning a major score for this week and they said specifically that they want it done before Stillman returns from taking care of his parents because they know that he'll be putting in a lot of time at the club and will be in the way. We have it on tape. Your man Stillman is in the clear."

"Did your operative say anything that could indicate that the murders were to get Derrick out of the way?" David asked him.

"We thought that too, but no," Fredericks said. "This big deal came up as a result of the murders. It was going to happen next week, but then they moved everything up because it became more convenient with Stillman gone. They adjusted their schedule as a result of the murders, not the other way around."

"It's great to hear that he's in the clear," David said.

"Thing is," Fredericks added, "Zoe Reese isn't working alone. She keeps referring to her partner and saying that she has to check with him. He's the brains of the two. Could be the bartender or one of the comics who's regularly on the bill. She's using a burner phone to call him and she hasn't referred to him by name yet."

Fredericks finished the conversation by telling David that he would contact him if he got any information that could pertain to the Spencer Police murder investigation. After disconnecting the call, David climbed up onto the bar stool next to Mac and passed on the news.

"So the assistant is the one dealing the drugs, but she has a partner who's pulling the strings from behind the scenes," David concluded. "They haven't identified him, but they know it's not Derrick Stillman."

"She's doing the dirty work and taking the chances," Mac said. "I wonder how loyal she'll be when the feds nab her." He answered his own question. "Depends on if the partnership is business or pleasure."

"It's amazing how quickly the honeymoon ends when threatened with twenty years of sharing a cell with a two-hundred-pound bruiser calling you 'Cupcake.'" After taking a sip of his beer, David set down the glass and turned on his stool to face Mac. "Are you seriously thinking that these murders go all the way back to Kate Coleman's death on that hilltop road in Hollywood?"

Mac shrugged. "Maybe, maybe not." He took another sip of his beer.

"What are you thinking?"

"Carson Drake," Mac said. "That's who I'm thinking about. He's been hanging over this whole case like Jacob Marley's ghost in Dickens' *A Christmas Carol.* He's not here, but he's certainly the catalyst for everything going all the way back to Kate Coleman's death."

"More like the serpent in the Garden of Eden," David said. "In exchange for promising to make him a star, he got Kate, Lenny, and Derrick hooked on drugs and the party scene. When she couldn't deliver, Kate ended up dead. Lenny ended up kidnapped, terrorized, and in and out of rehab ever since. Derrick became addicted, but cleaned up his act only to lose both of his parents. This isn't Charles Dickens, it's a Greek tragedy." Seeing Mac squinting into his beer glass, he put his elbows on top of the bar to lean in close. "You aren't listening to me. What are you thinking?"

"What if?"

"What if what?" David asked.

"Something Boris said…I was thinking the same thing but…what if it was more than that?" Mac took his cell phone out of its case and ran his finger over a phone number he had recently put into his contact list.

At the same time, David's phone vibrated. The caller ID read Bogie. He brought the phone to his ear and connected the call. "Yeah, Bogie…"

"How's your ribs?"

"Not great," David said while rubbing the brace around his midsection. "What's happening there?"

"There's a woman here to see you and Mac," Bogie said. "She saw the news about Zachery Harris' death and says she has information for the lead investigator in the Stillman murders. She drove all the way here from Delaware."

"Delaware?" David replied.

Deciding to think more on his idea, Mac set his phone down without dialing.

"That's what she says," Bogie said. "And she will only talk to the man in charge of the investigation in person. She claims to have evidence that'll bust this case wide open."

"Wide open?" While David was hopeful, he was equally doubtful.

"Her exact words," Bogie said. "Are you and Mac coming in?"

David looked over at Mac, who was smiling at the doubt in his face. "We'll be right there."

CHAPTER NINETEEN

"Zachery Harris' address, according to his driver's license, was in New Jersey," David noted during the drive back down the mountain to the Spencer police department. "He drove all the way down here from his place in West Orange. What does he have to do with this woman in Delaware?"

Not as perplexed by the address as the police chief, Mac shrugged. "With the Internet, people are connecting all over the world. My son, Tristan, has professors, fellow students, and colleagues in science who he considers actual friends and mentors, even though he's never met any of them. Whatever this woman has, she considers it important enough to get into a car and drive five hours to hand deliver it to us."

At the station they found a woman who appeared to be in her sixties sitting on the sofa in the reception area. At first glance, she resembled a character out of a comic book. Her shape was round. Her hair was a thick cloud of blue curls that encircled her head. Her face was equally round. Her pantsuit was steel blue, which matched her hair. Even her big eye glasses were round and blue.

As soon as she saw David and Mac, she jumped to her feet and clutched a valise to her chest as if she feared they would snatch it from her. A wide smile stretched across her wide face when she looked Mac up and down.

Bogie came out of his office to make introductions. "Chief, this is Rita Jarvis, she was a friend of Zachery Harris—"

"Not his friend," Rita interrupted the deputy chief before turning back to the police chief. She licked her lips. "I was Zachery's literary agent." She offered David her hand while clutching the valise with the other. "I take it you are the chief of police."

"Yes, I am David O'Callaghan." He shook her hand. "And this is—"

"Mac Faraday." They were shocked by the squeal in her tone. "Robin Spencer's only child." Her eyes wide with adoration, she pushed past David to step up to Mac. "I loved your mother."

Taken aback by her enthusiasm, Mac backed up a step. He could hear Tonya giggling behind him. "I'm glad," was all he could think to say.

"I was her number one fan," Rita gushed. "I read every single one of her books and short stories and saw all of her movies and went to see her plays in New York. I loved Robin. Half of my books have her autograph. I once stood in line four hours in New York to get her autograph on *Fatal Flight.*" Giggling she fingered her blue curls. "She liked my hair. She called the color stunning. I dye it myself." She brushed the fabric on her dress. "Blue was Robin Spencer's favorite color. Did you know that?"

"I'm afraid I didn't." Mac shot a glance to David behind her. The police chief's expression mirrored his own thought. *This woman is a nut and she's wasting our time.*

"It is such a pleasure to meet you." She offered Mac her hand.

Grasping her hand, Mac injected congeniality into his tone to ask, "I understand you knew Zachery Harris..."

"Yes, I did." Nodding her head, she continued to gaze into Mac's eyes. "You must get your eyes from your father. Robin's eyes were violet."

"My daughter inherited Robin's eyes," Mac said. "Tell me about Zachery Harris."

She paused, as if to recall the purpose for her visit. "I was his literary agent." She opened her valise and searched through the contents.

"So you told us already," David said. "Did he tell you why he was coming to Deep Creek Lake?"

"No," she said during her search. "He stopped by my place in Delaware on Thursday. I was surprised to see him, I mean, actually meet him. We've done everything via emails and phone calls. Even our contract was done over the Internet. That was how I fired him...with an email."

"Then you weren't his literary agent?" Mac asked.

"For his one and most likely only book." With a giggle, she shrugged before resuming her search. "I guess now that he's dead, *The Abduction of Lenny Frost* is his first and last book. I'll be lucky if I can get another book published after that fiasco. The publisher is looking to get their advance back, including my ten percent—" She sighed. "I should have known better."

She extracted a thumb drive from the pouch and handed it to Mac. "Zachery gave this to me and told me to find the police detective in charge of the investigation and to hand it to him personally if anything happened to him. I assumed when I saw on the news that he was killed in a police shoot out that 'something happened.'" Her hand still in his, she smiled. "Never in my wildest dreams did I imagine that the detective in charge of the investigation would be Robin Spencer's baby."

Mac extracted his hand from hers and examined the thumb drive. "Do you know what is on this?"

"No, Zachery made me promise not to open it. He said to just give it to the police. He claimed he had no one else he could trust." She licked her lips. "I guess this means that we're working together on this case."

"Not really." David reached around her to take the thumb drive. "Thank you very much for bringing this in. We're sorry that you drove all this way. We could have come to pick it up."

Gazing up at Mac, she replied, "No problem at all."

Glancing over the top of her head, Mac gestured with a jerk of his chin for someone to usher Rita out.

Bogie stepped forward to take her elbow. "Thank you very much for contacting us and bringing in this evidence. We have your contact information—"

"Oh, I'm staying at the Spencer Inn tonight. I was lucky to get a room." She wrested out of Bogie's grip and turned back to Mac. "Can I bother you for an autograph, Mac?"

Stunned, Mac stared at her with his mouth hanging open. "Autograph? Mine? Why?"

"You're Robin Spencer's son," she gushed while extracting a marker from her bag. "You are the offspring of a literary legacy. No one in my book group will ever believe I met you if I didn't get your autograph." She held out the marker to him.

Mac's cheeks felt like they were on fire when he reached out to take it. "I need a piece of paper to write it on."

"You can sign it on my chest." To their dismay, she unbuttoned the top of her blouse and held it open to expose the top of her left breast. "Just sign your name right here over my heart."

Unable to contain himself, David whirled around on his heels and went into Bogie's office. He slammed the door.

Tonya bit both lips. Bogie's mustache twitched while he fought to control his laughter.

Mac swallowed. *Let's get this over with.* With concise movements, he signed his name across the woman's breast as quickly as possible.

With the final sweep of his hand, she jerked forward and kissed him on the cheek before he had a chance to back away. "You have made me the happiest woman in the world, Mac!" She snatched the marker from his hand and practically floated out the door on a cloud of ecstasy.

The police station was enveloped in a stunned silence for a full moment after she closed the door. Bogie's office door opened and David stepped out. Mac's back was to him.

"Don't say a word," Mac said over his shoulder.

"About what?" David's laughter opened the door for Tonya and Bogie to join in.

"Be thankful, Mac! At least she didn't take off her girdle and throw it at you." Tonya doubled over in her chair.

Wiping the tears from his eyes, Bogie grabbed the countertop to hold himself up.

"No one is going to say a word about this to Archie," Mac ordered. "She'll never let me live it down."

"How much is our silence worth to you?" David asked while fighting to regain his composure.

"What do you want?"

David held up his hands to interrupt Bogie and Tonya from answering. "We should ask for something for the station."

"Yeah," Bogie agreed. "What do we need that we can extort from Mac?"

"An espresso maker in the break room," Tonya said.

"No," David said. "You're thinking small. You need to think bigger."

"Bigger than an espresso maker?" Tonya asked.

"I know!" Bogie snapped his fingers. "Just the thing. A helicopter."

"Yeah!" David grasped Mac's elbow. "That's what we want. You buy the station a helicopter and we'll forget all about your over-aged groupie."

Mac looked from Bogie, who was nodding his head with a wide grin on his face, to David, who was practically jumping up and down like a child anticipating Santa's arrival, to Tonya, who was looking at each of them with a grimace on her face. Clearing his throat, he folded his arms. "Okay, I'll buy the station a helicopter if you can answer one question for me."

"What's that?" Bogie asked.

"Who's going to fly it?"

His face blank of expression, Bogie looked over to David, who gazed back at him.

"I guess we'll settle for an espresso machine in the break room," David said.

Bogie agreed. "Sounds good to me."

 CB SO CR BO

"There's only one file on the thumb drive," David announced after inserting it into his laptop up in his office. Tonya wasted no time in ordering the espresso machine while Mac and Bogie followed David up to his office on the second floor of the station to examine the contents of Zachery Harris's thumb drive. "It's a video."

David clicked on the file's icon to open it up and turned the laptop screen around for Mac and Bogie to observe. He moved his chair around the corner of his desk to view it as well.

Zachery Harris's image filled the screen in a close-up headshot. It looked as if he had recorded the video with his computer's webcam.

"Hello, I am Zachery Harris," he told the camera. "If you are viewing this, then most likely, if my agent followed my instructions, you are a police detective investigating my disappearance, critical injury of some sort, or death. I don't know exactly what happened to me, or how it happened, but I can tell you who did it and why. That's why I'm making this video.

"They say the wise learn from the mistakes of the generation before them. Well, this is one of those moments."

Zachery shot them a crooked a grin. "Today is Wednesday night and I am making this video in my home in West Orange, New Jersey. Tomorrow, I will be leaving to go to Deep Creek Lake, Maryland, where I will be preparing for my next project."

He paused while a solemn expression crossed his face. "This Saturday night, I am going to kill Janice and Austin Stillman."

"It's a confession," Bogie said.

"That's what it sounds like to me," David agreed.

Shushing them, Mac leaned over to rest his elbows on his knees. "Listen."

"This was not my idea," Zachery said, "and I did not plan this on my own. The idea and orchestrator of the plan was someone else. It is because I don't trust him that I am making this video to make you aware of how this all came about."

Pausing, Zachery leaned forward. When he sat back in his seat, he took a sip from a beer bottle. After placing it down, he wiped his brow with trembling fingers. His eyes glazed over while he seemed to gather his thoughts.

"Let me start at the beginning," he resumed. "My father was Carson Drake, a great actor. I mean, he was a great talent. But, he wasn't very tall or big like the major stars. He knew he had the talent. He was obsessed with being famous and became desperate. The last time I remember seeing him, he was happy. He was on his way out—all dressed up in his best suit that he always wore when he was going to a big event to mingle with big names. I was like ten years old. I told him to break a leg and he said that this night, he was really going to do it. From here on out, he was going to be running with the big dogs. That's what he said."

Zachery's face twisted in grief. "That was the last time I saw him. The next thing I know, everyone was saying that my father was a monster who had kidnapped Lenny Frost, a big star, because he was jealous and that my father held him hostage for a million dollars, and then ran off—abandoning me and my mom and sister. Mom said it wasn't true. Lenny Frost's agent, Janice Stillman, had promised to represent her and my dad if he worked on this one project for her.

"A year later, when we found out that Janice Stillman was closing up shop and moving to the east coast, we put it together. Not only was my father the fall guy, but my mom was also. She was an actress and model. No one would work with her after Frost's kidnapping. The Drake name had become mud."

Grief turned to fury. "The last time I saw my mother, she said that she was going to collect what was rightfully ours. I admit she had had a lot to drink. She was drinking a lot after Dad disappeared. The foreclosure notice on our house was the last straw. I remember her smashing a bottle of vodka against the wall. She said she had proof of who was really the bad guy in all this. Dad had been set up, and she wasn't going to be the nice lady kowtowing to the big dog anymore. She was going to clear Dad's name and she didn't care who she was going to bring down to make it happen. She left… and five days later, she was found tortured to death, tied to a chair, and beaten to a pulp, in an abandoned warehouse in LA. The Stillmans won again."

Zachery stared into the camera in silence.

Feeling sympathy for the young man who had lost everything at such a young age, Mac, David, and Bogie watched him without saying a word.

"So you must understand why I don't trust my partner in committing these murders," Zachery said. "That's why I am making this video." He took another sip of the beer.

"Fast forward eleven years," he said. "My sister Sela has studied and worked hard to become a martial arts stunt woman. She's good at it, too. She works out at the gym every day. She also became hooked on steroids. But she's smart. She got help and ended up at the same rehab center in Hollywood where they shoot *Star Rehab*. The celebrities actually have group therapy with the average folks.

"By that time, Sela and I had both changed our last names, so her name was not Drake when she was in group therapy with none other than Lenny Frost, who had no idea that Carson Drake's daughter was sitting next to him when he confessed to killing a man. He gave no details except to say that it was self-defense. He was backed into a corner and felt like he had no option. If he was to survive, then he was going to have to be smarter. Life in Hollywood, Lenny said, was a case of survival of the fittest. If this man had kept his head and controlled his ambition, then he would not have had to kill him. Then, Lenny told them, he had to live with this killing on his hands and that that was what drove him to booze and drugs."

"Is he saying Lenny killed Carson Drake?" David asked.

As if to answer David directly, Zachery said, "Lenny Frost killed my father."

"What about the million-dollar ransom?" Mac asked.

David paused the video. "If Lenny killed Carson Drake in self-defense after he had kidnapped him, why didn't he simply tell the police that?"

"The money," Bogie and Mac said in unison.

"If Lenny had told the police that he killed Carson Drake," Mac said, "they would have expected to get the ransom back. If Lenny hid the body and made it look like Carson Drake had run off with the money, then everyone would have been looking for him and expecting him to have it. Who would ever consider the kidnap victim would have the ransom?"

"Wait a minute!" David said. "Carson couldn't have had the money for Lenny to take and keep for himself. It was never delivered to Carson. Derrick switched the bags."

Slowly, Mac shook his head. "But according to Lenny's statement to the FBI and his interviews with the media, he heard Carson Drake in a phone conversation with an accomplice saying that he had the money."

"Somebody somewhere is lying," Bogie said.

The corners of Mac's mouth curled up. "Exactly." He hit the button to resume play of the video.

"My sister played it cool," Zachery recounted. "She never said a word to Lenny at the rehab center. When she told me, we took time to make our plan. We pieced together what we knew about the kidnapping, how Janice Stillman had closed up shop a year later and moved out of the area. Suddenly, they had a lot of money. We remembered how optimistic Dad was when he left that night because he was going to do this one last job, and then Janice Stillman was going to be his agent. Then, doors would finally open for him. We also recalled how Mom figured out who was behind everything and ended up dead when she confronted them. It was Janice Stillman.

"Then, I made an appointment to meet with Lenny Frost. I didn't tell him who I was at first. He agreed to be interviewed, but he gave me the same bull that he had given to every other reporter about Dad taking off with the ransom to meet his accomplice and split the loot between them. After a couple of months, Sela and I both confronted him with the truth and what he had said in group.

"At first, he denied everything." A slow smile crossed Zachery's face. "Then, he came clean. He didn't know at the time that it was Janice Stillman who had kidnapped him. It was a couple of years after the kidnapping that he figured it out. Suddenly, she had all this money. When he confronted her about the trauma of being abducted and the guilt of killing Carson Drake, she came clean. He said Janice claimed that no one was supposed to be killed. But Lenny said Carson Drake was afraid he would tell and ruin his career and was going to kill him. That was why Janice was taking care of him—hiring him at the club and bailing him out of trouble when he needed her. At that meeting, Lenny cried and told us that killing our father had ruined his life."

Zachery paused to take a sip from his beer.

"Lenny agreed to be my source to write the book, but only as long as I didn't name him because Janice would cut him off. But then, after the book came out, the Stillmans sued my pants off. Lenny refused to come forward to tell how Janice had confessed to him about being behind the kidnapping. With no proof, I lost everything. My career—reputation—it was like what had happened to my mother all over again.

"Then, a couple of weeks ago, Lenny came to Sela and me with a plan." He grinned. "That's right. Lenny Frost came to us. It was his idea. We would kill the Stillmans for him. It would be our revenge on them. Janice Stillman had assured Lenny that he was in her will. He would inherit enough to pay Sela and I the million dollars that Janice had gotten in ransom from the studio, and he would have money left over for himself."

Zachery sat forward in his seat. "You probably want to know why, after all these years, Lenny suddenly decided he wanted revenge on the Stillmans. Well, I asked the same thing. He said that she was forgetting about how much she owed him for having him kidnapped and terrorized and then abandoning him as soon as his career was over. Sela saw it when she met him at the comedy club one night. He went over the deep end when Janice insisted on them bringing in a new comic who was funnier than him. That same night Lenny started asking us to help him get rid of Janice."

He sat back in his seat. His expression was one of deep thought when he took a few more sips of his beer.

"I don't trust Lenny Frost. Neither does Sela. Both of our parents made the mistake of trusting the wrong person and ended up screwed and dead. That may happen to me. That's why this recording is my insurance policy.

"Here is our plan. Lenny stole Derrick's key for his parent's summer place and had a copy made, which he had delivered to me. Derrick never realized his key had ever been missing before Lenny put it back. Sela is cozying up to Derrick Stillman to get the security passcode at the Stillman house."

"We figured that out already," Mac said.

"To make sure the police can't locate her, she got the key for the home of a friend who she knows is stationed overseas," Zachery continued. "I am going out to Deep Creek Lake to wait for Sela to call and give me the passcode. That may be difficult because Derrick Stillman doesn't drink. He doesn't do anything. But Sela is going to try to work her charms on him. Once she calls me with the passcode, then I am going to let myself into the house to kill them. Then, Sela is going to disappear and leave Derrick without an alibi."

A wicked grin crossed his face. "Meanwhile, Lenny is going to establish an alibi for himself—right here in Deep Creek Lake. We know that the police will be looking at him because he is going to benefit from the murders. He's going to be his usual jackass someplace and get recorded in some bar or get arrested picking a fight or something."

The grin fell. "You are probably wondering why I'm doing this." He cocked his head while looking straight into the webcam. "Someone once said you don't really realize how much you have until it is gone. Well, when you're a kid, you have less ability to realize how valuable everything that you have is. Like a dad, who may not have been a movie star, but certainly was great. Or a mom who was always so happy and loving until she lost the love of her life. Imagine having it all, and then having someone rip it all out of your life before you were even old enough to appreciate what you had. All of these people ripped everything out of my life—and since no one else will make them pay—I'm going to."

Zachery moved in closer to the camera. The corners of his lips curled. "If you, the police, get an anonymous tip, or somehow things go wrong because someone somewhere double-crossed me and Sela—look up Lenny Frost."

The video stopped with the image of Zachery, his face twisted up in a wicked grin, peering into the camera. Unblinking, Mac stared at the image.

"Lenny Frost killed Carson Drake in self-defense," Bogie said.

"He must have taken the money," David said. "He knew where it was. He was the one who told Derrick where to hide it."

"And that's why he didn't tell the police about killing Drake, so that he could keep the ransom for himself," Bogie said.

"All these years," Mac mused, "Lenny played the victim. He's such a brilliant actor, especially when it comes to playing the victim." He pushed up out of his seat. "He won his Academy Award playing a kidnap victim. Why not make a million dollars playing the same role?"

David closed out the video file and saved it to his laptop. "We need to talk to Ben about getting this video accepted as evidence for Lenny's role in these murders."

"We're going to need more than that video if we're going to get Lenny into a courtroom," Mac said. "Zachery Harris is dead. This video will be considered hearsay. Lenny's lawyer will argue that Zachery wrote Lenny's name in Janice's blood to incriminate him as some sort of revenge because he blames him for Carson Drake abandoning his family and disgracing them."

Bogie's mustache twitched. One of his eyebrows arched. "Who's to say that isn't the case? We only have the word of a killer that Lenny Frost was involved in this conspiracy. Lenny had an airtight alibi."

"Then why did he take those people hostage and order Mac to find the real killers?" David asked.

"The guy is crazy," Bogie replied.

"Crazy like a fox," Mac said.

"Do you believe what Zachery Harris is saying in this video?" David asked Mac.

"We need to find out what exactly happened in that pub when Lenny took those hostages," Mac replied.

"Good luck with that," Bogie said. "Every one of those hostages was way over the legal limit for alcohol when we rescued them."

"Not the bartender and his family," Mac said with a shake of his head. "They were there when Lenny took everyone hostage, and they got out before the drinking party started."

CHAPTER TWENTY

"Lenny Frost ruined my life." Jason Dalton was on his hands and knees in his modest living room, mopping up urine that had been deposited by the new addition to his family.

The puppy had been ushered into the backyard by Jason's wife, who was not speaking to him because he had promised the pet to their son. The Dalton's young son, the only happy member of the family, was chasing the puppy for all it was worth. Squeals of delight drifted in from outside.

"Do you know how long it takes to housebreak a puppy?" Jason asked. "Do you even know how?"

"They aren't physically able to hold it until they are four months old," David said. "So you need to make sure they get outside to do their business every two hours—"

"It's like having a baby all over again!"

David shrugged his shoulders. "Exactly. That's what puppies are. Canine babies."

Still on his hands and knees, Jason's shoulders drooped. "My wife refuses to have anything to do with this. She said I promised Timmy the puppy—but what was I supposed to do? He refused to leave that dog and I had to get him out of there. Whoever would have thought?" He sat up and glared at David and Mac. "Can I sue Lenny Frost for this? Compensation for pain and suffering as a result of his taking us hostage?"

"I'm sure somewhere you can get a crooked lawyer willing to take the case." Mac chuckled before turning to the reason for their visit. "Jason, we need your help. We're trying to sort out what happened leading up to Lenny Frost taking everyone hostage in the Blue Whale. You were the bartender. You were the one who Lenny first attacked."

"Because I grabbed the phone to call the police." With a sigh, Jason deposited the sponge into the bucket. Sitting back on his haunches, he rubbed his forehead while shaking his head. "What was I thinking? I wasn't thinking. I saw the newscast about the police looking for Lenny Frost, suspected of killing his agent and her husband. His picture was on the TV."

"That was actually on television when you were taken hostage?" Mac asked.

"I was really absorbed in it because it was happening right here in Deep Creek Lake," Jason said. "I didn't even look over at the door when someone walked in and up to the bar. He was standing right behind me. Then, they were interviewing that couple's son and he said that his mother wrote Lenny's name in her own blood. She declared that Lenny Frost was her killer."

Jason looked from David over to Mac. "I couldn't believe it. I turned to ask this customer behind me what I could get him and here I am, looking right into his face. Lenny Frost. The guy whose face was right on TV and the police are searching for him and he killed two people only a couple of miles away. Without even thinking, I grabbed the phone. He knocked it out of my hand. Then, I yanked open the drawer where we had the gun and he grabbed it from me. Next thing I knew, we were all taken hostages."

"Then," Mac said in a drawl, "Lenny Frost was behind you watching the newscast of the Stillman's son recounting what he saw inside the house when he found the bodies?"

"Exactly," Jason said, "that was how it happened. I have it all seared in my mind."

Thanking him, Mac motioned to David for them to leave. As they were parting, Jason was still in a state of disbelief. Indicating where he was kneeling in the middle of a carpet surrounded by pet stains, Jason sighed, "Little did I know then that within twenty-four hours, I would end up like this."

∽ ∾ ∽ ∾

"It's obvious that someone is lying," Ben Fleming said in response to Mac and David's report of where the Stillman murder case then stood.

"Of course," Mac replied with a chuckle. "It's a murder case. Someone is always lying when it comes to a homicide investigation. If everyone was sincere and functional, there wouldn't be any murders."

Their next trip was to the county prosecutor's office in Oakland, Maryland. The corner office was on the third floor in city hall.

Ben Fleming's handsome features represented his lineage. His ancestors had been tight with the Spencer family going back over a hundred years. His role in Garrett County was not only one of privilege, but also of duty and love for his country, state, and Deep Creek Lake. The brilliant lawyer and politician knew his way around cutting a deal, which often happened on the golf or tennis courts at the Spencer Inn resort. Fleming's charisma made it difficult for his less-sincere colleagues to know on which side of justice he fell, until all of the chips landed and justice prevailed.

Chelsea Adams was included in the meeting in Fleming's office, which had a view of the park outside the window. With Molly laying at her feet, the paralegal took notes of the discussion. Occasionally, David would reach over to pat Molly on the head or flash Chelsea a grin, which she would coyly return.

Ben flashed a wide grin with a mouthful of white teeth in response to Mac's observation. "Do you have anything besides Zachery Harris' statement in his video that Lenny Frost was involved in a conspiracy to kill Janice Stillman and her husband?"

Mac and David exchanged glances.

"We do," Mac answered, "but right now, it's not definitive."

"What do you mean that it's not definitive?" Ben asked.

"A theory."

Ben sat forward and folded his hands on top of his desk. "I always love to hear your theories, Mac."

"Because they're usually right."

"Almost always," Ben corrected him. "Tell me."

"Right now, Jeb Winkler, the federal agent who led the investigation into Lenny Frost's kidnapping, is taking a team up to the cabin where Lenny Frost claimed to be held during his abduction. They're taking cadaver dogs to search for Carson Drake's body."

Ben chuckled. "So they find Carson Drake's body and Lenny will go into full victim mode claiming he killed Carson Drake in self-defense. Who's going to argue with that? Besides, the statute of limitations for involuntary manslaughter ran out years ago. What good is that going to do us in these murders? The Stillman murders? The crimes in our jurisdiction?"

"There's no statute of limitations for murder," Mac said, "which is what Drake's death will be if it turns out the Stillmans didn't mastermind his kidnapping, but Lenny did and killed Carson Drake to make him the fall guy."

Ben looked from Mac to David, who said, "You should listen to him, Ben. It makes sense and explains everything."

The prosecutor sat back in his chair and folded his arms across his chest. "I'm listening."

Mac sat up in his seat. "Lenny Frost is not just a brilliant actor, but he's also just plain brilliant. Did you know he has a genius IQ of one sixty?"

"So he's smart," Ben said.

"Exactly," Mac said. "It's a fatal combination. It's been long proven that he's got an addictive personality, which means he's got to lie to keep his enablers, mainly Janice Stillman, supporting him. Who's a better liar than a brilliant actor? And being smart, he has come up with ways to manipulate things to get out of tight corners and come out ahead, not just once, but twice."

"How?" Ben asked.

"It all started when Lenny was 'dating' Kate Coleman." Mac held up his fingers to indicate quotation marks.

Ben and Chelsea turned to David.

"Who is Kate Coleman?" Ben asked.

"Didn't you have a crush on her?" Chelsea asked David.

"Like twenty years ago," David replied before explaining to Ben. "She was a pop star who the media and studio paired with Lenny Frost a couple of years before he was allegedly kidnapped."

"But he wasn't kidnapped?" Ben asked.

"You're getting ahead of the story," Mac said. "Lenny Frost and Kate Coleman were dating for the media. It was all a publicity stunt. But—" He held up his finger, "I think Lenny really did develop feelings for Kate Coleman, who, in reality, was dating his best friend, Derrick Stillman." He waved his hand. "This is total speculation on my part."

"Then it won't be admissible in court," Ben said.

Mac continued, "This is fact from more than one source. Kate Coleman and Lenny Frost developed drug habits, and Carson Drake was their source. Carson Drake was a drug dealer, blackmailer, and all around leech. One night when Lenny was out doing drugs with Kate Coleman, something went terribly wrong, and he ended up killing her."

"ME report supports that," David said. "COD is blunt force trauma to the back of the head. The rest of her injuries occurred after death."

"When he accidentally or purposely killed Kate, Lenny couldn't call his best friend Derrick to help him cover it up because she was his girl," Mac said. "So Lenny calls his go-to guy, Carson Drake, who helps him clean up his mess by making it look like an accident. Now, Drake has something to hold over Lenny's head, in addition to his drug addiction."

"Not to mention that Lenny owes him money for drugs," David said, "money that he doesn't have to pay him back."

"Harris said Lenny told those people in group therapy that he was backed into a corner when he killed this man in self-defense," Mac said. "I don't think he meant literally. I think he meant metaphorically. Carson Drake was putting pressure on Lenny to set him up with Janice Stillman as his agent, make him a star, and pay him back for the drugs he was giving him. Lenny couldn't deliver on any of that. Derrick stated that his mother considered Carson Drake a low-life and even blamed him for Kate's death. We can only imagine what Lenny thought when Drake threatened to expose him for being the culprit who killed America's pop sweetheart."

"In that case," Chelsea pointed out, "we're not just talking about him losing his star power, but about jail time to boot."

"So Lenny kills him?" Ben replied.

"While launching a new publicity campaign that extends his dying show for another year. He revived his career," Mac shrugged, "for a short time, and made himself a million dollars doing it." He chuckled, "He came up with an excellent plan that solved all his problems."

"Derrick Stillman reported at the time of the kidnapping that the last person he saw Lenny Frost with was Carson Drake," David said.

"If you flip it," Mac said, "the last person Carson Drake was seen with before his disappearance was Lenny Frost. It was Lenny Frost who called the studio to make the ransom demands. It was Lenny who called Derrick Stillman to give him instructions for switching the bags with the money. Most likely, Drake was dead long before Lenny made those calls."

"Derrick Stillman told me that Lenny Frost regularly stayed at the Stillman home," David said. "He had his own bedroom."

"After the kidnapping, Lenny insisted on staying with the Stillmans," Mac said. "That gave him access to the ransom that Derrick had hidden behind the access panel. Meanwhile, Lenny's performance as the poor kidnapping victim sent everyone in hot pursuit of a dead man."

"You have to admit," David said, "the plan is genius."

Ben sat up in his chair. "Do you have any idea how hard it's going to be to prove that Lenny Frost wasn't the victim, but the perpetrator in his own kidnapping?" Reminding himself and them that the abduction was a federal case, he said, "Glad this is not our case. What connection does Lenny's kidnapping, which you are saying didn't really happen, have with the Stillman murders?"

Mac said, "Sela Wallace, a.k.a. Drake, ended up in the same group therapy session as Lenny Frost, where he confessed to having killed a man in self-defense. Not letting on who she was, she put together the pieces and realized he was talking about her father. However, she interpreted it to mean that Carson was really trying to kill Lenny. Then, Lenny found himself blackmailed again."

"Why would Lenny confess to killing Carson Drake in a public forum like that?" Ben asked them.

"Because he's a narcissist," Chelsea said in a matter-of-fact tone. "To get attention. Lenny Frost is a sociopath, if not a psychopath, when you consider how many people have ended up dead because of him and his actions. Any remorse that he shows is only a great performance. Most likely, when he was in that group therapy, he had a great need, not desire, but actual need to be the center of attention, so he had to give a great performance. What better performance than confessing to killing a man?"

"Exactly," Mac said. "'Indirectly, that performance led to Janice and Austin Stillmans' murders. Sela and Zachery started putting pressure on him to help them prove that the Stillmans were involved in his kidnapping. Well, Lenny couldn't exactly do that because he was mooching off Janice Stillman, plus it wasn't true. So, he did what he could by being Zachery's anonymous source for his book."

"Feeding him a pack of lies," David said.

"When Zachery got sued and lost everything, then they really put the pressure on Lenny to go public with Janice's confession to him about being the mastermind of the kidnapping," Mac said.

"Which was a lie he had told Sela and Zachery," David said.

"Once again," Mac said, "Lenny was backed into a corner."

"Then Janice Stillman unintentionally threatened him," David said.

"How?" Ben asked.

"The DEA was investigating the Comedy Café for drug dealing," David said. "They thought Derrick Stillman was behind it. Turned out it was Derrick's administrative assistant, who is probably going to be arrested within the next twenty-four hours. She has a partner who has yet to be identified."

"I'm willing to bet it's Lenny Frost," Mac said.

"Sucker's bet," David said. "The feds have found evidence that the assistant has been spending a lot of nights in Lenny Frost's condo. They're lovers. She's not aware that she's not the only one. Neighbors say he has women going in and out of there all the time. One of them was Sela Wallace, who was using him as much as he was using her."

"See?" Mac replied.

David continued, "The feds asked Janice to use her influence to get an undercover operator into the club as a comic. Janice showed up at Sally Riggleman's audition and got her in. Possibility number one, this comic was a threat because she was better than Lenny. Number two is that it's entirely possible that Lenny sensed the comic was a fed."

"Lenny does have a one sixty IQ," Mac reminded Ben.

"So, when Zachery and Sela put pressure on him," David said, "Lenny saw a way for them to get their revenge, plus get Janice and her husband out of the way, and let him take possession of his expected inheritance."

"Then, Lenny would pay Sela and Zachery out of his inheritance to go away," Ben said.

"I don't think that was part of Lenny's plan," Mac said. "He's too smart to leave loose ends. He killed Carson Drake after framing him for his kidnapping. I have no doubt that his plan all along was to kill Zachery and Sela. Only they were smart enough to sense it—"

"At least Zachery was," David said. "He made that video."

"If they were really smart, they would have recorded their conversations and then taken it to the police and turned Lenny in," Mac said.

"They honestly believed the Stillmans were the master-minds behind Lenny's kidnapping," Chelsea said.

"Which was another one of their mistakes," Mac said.

"Do you have any proof?" Ben asked in a firm tone. "I'm hearing a lot of speculation, but nothing I can take to a judge and jury."

"The suitcase in Lenny's room," David said. "It had garbage bags and duct tape. Everything Lenny brought to the Wisp fit into one suitcase. I believe he planned on meeting Sela at the Blue Whale and then going back to his room to celebrate. There, he would kill her, and then stuff her into the suitcase and take her body someplace to dump it. Later, he would catch up with Zachery Harris and kill him."

"And I believe the suicide cocktail that Sela had in her purse was meant for Lenny," Mac said. "Their plan went south when Derrick Stillman got before the cameras and declared that Lenny had killed his parents and that his mother had actually written Lenny's name in her own blood. Lenny expected to be a suspect, but he had an airtight alibi. When he walked into the pub and saw that on the news, that Zachery had cemented his place as a person of interest by writing Lenny's name in Janice's blood, he knew that he was walking into a trap. The Drakes were framing him. Lenny had to act fast. The bartender grabbed for the phone and Lenny reacted. When he managed to take possession of the gun, he turned it into a hostage situation and called for Mickey Forsythe and the police to find the killers. Once again, Lenny Frost played the role of the victim." With a grin, Mac added, "But he's not flawless. Lenny gave himself away when I told him that we had suspects. He told us to call him after we arrested *her*. Not him, but *her*."

"How did he know our suspect was a woman?" David asked. "That, plus the video on YouTube, and Zachery's statement prove` they knew each other, when Lenny pretended that they didn't. A jury will ask why he pretended he didn't know Sela."

"The hostage situation was an act Lenny launched on the fly to divert suspicion from himself," Mac said. "He was confident that he would be cleared since he had an alibi, and that it would be assumed that he had been set up. Sela got out of there. Then, she and Zachery had to regroup to complete their revenge against Lenny."

Mac, David, and Chelsea waited for Ben's verdict on their theory.

"It's a great story," Ben said. "But where's the proof?"

"How about a confession?" Mac said.

"Do you think Lenny, as smart as he is, is going to give you a confession?"

"No problem," Mac said with a grin.

"What makes you so certain you can get him to confess?"

"He's a narcissist." Mac chuckled. "What fun is there in outsmarting everyone if you can't brag about it to someone?" He tapped his finger on top of Ben's desk. "We're going to make sure that when Lenny starts bragging, we'll be there to hear it."

CHAPTER TWENTY-ONE

"We're going to be right here, in the very next room," David assured Derrick Stillman while the federal agent adjusted the audio surveillance wire that was concealed in his sports coat. "We have a camera in Lenny's suite, so we'll see and hear everything. If there's any trouble, over a dozen agents and officers will be in that room in less than ten seconds."

"Lucky thing for us that Lenny didn't decide to head straight back to the city after the hospital released him," Bogie said. "It would have been more difficult to have set up surveillance in his condo."

"Not really." Jeb Winkler stepped up to Derrick to ensure the wire was not visible. "We got a warrant for surveillance as soon as we found Carson Drake's body. The gun used to shoot him was buried right along with his body. Serial number traces it back to Lenny's father. That and Derrick's statement got us everything we need."

Recognizing him from years before, Derrick smiled wistfully at the elder agent. "I'm sorry."

Jeb looked up from the jacket to meet Derrick's eyes. "For what?"

"For not telling you about what really happened back…" Derrick swallowed. "If I had, my folks…" He blinked back tears while gazing at the elderly man. "If I had told the truth—what price did you pay for my lies?"

"Doesn't matter now," Jeb said. "The past is gone. We can't get it back, nor can we change it. All we can change is the here and the now and what is to come."

"But because of my idiocy—"

Jeb clasped his shoulders. "We've all been idiots at one time or another. The trick is getting over it and making things right. That's the difference between you and Lenny Frost."

Mac slapped Derrick on the back. "It's going to be tricky getting what we need."

"That isn't what you said when you asked me to do this," Derrick pointed out.

Smirking, Mac shrugged. "In some ways, it will be easy. The sea of conspiracy surrounding the Stillman murders was filled with distrust and dishonor. Use that to your advantage, and he'll believe everything you say. His ego won't let him not tell you the rest, which is what we need to bust him."

"The tricky part is that you can't spoon feed him what we believe to be true," David said.

From across the hotel room next to the surveillance equipment, Ben Fleming agreed. "You need him to do the talking. Get him to give us what we need. If you say too much, the judge won't allow it."

Mac said, "Pretend you already know everything and get him to talk about it."

"That will be easy," Derrick said. "Lenny loves to talk. He loves to prove how smart he is."

"That's what we're counting on," Mac said.

 C3 80 C3 80

"It's show time," Derrick muttered for them to hear before rapping on the door to Lenny Frost's suite at the Wisp.

Almost instantly, the door flew open.

Champagne glass in hand, Lenny Frost smiled broadly at Derrick Stillman. "You're just in time, bro!" He took Derrick into a bear hug before leading him into the suite. "I was just pouring a glass. Join me." He gestured to the bottle of champagne resting in the middle of the table. Next to it was a gold foil gift box that had been sealed with a red ribbon and a large bow. An open greeting card lay inside the box where it had been tossed after Lenny read it.

"No, thank you." Derrick adjusted his sports coat, while checking to make sure the wire was not loosened during the hug. "I gave up booze a long time ago."

"Leaves more for me." Lenny shrugged off Derrick's decline of his offer and poured the champagne into his glass. "I tell you, God must have heard my prayers in that hospital, man, because this was waiting for me when I checked into the room."

"Who sent it?"

"A devoted fan." With a giggle, Lenny gulped down the drink until the glass was empty. With a belch, he refilled the glass before plopping down into the chair next to the table. Seeing his guest, he blinked as if he had forgotten Derrick was there. "How are you doing?" He draped a leg over the arm of the chair.

"Not so good," Derrick said. "Between making funeral arrangements for both of my parents and going over their estate…"

"Yeah, that's rough."

While Lenny's voice choked, Derrick saw no tears in his eyes. He moved to stand over him. "The night that my parents were murdered I was on a date."

"Yeah?" A wicked grin crossed Lenny's face.

"She had told me that her name was Madelyn Preston," Derrick said, "but then, after I got to what was her place, and we got all nice and…cozy, she told me the truth. Nothing like a little lovin' to bring out the truth in a woman, huh, Lenny?"

Lenny stopped drinking in mid-sip. "Are you saying she was married?"

Derrick grinned. "Let's just say she switched teams by the time I left her place."

"Switched teams?" A wicked grin crossed Lenny's face. "You mean you turned her into a lesbian." He laughed. "That's pretty bad. I wouldn't go spreading that around if I were you."

"You know what I mean, Lenny," Derrick said.

Lenny stared at Derrick, who returned his glare.

"You don't know anything," Lenny said in a low tone. With a chuckled, he sat back in the chair and took a big gulp of the champagne.

"Are you sure about that, Lenny?"

"She lied to you, Derrick," Lenny said. "You were always so gullible—believing anything that anyone told you."

"I saw the video on YouTube, Lenny," Derrick shot back. "You know the one, where you behaved like a jerk trying to heckle Riggleman. Madelyn, aka Sela, was right there next to you. What would you say if I told you that the police dusted my key for the summer place and found your fingerprints on it?"

"She arranged all of this to frame me!" Lenny rose up out of his chair. "No one is going to believe anything that she told you. She's dead. The police killed her when they caught her trying to kill me." He laughed. "Looks like I came out ahead in that deal."

"Well, it's a hollow victory for you, Lenny." Derrick stepped closer to him. "You're fired."

"You can't fire me!" the comic raged. "I've got a lifelong contract with the club. It's in your mother's will."

"No, it's not," Derrick said. "She changed her will before…" He stopped himself. "All you get is the condo and the trust fund." He yanked an envelope from his suit coat. "Now, if you don't want me to go to the police with everything that Sela told me, then I suggest you sign these papers turning it all back to me and get out of my life."

"What Sela told you was hearsay. No judge will allow it in court."

"It's all recorded," Derrick said. "Plus, I know about Kate."

Lenny's eyes widened.

"Sela's mother, Drake's wife, had told her everything."

Seeing the truth in his face, Derrick shoved his old friend down into the chair. The champagne glass shattered when it hit the floor. "You killed Kate!"

"It was an accident!" Lenny yelled back. "I just wanted to talk to her. All I did was tell her about how I felt, but she refused to talk to me and I grabbed her and she tripped and fell and—next thing I know, there's blood everywhere and she's dead!"

"So you pushed her car off the mountain road and made everyone think she had killed herself?"

"It was Carson's idea!" Lenny said. "I trusted him! Biggest mistake I always make is trusting anyone! Everyone I ever trusted turned against me. Carson had recorded everything when he came to her place, and then he edited himself out of it. Plus, it turned out, he saved my clothes that had Kate's blood on them. Then, he turned around and blackmailed me. He left me no choice but to kill him for the tape. Wouldn't you know it? Here, his wife had my clothes and knew what they were. I had to torture her for a full day to find out where they were so that I could burn them. I thought I was rid of that nightmare when suddenly their kids show up. It was like the spawn of Satan! Next thing I know, your mom was squeezing me out of the club with that second-rate bitch who calls herself a comic! But you know what?" He tapped his finger against his temple. "If you put your mind to it, then you can fix any problem. All you have to do is give everyone what they want—and they will trust you. That's when you let them have it. That's how you come out on top. First, you make them think they won, and then you bring them down."

"Is that what you did, Lenny? You brought my parents down? For what? They gave you nothing but their support."

Lenny jumped out of the chair and shoved Derrick. "Your dad always treated me like gum stuck on the bottom of his shoe." Turning around, he picked up a fresh champagne glass with one hand and the bottle with the other. "Like Sela—" Catching his chest, Lenny set the glass down. "You said she formed an alliance with you," he said while pouring the drink into the glass, "Well, let me tell you about Sela."

Staggering, Lenny turned to Derrick and held up his glass to him. "She formed an alliance with me…to kill her own brother." He dropped down into the chair.

Noticing how uneasy Lenny was on his feet, Derrick asked, "How much of that champagne have you had to drink?"

"I'm celebrating." Lenny held up his glass in a toast. "To retribution!"

"Retribution for what?"

"For betrayal."

"My parents and Kate did not betray you."

Lenny's good spirits dissolved. His tone dropped to a low, cold sneer. "Everyone I've ever met has betrayed me. It's the way of mankind. Once you learn to know and expect that, then it makes life much easier." He chuckled. "It even becomes kind of fun. A grown-up game of figuring out how to outsmart the other guy."

Lenny guzzled down the champagne and wiped his mouth with the back of his hand. The room fell silent while he shook his head. "Where was I?"

"You were telling me about how life is one big game of outsmarting the other guy," Derrick reminded him.

"Yeah," Lenny said while grasping his head and then his chest. "This champagne has gone straight to my head... anyway, for example, on Saturday, I went to the Blue Whale to meet Sela. But before Zach got there, I saw your face all over the news saying that I killed your folks. Zach had double-crossed me by writing my name in your mother's blood. The bartender recognized me, and that idea was toast." He looked into the empty glass. "But if things had gone according to plan, when Zach got there, we were going to go up to my room to toast with champagne." He flicked his finger on the bottle. "Sela had poison to slip into Zach's drink. I brought the suitcase that we were going to put his body in. After he dropped dead, we would just take him away. Then, when we got to where we were going to bury him—" He laughed.

"What?" Derrick gasped out. "What, Lenny?"

"I don't believe in splitting up families."

"You were going to kill Sela after she helped you kill her brother."

"Come on, Derrick. Don't you get it? You can't trust anyone!" Worked up into a full rage, Lenny struggled to push up to his feet, but instead dropped back down into his chair. "When are people going to learn? You mess with me and you'll get burned."

"Everyone I have ever cared about, you have ripped from my life!" Derrick was at Lenny's throat. "I'm going to kill you with my own hands."

Derrick grabbed Lenny's throat in his hands and squeezed. He was shaking Lenny by the throat when the doors to the suite burst open. As David had assured Derrick, a dozen uniformed officers and agents swarmed in with their weapons drawn. Seeing Derrick strangling Lenny, David and Bogie pried his hands away from Lenny's throat and pulled him back.

"It's okay, Derrick," David assured him while pushing him away from Lenny and back to the other side of the room. "We got enough. We got him for conspiracy and everything else. You did good."

His heart racing, Derrick paced the sitting room. Over at the table, Mac and Jeb Winkler were bent over Lenny, who was still slumped in the chair.

Bogie grabbed his shoulder mic. "We need the medical examiner to come to the Wisp…"

"What's going on?" David asked.

"He's dead," Jeb told David.

Mac sniffed the bottle of champagne while examining the card in the box.

"What?" Derrick grabbed his head with both hands. "Are you serious? I killed him?"

"There's no way he had time to kill him—" David objected. "We were in here—"

"When you drink this, make a toast to retribution for those betrayed," Mac read out loud from the card. "It's signed S.D."

"Retribution? Who's S.D.?" Ben Fleming asked for anyone who knew the answer.

"What's going on here?" a woman in a gray business suit with a nametag identifying her as the hotel manager pushed her way into the suite. Spotting David in his police chief's uniform, she made a beeline for him. "When we were asked to let you and your people pull this sting, you assured us that everything would be under control. Now I'm told that the medical examiner has been summoned. Is that having everything under control?"

Staying one step behind her, a chubby man in a dark suit had followed her in. He nodded his head vigorously in agreement with her every word.

Before David could usher her out of the suite in order to contain the scene, Mac grabbed their attention with a question. "Where did this champagne come from?"

"It was delivered for Mr. Frost," the chubby man answered.

"He ordered it?" Mac asked.

"No, Saturday morning a woman came in with it wrapped and with a note," the hotel employee said. "I remember because I spoke to her. She said that it was for Lenny Frost, but she left strict instructions that it was to be delivered to him on Sunday morning and not before."

"Today is Tuesday," Jeb noted.

"I know," the employee said quickly while ducking the manager's glare.

"Lenny Frost was in the hospital under observation from Saturday night until today," Mac said.

"Exactly," the employee said. "We had no address to send the champagne back to the woman. But we did have Lenny Frost's home address. I had given orders to my assistant to pack it up and mail it to him when Lenny's lawyer called us to make reservations for him to stay here tonight. So, I decided to have it sent up like the lady had requested."

"Lady?" David's eyes narrowed to a squint.

"What did this woman look like?" Mac asked the employee. "Would you recognize her from a photo?"

A grin crossed the employee's lips. "Oh, yeah. She was a real looker."

David pulled up the photo on his phone that Derrick Stillman had sent to him earlier. "Is this her?"

"Yep, that's her," he said with a nod of his head.

"Sela Wallace," David told Jeb and Mac.

"Also known as Sela Drake," Mac said. "S.D. She dropped off the champagne for Lenny before going to the Blue Whale. How much do you want to bet it was laced with a suicide cocktail?"

"Oh, dear Lord!" the employee stammered. "We sent poison up here to Lenny Frost's room?"

"It is not our policy to serve poison to our guests," the manager said.

"I'm sure it's not," Ben Fleming assured her.

"Then I didn't kill him?" Derrick asked.

"That's for the ME to decide," Mac said. "But I don't believe Sela trusted Lenny any more than her brother did. This bottle of champagne was her back-up plan. If they didn't succeed in making him pay the day after the murder on Saturday, then—even if he killed them, they could still get their final revenge on Sunday—"

"Thinking he had come out ahead in everything," David said, "just like we heard him telling Derrick, he'd drink the champagne—"

"Toasting his superiority," Ben said.

Mac looked down at the body of the once-great actor sprawled out in the chair. His lifeless eyes gazed up at the ceiling as if in search of the star that he had once been. Mac felt a tug of sympathy at seeing such an ending for someone who had achieved so much at such a young age, only to have thrown it all away during his descent into madness. "And serving up his life as retribution for his betrayal."

EPILOGUE

Spencer Inn Restaurant

Archie looked around the table at the six empty seats. She also took note of the equally quiet tables throughout the restaurant. At six o'clock on Saturday night, with the spring blossoms in full bloom, the five-star restaurant should have been hopping.

A smile came to her lips when she saw Mac making his way toward her. Since they had first met, Mac Faraday had come a long way. He used to be one of the worst dressed men in Spencer. Gone were his worn leather dockers, which Gnarly had chewed to bits, and faded jeans, though he had looked good in them. Mac had learned to embrace a more stylish image in tailored suits like the blue-gray one he was wearing with a matching silk shirt and tie.

Earlier, when Archie saw the suit he was putting on, she had slipped into a pale blue cocktail dress and gold jewelry.

They matched like every perfect couple should.

"Where is everyone?" she asked when he slipped into the chair next to her.

Confusion crossed Mac's face when he took in the empty tables around them. "I guess they all had places to go."

"Mac," she said, "this is Saturday night in the spring. The Spencer Inn is always busy this time of year."

"Now you sound like Jeff." He gestured for the wine steward to bring over the champagne and glasses.

"Shouldn't we wait for the others?" she asked.

"We'll have another bottle delivered when they arrive."

She checked her watch. "They should be here by now."

"Stop worrying." After Mac approved the taste of the champagne, the wine steward filled their glasses and hurried away. Mac held up his glass in a toast to her. "Do you remember the first time we came here?"

She picked up hers. "You choked on your champagne when I told you how much the bottle cost," she recalled with a smile.

"You also had to test the champagne because I knew nothing about it." He gazed softly at her. "You've taught me so much, Archie Monday."

"Thank you." Her throat tightened.

"This case with Lenny Frost made me see how very important it is to value those things and people who mean the most to you," he said.

"Poor Derrick," she said, "I feel so sorry for him. Lenny killed the love of his life and his parents. What's going to happen to him?"

"Legally, nothing," Mac said. "The feds aren't going to prosecute. They believe that he was as much a victim of Lenny Frost as everyone else was. Forensics found gunshot residue and Carson Drake's blood on Lenny's clothes, which they had taken into evidence after the kidnapping. That proves he shot Drake. They've also been going through all of the interviews that he gave about the kidnapping and are finding a ton of inconsistencies in his stories."

"Funny that no one noticed that before," she said.

"No one ever entertained the thought that a seventeen year old would be able to pull a caper like that and get away with it," Mac said. "Once they looked at it from that angle—"

"Because you pointed them in that direction." She reached over to grasp his hand into both of hers. "What made you suspect Lenny Frost was the mastermind of his own kidnapping?"

"Something he said while we were in the pub that didn't hit me right." Mac paused to take a sip of his champagne. "He said Drake's addiction to fame got him killed. But, that morning, I saw on a newscast that Carson Drake was Hollywood's D.B. Cooper. No one knew what happened to him. But Lenny not only knew Drake was dead, he knew what killed him."

"Zachery Harris had said in his recording that Lenny claimed he killed Drake in self-defense," Archie said.

"Why keep it a secret if it was self-defense?" Mac asked. "Lenny was brilliant enough to know that as soon as the police discovered he had shot Drake with his father's gun, they would question his story. I believe that's why he buried the gun with Drake's body up in the mountains and came up with this whole kidnapping scheme. Not only did he cover up a murder, but he made a million dollars doing it."

"I can't believe the cadaver dog found the body after fifteen years."

"Cadaver dogs have uncovered bodies that have been buried for close to thirty years," Mac said.

"I'll keep that in mind if I ever need to get rid of a body," Archie quipped while picking up her glass of champagne. While taking a sip, she eyed the empty tables in the five-star restaurant. They were the only customers.

Jeff must be having a stroke.

She was getting worried. However, she noticed Mac, the inn's owner, didn't seem concerned in the least. His eyes were only on her—exactly the way she liked it.

"Lenny made a career out of playing the victim," Mac said while brushing his fingers across the top of her hand. "It was his award-winning role in more ways than one. He won an Oscar for it when he was eight years old. He got a million dollars from the studio for playing the kidnapping victim when he was seventeen years old, and when he walked into that pub and saw that his conspirators were doing a number on him, he launched into the role of the victim being framed for murder."

"But that role was planned, wasn't it?" Archie said. "Lenny wasn't in Deep Creek Lake at the same time as the Stillman murders by accident."

"No, he planned that," Mac said. "He knew he had the motive since Janice had made him a beneficiary in her will. So he had to make it look like he had opportunity by being in the area. The media has been making noises about Cunningham trying to buy the movie rights for the Mickey Forsythe movies, so Lenny, realizing I lived in the area, decided to drag me into the case. As big as his ego was, it must have been a turn-on for him to match wits with me."

"But taking the hostages was totally unplanned, wasn't it?" Archie asked.

"You're right there," Mac said. "Lenny had an intricate plan in place. He told Derrick right before he died that he was planning to make Zachery and Sela disappear just like their father. But that broadcast and the bartender recognizing him forced his hand. He had to launch into his role of the victim in a big way and pull me into the case to identify the shooters trying to frame him. He assumed that once we discovered that he had an alibi and that his supposed meeting with Cunningham was a ruse, the authorities would conclude once again that Lenny Frost was a victim and look no further. He was wrong."

She kissed his hand. "What if Lenny had not walked into the Blue Whale right when that newscast was reporting their interview with Derrick?"

Mac forced his attention away from how her short pixie-like blonde hair was framing her beautiful face. "What do you mean?"

"Well, if Lenny hadn't seen that television report about Zachery writing his name in Janice's blood, who do you think would have won? Would Lenny have managed to kill both of them, or would they have killed Lenny?"

"They all lost," Mac said. "Justice won out in the end."

"Just like it should," she said.

"Lenny Frost has ruined every life he's ever touched," Mac said. "Zoe Reese, Derrick's assistant, was arrested in a major drug bust by the DEA on the same day that Sela poisoned him. They have a ton of evidence against her for running a drug operation from within the Comedy Café. She's singing like a pop star and naming names, one of them being Lenny Frost for being the brains behind the operation."

He chuckled. "If Lenny Frost wasn't nuts, he could have done great things with his life. According to Zoe, he came up with whole idea of dealing drugs out of the Comedy Café and how to do it under Derrick's nose, while making it appear like Derrick was the one running it. The drug dealers that the DEA arrested, they truly did believe that Derrick Stillman was the boss."

"I hope Derrick has proof that he's innocent," Archie said.

Mac was already nodding his head. "The money trail. Everyone believed Lenny Frost was broke. Well, Zoe led the DEA to a bank account that he had in the Cayman Islands where he had been building a retirement fund from his drug profits. He had two million dollars stashed away. Every few months, he would go on a binge and disappear. Well, actually, he was in the Cayman Islands making a deposit." He chuckled. "Guess when he opened that bank account."

"When?"

"The year after he was kidnapped," Mac said, "the month after he turned eighteen years old. He deposited a half a million dollars in cash when he opened the account."

"Could that money have come from anywhere else?" she asked.

"No other source that the feds can find," he said with a shake of his head. "Derrick claims that Lenny had made a big stink when he turned eighteen and discovered that there was only fifty-thousand dollars in his trust fund. By then, he was washed up as a star. We can pretty well assume that money that he deposited was the missing ransom. Unfortunately, there's no way to prove it. That bank makes it a policy not to check serial numbers, which I'm sure Lenny made sure of before making the deposit."

"You got to hand it to him," she said with a shake of her head.

"If Lenny had applied his intelligence to making the world a better place instead of…" At a loss for words, he shook his head.

"I guess the DEA isn't interested in cutting a deal with Zoe to prosecute a dead mastermind?" she asked.

"Nope," Mac said. "Another life that Lenny Frost has ruined. Do you want to know the irony?"

"What's that?"

"The motive for the Stillman murders was betrayal," Mac said. "Lenny felt threatened because Janice brought in a comic with more talent than him." He chuckled. "We thought that maybe he had made her for being an undercover agent. But, according to Zoe, Lenny never knew. No one had any idea. The motive for Lenny wanting the Stillmans murdered was because he was convinced Janice had betrayed him by hiring another comic—insane paranoia."

Archie rested her head on her hand and tilted it at him. "And you managed to figure it all out."

"I did have help." He brushed his thumb across her cheek.

"Another homerun for the good guys."

"I'm glad you're on my team, Archie."

"Same here." She leaned over to kiss him on the cheek.

When she pulled away, he turned his head and pulled her back to kiss her on the lips. Sensing that the moment was turning into a sensuous display, Mac gently pulled back and took her hand. "Archie…"

"Yes, Mac…"

"Before Robin left me everything, and—most importantly —before I met you, I had nothing. But I was a survivor. I knew that I could rebuild my life. If I lost everything that I own now—this resort, Spencer Manor, the money—if I lost it all tomorrow, I would be sad, but I'd survive." He squinted into her emerald eyes. "I'm not so certain I could survive if I lost you."

She blinked away the tears she felt coming to her eyes.

"I do love you, Archie Monday, and I am ready to marry you." He reached into his jacket pocket and removed a small ring box. "How's this for making it official?"

While she sat with her mouth hanging open, he opened the box to reveal a ring made of white gold and a single small diamond. Her mouth worked to find the words to respond while Mac took the ring from the case. Taking her hand, he slipped it onto her finger.

"In the journal my mother left me, she wrote about how Patrick O'Callaghan had bought her a ring and asked her to marry him after finding out that she was pregnant with me. He sold his car to buy it. She accepted his proposal." He wrapped his hands around hers.

"But they never got married," she said in a quiet tear-filled voice.

"Robin was only seventeen, and her parents broke them up," Mac said. "But Patrick, my birth father, insisted that she keep the ring to signify their never-ending love for each other. Even though they never married, they did love each other, and she kept the ring. I finally found it in the back of the safe in the study. I'm hoping that with this ring we will be able to have the endless type of love they had, and more, when we get married."

He searched her eyes for her response. When she said nothing, he added, "I've set the date, too."

"You set the date?" She gazed at the small diamond on her hand.

"I booked the inn for New Year's Eve this year for our reception. You book the church. Tell me the time and I'll be there. Oh," he added, "you have to tell me where, too." He flashed her a smile. "I don't want to leave you standing at the altar."

She giggled. "So that's what Jeff meant when he told me that you were trying to kill him. New Year's Eve is the biggest night of the year in the hotel-restaurant biz."

"So I've been told." He tightened his grip on her hands. "What's your answer, Archie Monday? Are you ready to become Mrs. Faraday?"

"Oh, Mac Faraday," she blubbered, "I was ready to be Mrs. Faraday the first moment I laid eyes on you." She threw her arms around him and kissed him on the lips.

When she pulled away, he asked, "Is that a yes?"

"Oh, I love you so much!" she said, and continued to say "yes" between kisses on his lips.

Holding each other tightly, they continued to kiss until the clearing of a throat made them realize that someone had come up to the table. Sheepishly, Jeff Ingles waited a few feet away. "Did she say yes?" he asked in a whisper.

Peering into Archie's sparkling eyes, Mac clutched her hand on which she wore the ring. "She said yes."

Jeff turned around. "It's yes! Let the celebration begin!" Patrons and employees flowed into the restaurant. Most of them stopped to congratulate the couple.

"Oh, Jeff," Mac stopped the manager on his way out. "A bottle of champagne for each table tonight—on the house."

Jeff visibly slumped on his way out. When he saw the despondent manager, David asked Mac, "Are you still trying to kill him?"

"I'm just keeping life interesting for him," Mac replied.

Chelsea, Doc Washington, and Catherine Fleming, Ben's wife, admired the diamond ring that Archie then wore. Even Molly sniffed Archie's hand as if to inspect the ring before turning to lick one of Gnarly's ears. David had decked out Gnarly in a service dog vest in order to let him join in the celebration. As long as the German shepherd laid low, hopefully Jeff wouldn't notice.

"When's the date?" Catherine demanded to know.

"New Year's Eve," Archie said. "And we are planning for you all to come."

"It's going to be a huge wedding," Mac warned. "Archie has six big brothers." He held out his hands. "And I mean big."

"And they all have families," she added. "Being their only baby sister, they'll all come, for sure."

Draping his arm across the back of Doc Washington's chair, Bogie chuckled, "Sounds like it's going to be an affair to remember."

Gnarly let out a bark as if to agree. Appearing to have forgiven him, Molly was still licking his ear.

"Would it be anything less than memorable with Mac, Archie, and Gnarly involved?" David asked. "I can tell you one thing, the only way I'm going to miss this is over my dead body."

"Hear! Hear!" Bogie called out.

Mac kissed his lady love while they all raised their glasses in a toast to the newly engaged couple.

The End
(Actually, this is only the beginning.)

For Mac Faraday's Next Case—

A Wedding and a Killing

A Mac Faraday Mystery

When Mac Faraday decides to do something, there's no stopping him...even murder.

Not wanting to wait until their big day to start their life of wedded bliss, Mac and Archie decide to elope and get married in secret at Spencer Church, where Mac's grandparents and great-grandparents had been married. However, before the reverend can say, "I do," the sanctuary erupts into chaos when Gnarly finds a dead body in the church office.

As they dive into the investigation, Mac and his team discover more questions than answers. What kind of person walks into a church and shoots a man for no apparent reason? When the victim's life turns up no suspects who would want to kill the quiet, mild-mannered accountant, the question becomes how do you solve the murder of a man who has no enemies in the world?

And then, there is the all-important question, when a murder is discovered before the reverend says "I do," are the couple married?

Coming September 2014!

About the Author

Lauren Carr

Lauren Carr fell in love with mysteries when her mother read Perry Mason to her at bedtime. The first installment in the Joshua Thornton mysteries, *A Small Case of Murder* was a finalist for the Independent Publisher Book Award.

A best-selling mystery author on Amazon, Lauren created the Mac Faraday Mysteries, which takes place in Deep Creek Lake, Maryland. *It's Murder, My Son, Old Loves Die Hard, and Shades of Murder, Blast from the Past , The Murders at Astaire Castle,* and *The Lady Who Cried Murder* have been receiving raves from readers and reviewers.

Lauren is also the author of the Lovers in Crime Mysteries, which is located in the Pittsburgh, Pennsylvania area, where she grew up. *Dead on Ice* features prosecutor Joshua Thornton with homicide detective Cameron Gates. The second book in this series, *Real Murder* will be released April 2014.

The owner of Acorn Book Services, Lauren is also a publisher. In 2013 thirteen titles written by independent authors (not counting Lauren's own titles) will be released through the management of Acorn Book Services.

A popular speaker, Lauren is frequently asked for advice about how to succeed as an author while running a business, cooking dinner, feeding dogs, and doing laundry. *Authors in*

Bathrobes tells budding writers the truth about what it takes to be a successful writer today: determination, hard work, a dependable laptop, a full pot of coffee, comfy slippers, and a durable bathrobe.

She lives with her husband, son, and two dogs on a mountain in Harpers Ferry, WV.

CHECK OUT
LAUREN CARR'S MYSTERIES!

Order! Order!

Numerous readers have asked the order of Lauren Carr's titles. All of Lauren Carr's books are stand alone. However for those readers who claim to be obsessive-compulsive, here is the list of Lauren Carr's mysteries in order. The number next to the book title is the actual order in which the book was released.

Joshua Thornton Mysteries:

Fans of the *Lovers in Crime Mysteries* may wish to read these two books which feature Joshua Thornton years before meeting Detective Cameron Gates. Also in these mysteries, readers will meet Joshua Thornton's five children before they have flown the nest.
1) A Small Case of Murder
2) A Reunion to Die For

Mac Faraday Mysteries:

3) It's Murder, My Son
4) Old Loves Die Hard
5) Shades of Murder (introduces the Lovers in Crime: Joshua Thornton & Cameron Gates)
7) Blast from the Past
8) The Murders at Astaire Castle
9) The Lady Who Cried Murder (The Lovers in Crime make a guest appearance in this Mac Faraday Mystery)
10) Twelve to Murder

Lovers in Crime Mysteries

6) Dead on Ice
11) Real Murder (June 2014)